Murder In Between
A Novel

"Gaylan Morray's imposing tactics, including but not limited to murder, occupied all his time and attention in their division. It never occurred to him he was ruling a miniscule kingdom. Though perhaps not a textbook psychopathic personality he was certainly amoral, manipulating people and the law to his own devices without shame or remorse."

Small towns, unique in character to cities, are seen as pristine places in which to live but not all are idyll. The town of Between is firmly held in the grasp of a ruthless bank president, striking fear or worse into any who oppose him. Most citizens of the town, having surrendered their autonomy to him, forfeiting power and property, sometimes life or limb, have become apathetic, giving free reign to his dominance. Not so complacent are Curtis and Phoebe Higgins who challenge Morray, struggling against his relentless oppression to maintain their livelihood and retain ownership of their farm.

Comment: "It's been a while since I've read a book with as nasty a character as Gaylan Morray. His methods make most bankers seem like choir boys. The novel was intriguing, interesting, and full of colorful characters. A good read." – Stephanie R.

Published by Winsor Bleu Editions
www.miriamnesset.com

Copyright © 2011 Miriam Nesset
#TXu 1-760-618

ISBN #978-1-4507-8662-1

See the web-site for other books
by Miriam Nesset
www.miriamnesset.com

Book design and photograph
by Miriam Nesset

Printed by Walch Printing
Maine, U.S.A.

For my daughter, Alison

Thank you to Lyn Anglin, Donna
Saywright, Alison Rowe, Pope Brock
and Carol McCracken for first reads
and editing, to LAS for the inspiration,
and a special thanks to Joan Martinez
for all her guidance and assistance.

Murder in Between is a work of
fiction. Any references to persons,
places or events are used fictionally.

MURDER
IN
BETWEEN

CHAPTER ONE

"What is it you want to talk with me about?" Phoebe thrust toward Gaylan Morray, president of the bank, as she strode across the lobby to his office.

"Lower your voice, Mrs. Higgins," the autocrat advised, meeting her at the door.

"Your secretary said it was urgent. I hope it's not about those papers again. I've told you before that I won't sign," Phoebe pronounced, looking down at the short, stout man with a spit-polished dome, much diminished in her presence.

"Just sit down—and relax, Mrs. Higgins," Morray ordered, staring up at her through wire-rimmed glasses.

Phoebe remained standing for a few more seconds before sitting opposite him, happy for the barrier of an oversized desk between them. Adjusting his bulk, he glowered across at her from his leather high-back swivel chair.

"This is not a social call," she stated, at eye level with him. "Tell me what you want."

He shoved some papers toward her and she knew right away what they were—what he wanted.

"Quit bothering me with those papers," she spit.

"So you still won't sign," he returned, a scowl deepening on his sloped forehead.

Phoebe had never been close enough to him before to notice the dark, bushy eyebrows sprouting over his glasses like they were trying to escape his wicked eyes or the black hair in wide nostrils that heaved when he spoke.

"Not only won't I sign, I'm not coming in here to talk with you about it again. As I've told you repeatedly, we own that acre outright. You do not have a right to it just because you want it so you can save yourself the continued strain of trying to get it. Nothing you do or say is going to make us sign it away."

"Oh, I'll make you sign. You mark my word," Morray exerted with a sneer.

"Is that a threat?"

"You call it what you want."

Between, the Dirk County seat, was so named because it lay midway *between* Herston and Dirkville. Herston Dirk, an early speculator and distant relative of Gaylan Morray's wife, had platted both Herston and Dirkville. A balefully greedy man, after selling most lots, he laid out a third town between the two, designated it the county seat and built a courthouse, hoping to clean up. After raising a house for his family he established a bank and several commercial establishments, setting himself up as the town's leader and, arguably, its wealthiest man.

Optimistic regarding Between's future, he surveyed lots far beyond advancement. The city limit sign, altered in recent years by bored local juvenile delinquents to read *Welcome to PRE-Historic Between,* still stood on its post two miles north of the central business district with no intermediate development. In the mid 1800s it was only through the determination of local powers existing at the time, specifically Herston Dirk, that the maneuvering of the county seat from Between to Dirkville had been thwarted—un-scrutinized efforts that supposedly included murder. His free-range strategies were less effective when it came to the railroad, however. Occupied with county business, surveying lots, nourishing bank capital, as well as lining his own pockets, he failed to hear of the railroad's anticipated arrival until deals were set and depots under construction in Dirkville and Herston. In a race against time his stepsister town faltered while the earlier established ones thrived and grew in population. This rare oversight was, for a time, the bane of Herston Dirk, adversely impacting his finances, tarnishing his reputation and, worst of all for everyone concerned, deflating his ego—but not for long. In the years that followed he regained through intimidation and subversion all he'd lost and more, leaving no question as to his authority. Such was the lineage of Between bank presidents.

A picturesque village, Between was cradled amid rolling hills, bordered on the east by Bullfrog Creek and on the west by French River—the kind of place where women groomed as ladies took turns pouring tea in their parlors afternoons from hand-painted porcelain sets, conversationally besmirching the character of anyone not in attendance. Their male counterparts gathered each morning over white ironstone coffee mugs at the local café to sort out world issues or generate gossip before going to their respective vocations. On the surface the town looked peaceful, a snapshot of well cared for lawns fronting practical white historic homes on elm tree-lined streets (at least until Dutch Elm disease altered the utopian scene). Beneath the picturesque serenity, however, lay a strong and malignant undercurrent of deception—borderline, if not totally illegal, doings by the town's movers and shakers, guided by the current president of First Enterprise Bank and his board of repellant cronies.

Most small towns have a sense of unity, like a large family of sorts. Between, however, was characterized by desultory parameters for normal and social clicks that defined the caste of its citizens. Long ago wrested of any say in the functioning of their community, most denizens had adopted an apathetic attitude without hope of affecting change, acquiescing to those perceived to have power and influence. Local partite politics went way beyond the usual friction between locals and outsiders, described by an attorney briefly practicing in Between as a battle between the aggressively ignorant and those with divine guidance syndrome.

Outsiders were not welcome in Between, especially those with the affliction of worldliness—their arrival garnering suspicion and angst. The natives, too enamored with their own ideas to inform themselves of others, huddled together like expatriates, setting fluid boundaries for normalcy. Originally lured by the charm of a quintessential small town, newcomers soon left—the relentless social or financial challenges too difficult to abide. Businesses were opened then closed on a continuum of predictable regularity. If you married a local you might eventually move from alien to stranger status after fifty years but your lot could never be further improved upon.

The only respectable way to leave Between was in a casket. Those who left of their own volition were dismissed as misfits—the locals refusing to accept the decision to depart from their community as anything other than poor judgment. A trail of gossip, suspicion, and character assassination usually accompanied the departee, their sullied reputation more than adequately excusing the perceived rejection to paranoid locals, oblivious to their collective neurosis.

In a large city it's possible to live in anonymity. People come, go, and do as they please without notice or concern. In small towns everyone knows your business. In Between it went far beyond idle curiosity. Locals passed judgment on anything or anyone straying from a contrived norm. This amorphous definition of *normal,* while applied however haphazardly to newcomers, blurred the limits of behavior for locals. As a result Between churned out eccentrics or worse, a hotbed for the generation of unusual characters. No one referred to them as odd, however, only *interesting.*

A beacon of hope, the L & W Railroad finally arrived in Dirk County in the late 1800s but found only a modest way station between Herston and Dirkville. The train at first came daily to Between, with scheduled stops at the grain elevators north of town. Since the agricultural economic base of the county had begun shifting to one more diverse in the 1960s, the elevators had stood empty and the train roared past, only stopping every Tuesday and for reasons unknown.

It was widely assumed locally that L & W stood for liquor and women. A house full of sorry women camped out in a dilapidated, paint-less house within a mile of the tracks and, though without license, the scofflaws sold gallons of liquor—but only to locals or rail-jumping vagabonds. In an occasional burst of occupational duty the sheriff, with a warrant from the judge, had tried to get the women to close up shop—his official visits taking longer than justifiable. It was all to no avail. The last time he'd attempted it, Gertrude, the most sorry, came running from the house wearing only bib overalls—her devoted pack of dogs at her heels. It took him a while to notice the shotgun held tight to her naked, bouncing breasts. Before he could reach the patrol car a shot rang out, his windshield shattered.

It was no secret that nearly every businessman in town, including the judge and mayor, had, at one time or another, frequented Gertrude's establishment—most unaware their escapades were common knowledge. The rest blatantly flaunted their extracurricular activities. Curtis Higgins had seen Gaylan Morray sneaking out of a motel in Dirkville one balmy summer afternoon in the presence of Sally Torrent, one of Gertrude's girls and his regular, oblivious to the indiscretion's possible tarnishing of his reputation.

Off the beaten trail, Between was isolated enough to allow those with perceived or actual power to wield their authority as easily as a prostitute her boa. The law was phlegmatic at best. Despite accumulating bodies over the years, no one had ever been convicted of murder in Dirk County. Judge Wilcox, a tall man with kestrel features and a pronounced dewlap, was best known for his erasable nature. Drunk or sober, he presided over the kangaroo court, dispensing legal improvisations in his black robes. Out of court he could be seen in black leather on his Harley.

The sheriff was a force, about six feet five inches tall and weighing over three hundred pounds. His uniform exhibited signs of stress—the tan fabric stretched to the limit across a broad chest and protruding belly. Sheriff Tagwell, an ardent advocate of corporal punishment, had an effluvial sense of justice and order. The perpetually menacing look on his face sent most people's nerves into spasm. Their fear was well warranted. His weapon of choice, an overused wooden baton, had dented more than a few heads. Repeat offender were rare. Judge Wilcox had billeted him as sheriff. However, as a convicted felon, he wasn't allowed to carry a gun. After all, the law is the law.

Most people that had been in, or more likely through Between, felt that any progressive plan for the town, and for that matter the county, should certainly list fluoride as a top priority. Going to Between was like stepping back in time fifty years. They say that communities are best preserved when they're poor and isolated, both criteria apt in the case of Between. Citizens rarely strayed from the city limits and, when they did, it was usually only to go as far as Dirkville or Herston, each twenty miles away. Occasionally the more daring citizens spent their vacations away from Between, venturing out in groups or multiple couples. There was a lot of money in Between but solely in the hands of an opulent few, gained through overfeeding on the poor. To say that anyone of authority or a modicum of power would be a big fish in this small pond would be a gross understatement. Communal apathy allowed selective domination to thrive into the 1970s, notwithstanding the occasional upstart's resistance.

"Don't you think it's rather inappropriate for a bank president to be threatening his customers?" Phoebe returned, in a much raised voice.

"If I were you, Mrs. Higgins, I'd shut my mouth," Morray warned. "Now take the papers home to discuss with your husband and let me know when they're signed. I'll pick them up out at your place anytime you like—or I can bring them to you if you prefer to discuss the matter with him first."

"There's nothing to discuss. I told you I'm not signing those papers—not now, not ever," Phoebe pronounced, pushing the papers across the desk like they were hot.

"You're biting off your nose to spite your face."

"Well it's my nose, my face, and my land," Phoebe threw back, rising to leave.

"We'll talk about this later—when you've come to your senses."

"I've come to my senses, just this minute, in fact. I think it might be time for an attorney to hear about your threats and unwarranted pressure to sell that land."

"Let me give you some free advice, Mrs. Higgins," Morray wheezed through clenched teeth, escorting Phoebe by the elbow to the front door. "You can't win against me. I'll have that piece of land—and your farm too—if it's the last thing I do."

"And it will be the last thing you do," Phoebe threw back in a husky whisper, before pushing open the door with so much force the rafters shook.

"Confounded woman! She's just impossible! What are you all staring at, anyway? Get back to work," he screamed at cowering employees.

The trouble had all started when Curtis, Phoebe's husband, a business major, bought an acre of land near the road into Dirkville on the north side of town. The land had never gone up for sale because he'd had the advantage of hearing about it before anyone else caught wind of it. His uncle owned half-share in it. When Uncle Ernest's business partner died, he decided to sell the land. Curtis planned to build a small office building there and open his own insurance agency, renting out three other spaces as income to help defray construction costs. He had complied with every directive of the county board but could never get his plans approved or a building permit issued because, at the eight meetings he'd attended over the course of two years, there was never a quorum and so a vote could not be taken. There were other meetings where a quorum was present, votes taken, decisions made, permits granted but he never learned of them until after the fact.

As droll as county board meetings could be, those of the town were often heated and steeped in controversy. When progressive citizens, bringing business before the board, realized their plans had been bashed, their ideas thwarted, by a board with blinders on and punitive intent, they often exploded in frustration. At the last meeting Curtis had attended, a woman tried to get the board to allow parking behind her business, presenting a rational argument. "The metered spaces on the street are limited to begin with," she maintained, "used up by ignorant business owners who stupidly park in front of their own establishments taking up spaces that should be reserved for their customers then bitching because they have no business." Told by the mayor that she needed permission from the board in order for her patrons to drive down the alley—the public alley—to land she owned, she had, for months collected surveys from her customers to prove more parking spaces were needed. "I will improve the land for parking and it won't cost the town a cent." Her request was denied, the Maelstrom that followed having no visible effect on the board.

"You've just made me close my fucking business," she screamed, slamming down her surveys on the table in front of the mayor and stomping from the room.

True to her word, within the month she closed her business and left town. It was of no significance to the mayor or the board. Someone else would come along to fill the void. They always did. Meanwhile, occupied vacancies filled in the gaps—hobby businesses or tax write offs, closed more often than open. New arrivals came in predictable waves. Seeing the potential of the town, they brought ideas for positive change with them, enthusiastically volunteering their time, energy and initiative. The altruistic rendering of their hearts and souls as catalysts for positive change took about three years to crest. Following repeated attempts to inject progress into an ultraconservative, archaic mindset, they sold their properties, forfeited leases, and left town. And so it was that Curtis, in total frustration, eventually gave up on building plans. Fortuitous events led him to his first love, full-time farming, but he refused to sell the land in spite of constant pressures brought to bear.

The bank, run by Gaylan Morray, a ruthless narcissist and sanctioned by a board consisting of local attorneys, representatives of law enforcement, government and business leaders, had organized an illegal holding company. They were not an august group in any flattering sense. Flying under the radar of state inspectors, over decades their suborned preemptions had allowed them to routinely foreclose on properties, especially farms, for personal gain, gathering them up like tulips from a spring garden bed—morally oblivious to the lives ruined, hungry babies, suicides, and other carnage associated with their fiendish collusions.

One poor fellow, whose two hundred acre farm had been ingested, was publicly very vocal about the bank's complicity. Distraught and financially ruined, he eventually shot his wife then, in a botched effort, tried to hang himself. The rope broke. Out on bond, he tried to gas himself in the garage but ran out of gas. The third time appeared successful. He jumped from the railroad trestle onto the muddy bank of French River. The county coroner briefly questioned the ability of a right-handed person to slit their own throat right to left, especially with a broken right collar bone, but was somehow persuaded to note suicide due to impact trauma as the cause of death on the official certificate.

Rarely did a year pass when a body wasn't pulled from French River or Bullfrog Creek. Their isolated locations and the loose nature of county law enforcement had gained these waters a reputation as depositories for the unwanted or troublesome, contributions sometimes coming from distant parts of the state or adjoining states. More than not the law turned a blind eye if anything questionable occurred, overlooking persistent details unless there was a need to manipulate them toward an alternate result. For those that fell on hard times, unable to get their financial feet under them, creative solutions were found for their economic woes. If they fell behind on their mortgage payments, foreclosure was always the first line of offense. In a couple of cases, however, a fire conveniently broke out, destroying the house. The owners, convinced to be satisfied with narrowly escaping prosecution for arson, and one time murder, chose to live elsewhere, forfeiting their properties.

"We have got to change banks, Phoebe fumed," storming into the kitchen where Curtis, on a rare break from farm work, sat sipping a cup of black tea.

"You know that's not possible. I'm not driving twenty miles to do banking. We've been through this a million times. Why do you continue to pursue it? You didn't talk to Morray again when you went to the bank did you?"

"Yes, as a matter of fact I did have another asinine conversation with the little troll—more like a yelling match. He's so crooked that when he dies they'll have to screw him into the ground."

"Oh, for God's sake, Phoebe, let it go," Curtis laughed. "You'll only rile him into doing something depraved enough to surprise us all."

"It's not funny, Curtis. I can't let it go. Every time I go in the bank he shoves those papers under my nose and insists I sign them. He seems to think you'd sign if I would. I'm not letting him get his hands on that land, Curtis. There's some reason why he wants it so badly."

"I've told him I won't sell either but he persists. Word has it he wants all the land he can get his hands on, so what makes you think there's a pressing reason for wanting that piece?"

"You mark my words there's a reason all right. He knows something we don't."

Curtis shifted in his seat, got up, stretched then went out through the mud room, letting the screen door slam behind him. There was no dealing with Phoebe when she was foaming at the mouth. He stood ten paces from the house on a rise that overlooked his—their—farm, surveying his realm, nearly three hundred acres of prime land spreading out behind the house and outbuildings. It was one of the best farms in the region, most being limited in size by rocky soil and hilly terrain. His pride expanded as he stared at the barn, stable, outhouse, pole barn, well house, granary and sheds for holding wood and equipment. Within the year he hoped to add metal corn sheds to the collection, the following year driers for shelled corn. Though profits were slim, he tried to make improvements each year. The farm had been in rough shape when he'd taken it over but years of hard work were everywhere evident.

Their farm abutted one owned by Jesse Tate on the west, the properties separated by a dense hardwood and pine forest. On the other side was a farm worked by George and Meredith Simons. Both equally desirable farms were cradled in the same pocket of prime agricultural land. The Simons had been tenant farmers for years but when Milfred Langton, the owner, decided to sell the farm, they quickly got their funds together and applied at the bank for a mortgage, setting off a series of *happenings* that eventually squeezed their finances dry. They lost their down payment money paying for damages to machinery and crops. Without a substantial down payment, the bank naturally refused them the loan for lack of security. With the bank as new owners and their meager remaining funds needed for operating capital, the Simons were eternally consigned to tenant farming. George Simon wore a defeated look on his weather-worn face and his wife turned to drink, relegating the raising of their three children mostly to fate.

Jesse Tate, not the brightest flame but honest and fair,

was a good man. Wound tighter than an eight-day clock, he was nervous, twitchy, and always in a hurry. He didn't so much walk as flit. His sunburned face wore deep gullies that ran vertically from crow's feet to his chin like arrows pointing out a leathery neck. What little hair he had was graying and large bovine eyes were the only remaining evidence of an earlier innocence. Any harshness was acquired, undoubtedly the result of what life had dealt him. His wife, Tootsie, had died following the birth of their son. Jesse never remarried and raised his son, John, alone. At the age of seventeen John was killed coming home from a basketball game, hit by a drunk driver the sheriff had said. Nothing was ever the same after that.

Slight of build, but muscular, Jesse ran the hundred-acre farm with only the intermittent help of a hired man named Pete Irvin who he let live in a shack at the back of the property. Pete, a mentally challenged man of forty-something, had wandered the streets of Between following the death of his devoted mother, ragged and without notice or aid before being taken in by Jesse several years ago.

Jesse often borrowed tools or checked to see if he had plowed, planted or harvested as much as Curtis, but they didn't socialize and rarely conversed. He'd had several run ins with Gaylan Morray who had tried to screw him out of his small farm more than a few times—finally able, through coercion, to get the mortgage when Jesse was emotionally weakest following the death of his son. Jesse hated the man so much he told Curtis he'd wait twenty years for just one chance to kick his ass. Mortgage in hand, Morray pretty much left Jesse alone, an anomaly in and of itself but, as Curtis was soon to learn, it was because he had bigger fish to fry.

Gaylan Morray had come from nothing. Raised in the next county to the north, he harbored endless resentments toward his parents, upbringing and, in particular the rural life from which he had done everything in his power to distance himself. His mother left his father, a farmer, when he was three. He had few remembrances of her but many of his stepmother, a cruel and heartless woman of social advantage who had married beneath her and never let any of them forget it. Her dowry, a haughty and spoiled daughter a year older than Gaylan. Within a year of the marriage a half-sister was added to the brood, soaking up the droplet of love in his father's heart. Being overlooked for a stepsister and half sister, abandoned by his mother, and treated cruelly by a stepmother, he grew into a young man extremely depreciative of women.

Morray's childhood memories consisted of abuse, deprivation, lack of attention or love, endless work and hardship and, worst of all, an emotionally sterile father who neither defended nor nurtured him. Rupert Morray, easily the stingiest man alive, hoarded what little money he could garner while his family lived like paupers. Taking seriously, but loosely, the words of Will Rogers, he proclaimed his meager fifty acres as the only thing of value in his life, protecting it like every cup of dirt could be alchemized into gold and driving his family to exhaustion in maintenance of the modest farm.

Gaylan left home at sixteen, sickened by the idea of farming and resentful of anyone choosing a farm life. Despite all his efforts in aspiring to the complete antithesis of his hated father, deeply imbedded beliefs clung to him like moss to rocks, influencing his dealings with others and firmly anchoring the notion that only land had reliable value. In eternal rebellion against his soon deceased father, he vowed never to let anyone or anything stand in his way again, setting a course for power, influence, and wealth with blinders bridled.

After years of struggle in the business world, he managed to get a foothold, landing a job as teller at the bank in Between. Opportunity came in the form of a woman—a widow with a small son. Edith Dirk DeMar was the daughter of the president of First Enterprise Bank. Managing to curtail his misogyny through the nuptials, Morray acquired wealth and position in one fell swoop with their union, heir apparent to the bank presidency. His father-in-law, grandson of Herston Dirk, was a harsh man of obvious cunning, heartless, except where his daughter and grandson were concerned. From him Gaylan acquired the tools of strategy, deception, and coercion necessary to begin building his *empire.*

Like many *nouveau riche* Morray had deep pockets and short arms but was best known for his cruelty. He did not wear the exclusive title *anus horriblis*, however. His two abhorrent sons, Owen and Clyde, were collateral or worse but, in their defense, mere henchmen. Incapable of intelligent thought, they lacked the perceptions to communicate above the level of moron much less conceive of the devious tactics predators touted. Though opposites, they cohered, sticking as close together as ticks on a hound dog. Some people referred to them as Tweedledee and Tweedledum, more as Tweedledum and Tweedledummer. They couldn't squat without their father's instructions. Knowing nepotism, and their lack of intelligence, would be his undoing, Morray kept his sons a safe distance from the inner workings of the bank, obedience training them to do his bidding without question.

Owen was tall and lean, rawboned, like someone who'd been left on the rack too long. He had a dull normal look stamped on his flat, expressionless face, a weak chin, blond straw-like hair and a large nose. His Adam's apple bulged out the collar of his tattersall shirt (the only kind he'd wear) which he insisted on keeping buttoned at the throat. Clyde, on the other hand, was quite obese, waistless and, like his father, truncated. His small feet looked unlikely to support his bulk. He had shaggy eyebrows and greasy dark hair that ran down the back of his thick neck, disappearing into his shirt collar and presumably covering his barrel-like back. Besides a very feminine nose, his only discernible facial feature was dun-colored eyes that held a feral expression.

Though it was difficult to separate the two sons as to character, on closer inspection one could see that Clyde was the dominant of the two. Considering facial features alone, he looked most like his mother. In all other respects, save intelligence, he emulated his father. The younger of the two by only a year, he engineered all activities for him and his brother in a futile attempt to gain the impossible approval of their stern and heartless father. Owen was of a somewhat softer nature but easily manipulated and the duller of the two. Both boys grew up fully entitled, observing close hand and approving of the effect their father's actions had on people but not bright enough to be jealous of his power and influence. Morray demanded, and got, their unconditional loyalty. Their mother's love, their only salvation and upon which they unconsciously depended, was resented and scorned.

Edith Morray was a holy woman, gentle and plump with blue-hair, thick ankles, porcelain skin and a coquettish smile. Gaylan's banking practices were not unlike those of her father so she never questioned his methods. Her time was totally occupied with the care and maintenance of a gracious and respectable facade. Though Gaylan had married her with the assumption of inheriting the bank in addition to the presidency, as opposed to any leanings toward love, it eventually came to light that Edith's father had neither liked nor trusted him. Having only a much cosseted daughter, upon his death, Franklin Dirk made her and as heir, her son, fifty-one percent shareholders in the bank. Gaylan had not counted on this close scrutiny of his intentions, leaving him no options but loyalty and devotion, however forced.

Edith seemed oblivious to his pretensions. Reared with the proverbial silver spoon, she lived a privileged life, indulging in manicures, beauty salons, and tea parties, driving her Corinthian Blue Cadillac to friends' houses or entertaining them in her own palatial estate cantilevered out

from the highest hill in town. She was often quoted as saying her house was modest but you had to wonder what
standards were used for appraisal. Her interest in the bank
extended only to the income provided, control it allowed
her to wield over Gaylan, and a respectable position for
her son.

Vincent DeMar, Edith's son by her first marriage, was
greatly favored by her for his intelligence and kind heart.
Edith had made sure that Vincent's father, a fallen war
hero, was the model for his character development, not her
husband, and he'd turned into an ethical and honest person. He was the scorn of his stepbrothers—a ball and
chain to his stepfather, who was eventually forced by
Edith to seat him as vice president of the bank. Despite his
position, Vincent was not privy to the operations of the
bank, serving only as a teller and gopher, excluded from
all board business. Vincent neither knew nor wanted to
know of Morray's dealings and kept a low profile.

Gaylan Morray's imposing tactics occupied all his
time and attention in their division. It never occurred to
him that he was ruling a miniscule kingdom. Rarely at
home, if he didn't have some poor sucker in a choker
hold, squeezing the financial lifeblood from him, he could
be found in the office of one of his unsavory associates,
smoking a stogie and drinking Jack Daniels. The plots
hatched in those smoke-filled rooms made gangsters look
like amateurs. Though perhaps not a textbook psychopathic personality he was certainly amoral, manipulating
people and the law to his own devices without shame or
remorse. His bank held mortgages on almost every house,
farm, and commercial property in south Dirk County to
use as leverage. He so intimidated the citizenry of Between that no one dared to question or confront him and it
didn't take much to compel everyone, in fear of losing
their property, to do as he asked.

Because he had very limited contact with Morray,
Curtis Higgins had no reason to be afraid of him, despite

words of warning from Jesse and others. He and Phoebe owned their farm free and clear, thanks to his generous father who had farmed it for forty years then willed it to them. The money he had been able to scrape together to begin farming paid for its operation the first few years, as well as the new house. His mother had lived with him and Phoebe until her death three years earlier. And, they owned the acre out by the highway, also a paid-for asset. He was too honest and guileless to conceive of impalpable strategies that might become his undoing—slow to burn and slow to suspect trouble brewing.

Looking out over the farm, the sun beating down on muscular, tan arms crossed over his broad chest, he felt pretty self-satisfied. He and Phoebe had put in ten hard years to turn the modest farming operation inherited into one of which his father had only dreamed. Phoebe was the ideal farm wife, a hard worker and true partner. While he was competent and capable, albeit sometimes too contemplative, too careful, Phoebe was an efficient and productive doer. His dad used to say "she never does anything in halves, just throws back her head and goes." Her parents had been killed in a car accident her junior year of college. Following their deaths her only sibling, a brother, moved back to the west coast where he'd attended college and they had seen each other only twice since. Their upbringing, characterized by extreme dysfunction, had not been very stable. While her brother, Harry had chosen to wallow in it, using it as an excuse to drift, for Phoebe it served as catalyst. She worked to pay her way and finish college, majoring in elementary education. Her home was in Carterville, two counties west, but she did her practice teaching in Between.

She and Curtis had met when he came home from college for a holiday. They saw each other only socially at first but soon he was coming home every weekend. The attraction was her slight, tall frame, sparkling blue eyes and dark hair, but it was her sense of humor and wit that reeled him in. Curtis was as tall as Phoebe but stocky in frame, with brown eyes and a towhead. His rugged, masculine good looks admittedly drew her but it was his empathy regarding the loss of her parents, his pure heart, that convinced her of their compatibility. They started dating, before long becoming serious. A marriage ceremony followed graduation.

Married life began in an apartment above the newspaper office. Phoebe taught school, second grade. Curtis pursued a career in insurance, working several years for a company in Lynchford. He never liked the work or commuting to the city hence the appeal of starting his own agency. They had planned to raise a family but Lily was a surprise. Soon after giving birth Phoebe quit teaching, proclaiming her desire to stay home with her child and any others that might follow to bless their lives. Curtis continued in a job he hated to support them, growing progressively more dissatisfied. When his dad died, leaving the farm to him, they found themselves at a critical juncture in their lives. After rehearsing in solo a rebuttal to every conceivable objection she might throw back at him, he screwed up enough courage to tell Phoebe that he wanted to farm. Instead of opposing the idea, she encouraged him to take it on, assuring him she would always be at his side.

They raised hogs and beef cattle, steering clear of the twice daily tether of dairy farming. Even without milking there was never a reprieve, but Curtis loved farming. The beef cattle or hogs needed constant attention, the vet often called to tend a sick animal, assist with a difficult birth or the multitude of other problems associated with animal husbandry. There were crops to plant, spray, cultivate or harvest, hay to cut and bale or repairs to fences and outbuildings. In the winter, when you'd think he might find some idle time, he overhauled machinery, ordered seed and other supplies along with the daily chores of hauling hay to the livestock, mixing feed, insuring wells and pumps were operational, and chopping ice on the watering tanks. Between chores he served as general contractor for the building of their new house.

The house was modest, vernacular in style, but exactly suited their needs. It stood toward the front of the farm, set back a logical distance from Digbert Road, a gravel road running past the house which led into town toward the east and to Herston, going west. Of Cream City brick construction, the new house was sturdy and easily maintained. The one hundred year old farmhouse it replaced had been replete with wildlife. Even with several cats around, mouse and rat droppings could be found in any cupboard or drawer, on every shelf and in every corner. Bats had taken up residence in the attic, at times swooping down into the kitchen. When a snake slithered its way through the pantry one day, presumably in pursuit of a bat or rodent, Phoebe mutinied, demanding something be done about their living quarters.

The back of the house had a southern exposure, sunlight streaming in to make the kitchen a warm and homey room. It was the hub, control central, with a large harvest table upon which were served three square meals a day. The table also accommodated canning and freezing operations, game-playing, puzzle projects, hair-trimming, sewing, pie-making and science experiments, as well as serious discussions and arguments. The rest of the house existed mostly as sleeping quarters, four bedrooms and a bath all upstairs. Books lined the large bookcase in the living room, the cupboards beneath bulging with puzzles and board games. A lonely television sat in the corner. The family gathered in front of it for occasional favorite programs but it was typically idle. Off the large kitchen on one end was a small office and, in the other direction, a laundry room, pantry, and second bathroom. An entry way and mudroom extended off the back of the house, a porch across the front.

Spring had come early. Winter wheat, planted in the

fall, would soon be ready to combine. Crops were in, the first signs of growth thrusting their green shoots upward toward the sun. The machinery was repaired and in good working order, the large fuel tank full, fences mended, feeder cattle fattening, brood cattle content with a pasture nursery full of calves, several new batches of piglets suckled their enormous sow mothers, the new house finally completed. He considered himself well on the way to becoming a successful farmer, sufficiently providing for a family of six.

Lily, the oldest child, had bloomed into a seventeen year old winsome beauty with dark hair and blue eyes like her mother. She was active, popular in school, and a stellar student with her sights set on college—also a great help on the farm, especially to Phoebe. After graduation the next spring, she would work away from home to earn college expenses for the fall. Though a gifted artist, she aspired to become a home economist, a farm kitchen the perfect lab in which to hone her skills. She, and her brother, Bart, the second oldest, raised a calf each year to exhibit at the county fair where they always won a blue or red ribbon. Lily was planning on entering the pie contest, hoping to woo the judges with her latest creation: Blackberry-Rhubarb Caramel Delight. Bart and Judd, the second boy, served as protempore judges, devouring whatever toothsome dish she put before them. The fact that they'd eat anything did not in any way diminish their accolades to Lily.

Bart, fifteen years old, was a sophomore in high school. Most times Phoebe couldn't tell him apart from his dad from the back. He also had his dad's taciturn nature. Bart would like to have been on the football team but farm chores and late summer crops to harvest prevented his participation. As a concession he went out for basketball but it was not his forte. His large, muscled, compact frame was less than agile on the court and he did more bench-warming than playing. The coach put him in for the last two minutes most games when they were ahead by a mile. He was a good son, gave his parents little grief, and worked hard on the farm alongside his father and brother. He wanted to be a farmer on Tuesdays and Sundays, a mechanical engineer the rest of the time.

Judd came next. Though only thirteen he was already a great help. Unlike his brother, he was tall, lean, dark-haired, and highly energetic. His passion was model airplanes and he wanted to be a commercial pilot some day, after he'd done a tour of duty in the Air Force—a subject Phoebe avoided. In addition to farm chores he had culled a suckling pig in early spring to raise and show at the county fair in early September. His pet turtle, Sheldon, had recently met his demise and Judd fervently transferred his reptile affections to the porcine. Prudence, a Hampshire hog, possessed the beauty befitting her name. Never was a shoat so nourished and preened. Her black body had a sheen you could see yourself reflected in and the white band across her shoulders was beyond spotless. The blue ribbon was sure to be hers if her hide wasn't scrubbed off by fair time. Once she'd reached her full grown weight Judd often let Jenny, his younger sister, ride on her back around the farmyard to entertain the family and give his pet pig some exercise. Much to the chagrin of Phoebe, Prudence was more likely to be found in the house than the hog pen—and often in Judd's bedroom.

Jenny, the trailer, was eight years younger than Judd. She had an angelic, almost fey personality. Very petite, she carried her weight, never complaining about the work she was able to do—and riding her pony, Tess, every free moment. For Christmas she'd gotten a new saddle and pair of cowboy boots. It was the pinnacle of her young life. The incontrovertible apple of her father's eye, she basked in his affections, at times the envy of her siblings. Blond curls cascaded down her back nearly to her waist, springing up and down as she rode Tess around the training ring. She had just finished kindergarten and couldn't wait for school to start in the fall when she'd be in first grade, riding the bus with her older brothers and sister.

In addition to hogs, cattle, Tess and Prudence, there were stray cats too numerous to name along with incessant batches of kittens, and Max, a golden retriever that stunk to high heaven but was affable and gentle. The children loved him but his heart and soul belonged to Curtis who had found him as a puppy, starved and abandoned, on Digbert Road and nursed him back to life. Max abided the attentions of the other children but, in Curtis' rare absences, Judd served as surrogate. Though worthless as a watchdog, a more devoted animal could not be found. Never leaving Curtis' side, he rode on the tractor, wagon, ATV or truck, walked the fields or farm yard with him, and at night slept on the floor next to his bed.

When Gaylan Morray realized Curtis and Phoebe Higgins had inherited the neighboring farm to the Simon's, his plan to have both farms thwarted, he considered it no more than a temporary setback. Patiently waiting, like a cat at the cupboard, he monitored the gradual improvement of the farmstead, plotting, like a military strategist, the most opportune time for transferring it to his greedy hands. It was the middle of June when evidence of his noisome scheming first showed up but, as the first clue, was not blatant enough for innocents to immediately suspect how corroded their daily lives would become. Bart, helping his dad with chores after school, made the discovery.

"Dad," Bart called out from the south pasture, when he saw his dad coming from the barn. "Come and look at this."

Curtis hopped off the tractor. Ordinarily he would not have been so easily diverted from his task but something in Bart's voice elicited a gut reaction.

"What is it, son?"

He needn't have asked. Near where Bart stood, adjacent to the watering tank, two brood cattle were lying on their sides. Instinct immediately kicked in.

"Get those other cattle away from the water tank," he ordered.

"Are they dead?" Bart questioned, as his father inspected the cattle then slowly rose to a standing position.

"Afraid so—go ask Mom for two clean Mason jars. I need to take samples of water to the county agent for testing—and tell her to call Doc Shepherd."

Bart was off and running before the finish of the sentence. The cattle, attempting to get to the water, began pressing forward and could easily have trampled Curtis but he picked up a large stick from the ground, prodding them back while trying to figure out a means for their containment until the water could be tested. Bart soon returned with the Mason jars. Curtis collected water from the tank then from the well, setting the jars on the ground under a nearby tree.

"The cattle won't be too happy being kept from their water supply. We'll need to do some refencing to hold them until we know for sure what's wrong. Go get the wire cutters will you? I think they're in the machine shed."

While Bart was gone, the vet arrived. Drake Shepherd, practicing veterinary medicine for years, was quite elderly—a tall man with deep set kindly eyes and a cool composure. Without asking any questions or even addressing Curtis, he knelt to examine the two dead animals.

"You can take the water samples I took back to your lab or I can take them to the county extension office for testing," Curtis offered.

The vet was silent as he continued poking, probing, lifting the eyelids of the dead animals, prying open their mouths—immense, blackish tongues lolling out.

"They've clearly been poisoned," Doc announced, concluding his inspection with a shake of his head.

"Is there a grass or some invasive plant around here that could be the source of the poison—or an insect?" Curtis innocently asked.

"No, I don't think so. I'll run some tests but I think its strychnine."

"Strychnine?"

"Yes, it comes from plants all right but is a crystalline alkaloid. Because it's colorless and odorless it's hard to detect. The symptoms usually begin appearing within fifteen minutes for pets and people but, with a large animal like this, it would take longer. By the time the symptoms are full blown enough to know what the problem is, it's too late. Don't know how it got into the water but I'm pretty sure that's what it is. You're wise to have separated the other cattle. Let me know if you see signs of trouble in any of them—restlessness, trouble breathing, twitching or even seizures—and I'll come back for another look. Curtis—someone had to put that in the water," Drake advised. "It didn't just happen naturally."

"But, who would do such a thing—and why?"

"I don't know but you better think on it. Someone is going to great lengths to pull a really cruel prank or has it in for you," Drake posited, removing his red baseball cap and scratching his head.

"I'll puzzle it out but I can't think of anyone," Curtis said more softly, as he saw Bart coming toward them.

"I'd give it some serious thought, Curtis," the vet advised privately, before leaving, nodding to Bart in passing.

"What did he say killed the cattle?"

"Doesn't know," Curtis lied. "This refencing is going to take several hours. We'll need to make sure the enclosure keeps the cattle away from this tank but allows them to get as close to the barn as possible. When we're finished we'll haul that other smaller trough from the barn out here, put it right up next to the fencing. You can run the hose from the tap in the barn so the cattle at least have some fresh water this evening. I'll have the water tested tomorrow then we'll know if it's just bad in the tank or also in the well. If it's not in the well we can let them water here again once the tank is cleaned thoroughly."

"If he doesn't know what it is what makes you so sure it's the water."

"Has to be. Can you carry on here while I go talk to Mom?"

"Sure thing, Dad," Bart solemnly responded.

By the time Curtis got up to the house it was full of kids, theirs along with several of the children's friends. He didn't want to say anything but always alert Phoebe noticed his look of concern and began to question him.

"What did the vet have to say? What's wrong with those cattle?"

"Something in the water upset them, I guess."

"You guess? They're more than upset if they're dead. Doesn't he know what killed them?"

"He's going to come back if we have any more problems with them. Can we talk about this later?" Curtis questioned, gesturing toward the kids.

"Sure," Phoebe responded, picking up on his meaning.

Someone messing with their feeder cattle would be bad enough but if their stock of brood cattle got depleted, it would take years to build up the herd again. At supper, Curtis was distracted, something clearly wrong. He had managed to convey to Bart ahead of time not to discuss the dead cattle, saying he didn't want the younger kids upset, but the absence of the usual bustle of conversation at the supper table only made the situation more awkward. Judd, having formed a question in his head, opened his mouth to ask but one look from his mother made him shut it. After dishes and clean-up the kids went to their respective rooms to do homework. It wasn't until Curtis and Phoebe were ready for bed that he told her everything about the situation.

"I still can't believe anyone would do something like that to our cattle, Phoebe. We don't have any enemies in town," Curtis concluded.

"Oh, no? How about Gaylan Morray?"

"As nasty as he is, I don't think he'd stoop this low."

"Oh, of course not," Phoebe sarcastically blurted. "He only ruined the Simons with similar pranks."

"Where did you hear that?"

"Mildred Sellerman told me. She used to be good friends with Jennifer Simons."

"But why? What does Morray want from us? We own our farm."

"It could be that acre of land or maybe he wants the mortgage on our farm. You know very well he tried to squeeze Jesse out of his farm through orchestrated mishaps. The stories of ruin in this county are replete with his *stoopings*."

Because it was a sleepless night, on Saturday morning Phoebe would like to have slept in, but the work wouldn't wait. It was still dark outside when she scrambled from bed. Curtis and Bart were already up, probably checking the cattle. She roused Judd then went down to the kitchen where she found Lily cutting up rhubarb for her next pie experiment. Smiling, she affectionately patted Lily on the back as she worked. Jenny, the sleepyhead of the family, was still in bed. Phoebe fixed breakfast as the first glimmers of morning light peaked through the windows. She was putting fresh biscuits on the table when Curtis and Bart came in from chores. Curtis didn't see Lily who had gone to the pantry.

"We counted two more cattle missing which, in the semi-dark, we couldn't find."

"Cattle are missing?" Lily inquired, emerging from the pantry.

"We'll find them when it gets lighter," Curtis offered, giving Bart a look.

Phoebe busied herself, absently filling serving dishes from the stove. The early birds of the family gathered at the kitchen table, sitting again in uncomfortable silence through the meal. Jenny straggled in as they were finishing.

"I'm going to the back pasture again to try to find the

two missing cattle now that it's lighter," Curtis announced, rising from the table.

"I'll come along," Bart offered.

"Me, too," Judd exclaimed.

"No, son, you need to help Mom with the garden this morning. We'll be back shortly and you can help us then."

Curtis and Bart got onto the three-wheeler and drove to the far reaches of the free-range pasture where they'd corralled the remaining cattle. It was now light enough to aid in their search and, in the brushy understory of the woods, they found two more cattle down—one dead, the other gasping for air then dying as they helplessly watched.

"What on earth is going on?" Bart asked.

"I'll check on the rest of the cattle while you take the ATV to the house to call Doc Shepherd, Bart. Ask him to come right away—and ask him if there's anything to be done for the other cattle—an antidote or precaution—in case any have drunk the water."

While Bart rode off Curtis looked over the rest of the cattle, thankfully finding none with the symptoms the vet had outlined. He was used to dealing with livestock maladies of all sorts but not poison. Thinking about what Phoebe had said the night before, he wondered if Gaylan Morray might have anything to do with his dead cattle. An inchoate thought, too distasteful to entertain, surfaced as Bart flew in on the ATV.

"Doc Shepherd can't come now," Bart solemnly announced, dismounting.

"Did he say when he could?"

"Let me rephrase that, Dad. He won't come—now or later."

"What do you mean *won't come*?"

"I asked him that and he said he couldn't say but that he wasn't in a position to come to help again."

"In a position—that's his job for Christ's sake."

Bart, unused to hearing his dad curse, stared at the

ground in front of him as though counting each blade of grass.

"What does he mean, Dad?" he finally asked.

Anger surfacing on his usually calm face, Curtis leapt onto the ATV and sped toward the house.

"We'll dispose of those dead cattle later," he called back, ignoring Bart's question. "Get the others fed."

By the time he reached the house, he was ready to explode in anger. Striding through the mudroom, he passed Phoebe, alone in the kitchen, grabbed the wall phone and called the vet.

"Drake, what is this about not being willing to come to the farm to inspect my cattle?"

"I just can't, Curtis. I hope you'll understand."

"Understand, hell. I understand that you've been our vet for ten years—and my father's before that. Where's your loyalty, man?"

"I'd like to help but I've been warned not to—my house, my practice, even my family is in jeopardy if I come to your farm."

"Warned by who?"

"I can't say—without the same penalties."

When Curtis hung up the phone his face was the color of a pomegranate. Phoebe handed him a glass of water, hoping to cool him down, but he threw it against the sink, shattering it.

"Stop that, Curtis. You know as well as I do who's responsible for this. You just refuse to believe it."

Phoebe urged the children to their chores when they came into the kitchen, drawn to the eye of the storm. There was no doubt in her mind where to lay the blame for their dead cattle. Why Curtis wouldn't believe it, she couldn't say, although he was notorious for avoiding confrontation. He did not ignore difficulties and could handle most but was often stubborn as to the cause. Some of their problems had been due to their ignorance as novice farmers but this was different. Their inexperience could not be blamed. Phoebe couldn't think of anyone on earth she hated—Gaylan Morray being the exception. Though not a complete miscreant she was not religious, but felt certain that if God existed he would certainly understand her loathing.

CHAPTER TWO

Farrowing hogs, newborn calves, as well as extensive refencing, kept Curtis busy for days. When next in town he casually inquired at the bank as to Gaylan Morray's whereabouts at the time of the poisoning, his alibi of being out of town, erasing suspicions. He was not successful in convincing Phoebe that Morray was not the subversive, however. No further problems immediately surfaced, they soon grew too busy to dwell on the matter and, over the next several weeks, her paranoia subsided. Late spring Phoebe planned her garden, deliberating as to the assistance she'd need.

School let out and the children were each assigned their summer chores. Judd and Bart had earlier cultivated the family garden, preparing the soil for seed. After poring over organic gardening magazines and journals all winter, Phoebe was quite ardent about trying a new approach, teaching Lily, Jenny, and the ever-reluctant Judd, the art of companion planting. Daily life became a whirlwind of activity as the summer days slid quickly past. Throughout June and into early July occasional signs of trouble surfaced but at first they didn't add up to anything more significant than typical farming mishaps.

Curtis and Bart refenced the portion of the pasture that had been gerrymandered, the brood cattle again able to drink from the tank by the well. Curtis tested the water in the tank and well on a daily basis with a kit acquired from the state office of agriculture. Thankfully, no more cattle died. The larger problem became their free ranging, occasionally straying into Jesse Tate's fields, trampling the corn, and evoking his anger.

"Curtis Higgins, ya keep yer damn cattle to yerself or I'll start shooting em. I've tried to be the neighborly sort but for crissake they're trompin my corn crop."

"I don't know how it happened," Curtis defended. "I'm sorry."

"What do ya mean ya don't know how they got out—the damn fence is down. I can see it plain as day. Ya need to keep it repaired."

"The fence is down all right but look how it's laying, Jesse—in, like it was torn down instead of out like it would be if trampled from inside by the cattle. It almost looks like someone intentionally tore down the fencing."

Jesse walked around the downed fencing, inspecting the way the fence posts lay on the ground with the barbed wire still strung between them.

"That's true enough I can see," he offered, professorially scratching his stubbly chin. After a lengthy deliberation, he drew his conclusions. "Someone's fooling with ya, I'd say. This looks a little too familiar. I'd watch ma back side if I was you."

"You think someone pulled down the fencing, don't you?"

"Suspicions—only suspicions. Think on it now for a spell and you'll know. You heard about the fencing problems at the Simon's farm and the same thing happened to me once. Meanwhile—keep those cattle out of my fields."

"It won't happen again, Jesse. I promise."

But it did happen again—twice in July alone. Jesse tried his best to be understanding but it took all the cajoling Curtis could manage to coax him into taking the incidents in good humor. Even seeing the tire tracks along the broken down fencerow Curtis had difficulty believing he was the victim of foul play. If the cattle weren't in Jesse's fields they were wandering down the gravel road past the house, getting into nettles and mustard that grew alongside in the ditches. Sometimes the downed fencing lay inward toward the pasture, occasionally outward, but always the barbed wire was intact.

The remaining cattle appeared particularly healthy that year and the hogs and feeder cattle were nearing their market weight already by the end of July. Curtis, who kept close tabs on his livestock, noticed a hog and a beef cattle missing. A thorough search through the pastures didn't reveal any dead animals so he decided to assume the animals had wandered off and died elsewhere. At times he thought he heard someone in the woods. Once, when he went to investigate, he found Pete Irving scrounging for firewood, raising suspicion for a time about his possible involvement in their problems. Twice, tools or equipment had been moved or misplaced in the barn. Thinking he or one of the children had been careless, he said nothing.

Every member of the family was engaged in the farm's operation. Bart was Curtis' right hand man. When Judd wasn't tending Prudence he worked alongside them, balking when relegated to what he considered women's work—the weeding of Phoebe's immense garden. Her ideas for companion planting proved to be very beneficial in terms of keeping weeds and troublesome insects at bay, however, and for that improvement Judd was happy. Phoebe supervised the canning and freezing but much of it fell to Lily. Jenny, still too young to be of great help, was often given the slack to pamper Tess and dream of a winning entry at the 4-H Horse and Pony Show in September.

It was hot, even for August, daily chores arduous in the intense heat. Curtis noticed his supply of feed corn depleting faster than expected—odd since he had stored more than usual. The granary stood behind the barn, right next to the pole barn and near the woods. Though he was careful not to drop corn when loading it into the wagon, sometimes the next day he'd find loose cobs on the ground. Still, he didn't make an issue of it, reminding himself to be more careful. The diesel smell up near the storage tank by the barn was easily accounted for by presuming it to be the result of Bart overfilling the tractor. When the smell persisted he inspected more closely, discovering a pinhole through which their fuel was slowly leaking. If undetected their supply of diesel fuel would have become depleted. The tank had rusted before, a pinhole the logical wear and tear that was all a part of farming. He got out the welder and a patch of metal, made the necessary repairs, and had the tank refilled. Eventually, accumulating evidence reached a critical mass, arousing his suspicions. Still unwilling to worry Phoebe, he said nothing. It wasn't until late August, just before school started, that an incident occurred too blatant to continue to deny they were the target of treachery.

"I'm going to run into town to get school supplies for the children," Phoebe announced at breakfast, as Jenny straggled into the kitchen. "School starts in a week and you kids need notebooks and other things the first day."

"Get me a three-ring binder will you, Mom—and a ream of college-rule paper?" Lily requested, handing her a list. "It's taken me three years but I'm getting the hang of how to organize my notes. With a three-ring binder I can use dividers to separate subjects instead of shuffling three or four different notebooks around."

"That's a good idea," Bart spoke up. "Get me one, too, will you?"

"Where are your lists, boys? Run upstairs and get them for me."

"I need a three-ring binder, too," Jenny chimed in, her mouth full of food.

"You don't need that in first grade," pronounced Lily.

"And, you'd better start practicing getting up in the morning if you're going to school. You're not in afternoon kindergarten any more," added Judd, getting up from the table to follow Bart upstairs.

"When the dishes are done could you please start on the sweet pickles, Lily," Phoebe requested. "Just get everything ready, wash the jars and pack the slices in ice. Use that large stainless steel bowl we use for popcorn. I'll help you when I get back. Jenny, you help Lily pick cucumbers before you start on that pony."

"She's not a pony, she's my sister," Jenny puckishly stated.

"Well that explains why you treat her better than your

real sister," Lily teased.

Phoebe never worried about leaving either Lily or Bart in charge at home since they were both prematurely responsible. All her children were trustworthy and respected each other, despite the occasional rivalry and fights typical of siblings. Driving to town, the morning sun's rays darting at her through the trees, she counted her blessings and not for the first time. She couldn't have asked for a lovelier or happier family. In town, at the Five and Dime, she bumped into Mr. Boardman, the eighty-five year old retired principal of the elementary school where she'd taught. She and several of the other young female teachers had been chased more than once around the desk of the old lech.

"How are you today, Mr. Boardman? Hot enough for you?"

"Hotter than Dutch love. Say—if you're not taken maybe I could have a go at you."

"Mr. Boardman, how you talk. Anyway, I've already been taken," Phoebe added definitively, flashing her wedding ring in his face and fighting a flush rising into her throat.

"I know that dream," Mr. Boardman lustily pronounced.

The blush on Phoebe's face deepened to crimson as she made her escape down the outer aisle of the store. Burying her nose in the kids' lists she quickly rounded up all the necessary supplies then, after checking to make sure Mr. Boardman had left, paid for her purchases at the front counter.

"Hey there, Phoebe," a familiar voice rang out, as she exited the store.

"Hi, Agnes. What brings you downtown?"

"What? You're the only one around here that shops?"

"Thought so," Phoebe laughed, giving Agnes a hug.

Agnes Warner was an artist that lived at the east edge of town on the way to Dirkville. She and Phoebe had met, quite accidentally, at a church bazaar. Neither of them went to church regularly but both had been drawn to the bazaar because of a well known water color artist that had contributed two paintings for the annual auction. Standing next to one another in the narthex admiring the paintings, they had started a conversation after several minutes that proved their common ground not only in art appreciation but many other aspects of life. Agnes was a relative new-comer to Between and a bit older, so their paths hadn't crossed before, though they'd gone to the same college. Concluding they were kindred spirits, they became friends.

"How is everything down on the farm?" Agnes asked.

"Fine, I guess. Farming has its problems but they seem to be escalating lately," Phoebe related, before telling Agnes of the incident with the cattle. "We suspect Morray may have his hand in it but no one else will implicate him."

"You've been asking the wrong people then. You wouldn't be the first to suffer at his hands. Not that many people talk to me around here, but I hear things. He's about as crafty and devious as they get. What will you do about it?"

"We've decided to go to the sheriff or the state police."

"Good luck with that—a waste of breath and time, I can assure you. It's suspected that Jeff Ritter, of the state police, is one of Morray's yes-men and Tagwell's in his pocket for sure, so I doubt you'd get very far with either of them."

"How come we always seem to be the last to hear of these things?"

"You think much too well of people and aren't looking for problems, I'd guess."

"Jesse Tate's had trouble with Morray but we never suspected we were on his *list* until the incident with the poisoned cattle. What would make a person like him so viciously mean and greedy?"

"I've heard he came from nothing—with lasting and extensive effect, apparently. Maggie McIntyre told me Shirley Ward told her that he grew up on a farm, hates farmers, and had a deprived childhood. Her parents knew his stepmother before she remarried, to Morray's father. A past like that could pretty well warp a person's sense of justice and decency if they let it. It appears he's hardest on farmers but occasionally I hear of people in town he's given the shaft to. How are the kids?"

"They're all fine. They'll be going back to school soon. Jenny is so excited about going into first grade she can hardly stand it."

"They'll show at the county fair again in September, I suppose."

"Lily will enter the pie contest. She and Bart have raised a calf and Judd singled out a pig in the spring. He's so wrapped up with his pet porker he hardly thinks of little else but winning that blue ribbon. I keep wondering if it's healthy to get so attached to any animal, much less a pig."

"I'm sure it's fine—a stage, if you will. I saw my kid's stages only in retrospect—the bane of parenthood, I'm afraid."

As Agnes was talking, out of the corner of her eye Phoebe saw Owen Morray's head poking out from around the corner of the Five and Dime just before Clyde pulled him back. Turning, she saw them get into their blue truck and drive down the street.

"Those two are almost as much of a problem as their dad," Agnes appraised, turning to watch them drive off, "but too stupid to operate on their own so you can be sure Morray's the one giving the orders. Gotta run. You be careful. Morray's no one to be trifled with. I haven't heard yet of anyone that outmaneuvered him. Why don't you stop over for a visit one of these days and we'll have a nice cup of tea together."

Leaving Agnes, Phoebe walked down Main Street to

the bakery. Whatever pastries her family usually had were homemade but she'd been too busy with the garden to bake and they were all getting rather tired of Lily's pies, not all of which turned out well. Perusing the clear glass convex case and tiered shelving, she looked for just the right family treat.

"Hi, Gladys," she sang as a middle-aged woman shuffled toward her.

Gladys, yet single, chocolate icing running down the front of her blue uniform, stood behind the counter without answering, one arm akimbo the other holding a rolling pin. Always with a stern demeanor, she looked like a prison matron waiting for you to get out of line so she could whack you. Her pocked, ruddy complexion greatly detracted from her looks, whose redemption solely depended upon a head of curly titian hair. Today, even that asset was obscured—a blue bandana partially concealing the lumps and bumps of curlers.

"I'll have that cake in the middle—white cake with coconut frosting is it?"

Gladys said nothing as she pulled a box down from the wall shelf behind her and, without divulging its flavor, hoisted the chosen cake into it. Visibly bored, she wound some string around the box then tied a knot and handed it over to Phoebe.

"Three bucks."

"All right. Here you are, Gladys. Have a nice day."

Phoebe thought about Gladys and Mr. Boardman as she made her way out of the store—one void of personality, the other totally outrageous. *Two more to add to the cast of local characters*, she mentally tallied.

Outside the bakery door she bumped into Mrs. Norma Wedgefield who, along with her husband, Walter, operated a neighboring farm several miles down Herston Road from Curtis and Phoebe. With her trusty wide-rimmed straw hat, stooped shoulders and chubby piano legs, Mrs. Wedgefield looked like a dolmen. Phoebe knew her only casually, and saw her very infrequently, so decided to keep things light and not mention their recent difficulties. Norma was a rather giddy sort, the obvious compensation of a woman married to a domineering man. Phoebe suspected she wouldn't know trouble if it looked her in the eye. The Wedgefield farm was small, with rocky soil. It had been difficult to eke out a living on it so Phoebe doubted they had experienced Gaylan Morray covetous maneuverings. They talked in front of the bakery for some time about the weather, their children, the low market prices then the weather again, walking slowly down the street to their parked cars, where they parted.

A mile from the house, engrossed in trying to sort out her inane conversation with Norma, happy her marriage was a true partnership, Phoebe was startled into the moment by a truck roaring down Digbert Road toward her—dust swirling behind it. The driver was taking his half of the road from the center and didn't appear to see her. At the last moment the truck swerved over to the right, narrowly averting an accident. The truck was blue and Phoebe thought she saw Clyde and Owen Morray in it as it passed but, focused on trying to keep control of her car, couldn't get a good look. By the time she could dust obstructed her view. When she got home Lily and Jenny were sitting at the kitchen table playing cat's cradle, the deafening blare of the radio in the background. The huge stainless steel bowl, filled to the brim with iced cucumber slices, sat on the counter by the sink. Phoebe turned down the radio then laid the school supplies on the table. She had just begun showing them to Lily and Jenny when they heard the scream. It was most certainly Judd.

With Lily and Jenny at her heels, Phoebe ran toward the barn, the pulse of fear beating in her chest. Judd was no where in sight. Not until they heard him crying did they realize the sound was coming from the direction of Prudence's pen behind the barn. They reached Judd concurrent with Curtis and Bart to find Max, standing outside the fence, and Judd sitting in the grass inside the pen holding the head of Prudence in his lap. Prudence's belly had been slit wide open, her guts flowing out onto the ground at Judd's feet. Curtis leaped over the fence, tore Judd away from the dead pig and handed him over the fence to Phoebe in one fluid movement. She held his heaving body against her chest for several minutes as they all stood aghast looking at the scene. Then, urging Jenny and Lily in front of her and holding Judd's hand, she piloted them toward the house.

"Now, will you do something?" she screamed at Curtis, over her shoulder.

Curtis was too stunned at first to move or say anything. He called to Max who came to stand loyally at his side. By the time he'd composed himself enough to respond, Phoebe was half-way to the house.

"What does she mean?" Bart asked. "Did someone do this deliberately?"

"It would appear so," Curtis numbly responded. "Judd sure didn't do it and pigs don't commit suicide."

"Who do you think did this?" Bart asked his dad.

"We don't know. Anyway, I want you to stay out of it. It doesn't concern you."

"If it concerns Judd, it concerns me. Are the dead cattle a part of all this?"

"Stay out of it."

"Dad, aren't we already involved? That was Judd's pet."

"Let me handle this, Bart. Help me take care of that pig, will you?"

"Why can't you tell me what's going on?"

"Your mother and I aren't sure what's going on, so we're not about to involve you kids. End of argument. I'll be right back. Go get the tractor."

Bart wanted answers but knew he wouldn't get any. Obediently, he headed toward the pole barn to get the tractor.

It was obvious to Curtis that the guilty party had to have come from the woods behind the barn. He walked to the edge of the farm then into the woods with Max at his heels. Slipping on the waxy pine needles, he made his way through the trees to a deeply rutted dirt road. Max became quite anxious, running around sniffing the ground and barking. Sure enough, there were fresh tire tracks.

By the time he returned to the barnyard Bart was there with the tractor. At his father's direction, Bart lowered the bucket to the ground near the pig. Together they managed to roll, push or shove the pig into it then scoop up the entrails with a shovel. Hoisting the immense pig into the air, Curtis turned the tractor and drove to the field on the other side of the barn. He wasn't sure whether to go ahead and bury her, getting her out of Judd's sight, or wait to see if his son wanted some part in her burial. He left the pig in the bucket, joined Bart and, together, they walked silently to the house.

"How's Judd?" Curtis inquired, as they entered the kitchen.

"He's upstairs crying his eyes out," Phoebe responded. "First Sheldon dies, now this. Go to him, will you, Bart. He could use a friend right now. What a mean prank," she offered, glancing at Curtis.

"Prank? You think it's a prank?" Bart blurted.

"Maybe you boys can go fishing later—as a distraction," Phoebe offered, ignoring his question.

Bart left in a huff to go upstairs, feeling like a small child. It was upsetting that his parents didn't trust him enough to tell him what was going on. *Maybe they don't know either*, his thoughts defended.

"Jenny and Lily, get this stuff off the table and put some lunch together will you? Whatever you'd like to fix is fine. There's sandwich meat in the fridge, fresh bread in the pantry, and a coconut cake in that bakery box. I was saving it for supper but I think we'll have it for lunch instead. Dad and I need to talk."

"You don't really believe it was just a prank, do you?" Curtis began, once they were behind closed doors.

"No, of course not but I don't want the kids to know."

"I don't know how long we can keep things from Bart. Since he was witness to the poisoning of the cattle, too, he's asking a lot of questions. I found fresh tire tracks near the woods. I can't believe someone did this and that it could have happened virtually under our noses. Bart, Judd and I were working in the back pasture when we heard Max barking. At first, I assumed he'd treed a squirrel but it sounded like he was up by the barn. It wasn't like him to leave us and go off on his own so, when he kept barking, I sent Judd to investigate. I should have gone myself."

"You did what you thought best, that's all," Phoebe consoled.

"Who would do this, Phoebe?"

"I have a pretty good idea and so should you."

"I guess I do," he reluctantly conceded. "But we have no proof."

"I didn't think much of it at the time but I saw Owen and Clyde Morray in town, snooping around the Five and Dime. I think they overheard me talking to Agnes about Judd's prize pig. They nearly ran me off Digbert Road when I was coming back from town," Phoebe offered. "It couldn't have been more than ten minutes later we heard Judd scream."

"We can't prove that it was them. It's our word against theirs and you know how that would go."

"You know as well as I do that they did this—and on Gaylan Morray's orders. I'd have to say that sneakiness might be the one thing those blithering idiots excel in. The question is—what do we do about it?"

Curtis solemnly nodded, marching orders received. Within the hour he had showered, put on clean clothes, and was headed for town—to the bank, to be precise.

"Are you responsible for the problems on our farm?" Curtis fired at Gaylan Morray, bursting into his office.

"What problems?"

"You know very well what problems."

"I don't know what you're talking about and if you can't change to a more civil tone, please leave my bank."

"I'm going to the sheriff—to have him investigate. Killing cattle is one thing but that pig was my youngest son's beloved pet."

"What happened to the pig?" Morray disingenuously offered.

Curtis didn't answer. Turning on his heels, he rushed from the bank, without seeing Morray pick up his phone, then drove to the sheriff's office.

When Curtis arrived at the County Sheriff's office, Sheriff Tagwell was on the phone. Soon he hung up the receiver and strode from his office, his vast beer belly preceding him. Curtis found himself mentally reviewing local gossip about the man advancing toward him. It was hard to picture him with any woman, much less having sex, but years earlier an incident had occurred that was the scandal of the town. Tagwell had apparently arranged a *meeting* with one of the women from the house out by the L & W tracks early one afternoon when he was supposed to be on duty. Not wishing to be found out, he drove them in his squad car to an isolated spot along Bullfrog Creek. He parked and, with the meter running on Dottie's favors, wasted no time in initiating sex. Unknown to him, in pulling down his trousers his knee hit the button of his radio dispatch unit, turning it on. While he made lurid comments, enjoying unabashed, passionate carnal relief, his deputy and a couple of his loitering friends listened in back at the office, boisterously hooting. The office secretary, often a victim of sexual harassment by the sheriff, also secretly listened in then told everyone she knew. When the scandal became full blown she used the opportunity to file a law suit against the sheriff. It didn't end well. Her sullied reputation fabricated, she was fired for insubordination—the disgrace driving her from town.

"Sheriff Tagwell, my son's pet pig has been killed—its stomach slashed open."

"Cut it on a fence wire, did it?"

"No, not a fence wire. Someone did it for her."

"Someone slit her belly? Who do you think mighta done it?"

"I don't have any proof but I think Gaylan Morray did it or, most likely had it done by one of his mutant sons."

"You don't really believe that? What reason would he have for killin' yer pig?"

"I expect you to help me figure out who did this. Several of my cattle were poisoned earlier in the summer as well."

"Poisoned, you say? Are ya sure it was poison?"

"Yes, I'm sure. Doc Shepherd said it was strychnine. Will you come or not?"

"Well, I'll come out this afternoon and have a look see—see if there's any evidence of foul play."

"There's a dead pig with its belly slashed open. Isn't that enough evidence of foul play for you? You need to take a cast of those fresh tire tracks in the woods and compare them with the tires on Clyde and Owen Morray's truck. My wife saw them driving away from our farm just moments before we discovered the slaughtered pig."

"Well, I'll have a look see."

"See you sometime this afternoon then?"

"I'll be there quick as I can. I've gotta lot of things to do here first," he said, yawning, absently scratching his groin.

Curtis started to get an image of all they might be up against as he drove home but wouldn't allow it into full focus. *If the sheriff is as indifferent as he seems, we're probably on our own,* he concluded. At home, he conveyed to Phoebe first his conversation with Morray then the sheriff.

"Why on earth did you bother with the sheriff? Agnes told me it's well known he's in cahoots with Morray."

"I was supposed to already know that? Maybe she's wrong. It's his duty to check these things out."

The sheriff didn't come that afternoon, or the next. He never came to investigate. The pig was ceremonially buried, Judd finally consoled, and life went on.

School started, the usual schedules prevailed, and things returned to normal for a time. Lily, a senior, relished the status that came with being on top of the heap. Bart enjoyed his studies, especially math, and, knowing he'd never excel in the sport, notified the coach that he would not be on the basketball team. He thought he might like to go out for wrestling when the season rolled around. Judd got immediately involved in middle school student council, enjoying a leadership role, and was voted class treasurer. Jenny, finally achieving her short term goal of being a first grader, was content to ride the bus with her siblings, otherwise focusing her entire attention on the training of Tess.

The county fair they always looked forward to participating in became the next disappointment. All Lily's pie making practice was for naught. She didn't win a prize because the judges, wives of several businessmen in town, disqualified her for using too many ingredients—not only a previously unknown rule but a totally arbitrary and capricious decision. She and Bart also did not win a ribbon, of any color, for their calf, Bonnie they'd so lovingly nurtured. Judd, his wounds still fresh, couldn't stand to be anywhere near the hog pens and hung out around the grandstand or rides most of the time. The lackluster fair lost its appeal after the first two days and they all stayed home for its duration.

Early September the whole family watched excitedly as Jenny and Tess won best of class at the 4-H Horse and Pony Show. Their reprieve from problems, however, was ephemeral. Two weeks later, after the kids had left for school, Vincent DeMar called from the bank to tell Phoebe she was overdrawn and needed to come in to straighten things out. Phoebe thought it odd that her account was overdrawn because she had only written three checks and there had been plenty of money in the account to cover the total. Suspecting another ruse by Gaylan Morray to get her to sign the papers selling their acre, she got dressed then put some lunch together. She'd rather have been boiled in oil than go to the bank and risk seeing *him* but, if by any chance her account had problems, she also didn't want to jeopardize their standing, giving him ammunition to use against them.

"I've got to go to the bank," she told Curtis over lunch. "They say I'm overdrawn."

"How can that be? I just put five thousand in your household account last week. Have you been on a shopping spree, Phoebe?" Curtis teased.

"You know I haven't," she defensively replied. "I've only written three checks—small ones."

"Well, go on in and see what all the fuss is about. It's probably a misunderstanding. Want me to go with you?"

"No, you have enough to do. I'll handle it."

"Well all right but I'd try to avoid Morray. You have a way of ruffling his feathers," Curtis commented, carrying his dishes to the sink.

"Really?" Phoebe questioned, with a mischievous sparkle in her eye.

"That wasn't a compliment. I'd better get back to work. That corn is just about ready to harvest—won't be another week."

"I do wish we'd change banks. I hate going in there."

"We've talked about this before," Curtis shot back, as he left for the barn.

Phoebe tried to reason out what the problem might be, as she drove to town. Simple accounting had never been a problem for her. Once in town she had to wait in line on Oak Street with the other cars while Zelma Hutchison, Gaylan Morray's half-sister, backed her car from the driveway out onto the busy street. If anyone honked she'd immediately seize up, get out of her car in a huff, and hurl curses at them, further delaying traffic. "You know I back out of my driveway every morning at this time so quit honking your damn horns." Possessing the same sense of entitlement as her half-brother, she threw her weight around town like a wrecking ball.

She was even shorter than Gaylan—her spherical frame apparently an inherited paternal trait. Her red dyed hair, more like deep pink, was piled atop her head and ratted like a mound of cotton candy, transparent in the sunlight. Her makeup was so thick it could only have been applied with a trowel. The corset, she was never without, so inhibited her chest cavity that she breathed in short pants. In her company you found yourself taking deep breaths on her behalf. Her dress fit like a doublet, her large bosom pushed up to her chin, a slit of cavernous cleavage extending from the ruff around her neck. With a crown of reddish hair, overly made up face, and enlarged chest, added to her bellicose personality, she might have been mistaken for Carroll's Queen of Hearts.

Thomas, her husband, had run his own accounting firm before having a fatal heart attack. He left her dripping with money and as sole custodian of their dog, Hoover, who followed her everywhere, running behind the huge, square, white Lincoln Continental and barking. If he failed to follow her home, which he often did, she'd call whatever establishment she'd last visited, have him put on the phone, and order him home.

At least half intoxicated most of the time, she routinely crashed her car into those parked or menacingly aimed it at timorous pedestrians as though for target practice. One of the few people to venture out of Between, she frequently drove to Dirkville or Herston to go shopping. She was a shopaholic, her house a grossly over-furnished obstacle course stuffed to overflowing with items purchased on endless shopping forays. In an ongoing attempt to achieve a fashion look other than dumpy, she never wore the same outfit twice. The entire third floor of her immense house, converted to a walk-in closet, bulged with dresses, suits, and accessories.

Sometimes, though rarely, her friend Fiona Partridge rode with her. Fiona was the town scold. She didn't cotton to redemption, passing judgment on everyone. In fact, those who escaped her acrid assessments felt positively shunned. Zelma was a terrible driver and the harrowing car rides must surely have been the cause of Fiona's nervous tic. Despite having difficulty keeping the car on the right side of the road, Zelma drove at top speed along the back, curving roads leading to Dirkville or Herston instead of the main highway. Once there, her elevated position in life less known, her more amenable side surfaced for the short term. Sanctioning red lights as only for others, she'd stop at them then proceed into the intersection when no cars were coming—or were coming too slowly. The rookie cop that once stopped her, asking for her license, gave her a ticket. She tore it up in front of the Dirk County judge, demanding, and getting, it thrown out as well as the immediate dismissal of the policeman. After that she stayed off the main streets of Dirkville and Herston, finding her way to various businesses by going through connecting strip mall parking lots.

Phoebe missed the turn into the bank parking lot thinking of Zelma, and had to go around the block. Noting Morray's Jaguar in its usual spot in the back, a shudder ran up her spine. Whenever she saw Morray's silver Jaguar going down the street, unable to see him hunkered down behind tinted windows, it looked like a phantom must be driving it. She had often wondered how he managed to reach the steering wheel with his short arms, much less see over it. After parking the car she walked through the front door of the bank building and headed toward Vincent, standing behind the counter. Vincent said nothing, motioning with his head to direct her attention across the lobby where Morray stood by the door to his office tapping the face of his pocket watch like he was the Mad Hatter, she, late for an appointment.

"Come into my office, Mrs. Higgins," he ordered, stuffing the watch and chain into the fob of his trousers.

"Vincent called me. What is this about my account being overdrawn?" Phoebe asked, as she crossed the lobby."

"Have a seat," he commanded, closing the door once she'd entered his office.

"According to my bookkeeping everything is in perfect order."

"Yes, yes, well—I just talked to the accountant and it appears that it was our mistake—an oversight. Your account is fine for the moment but you need to be very careful."

"I am careful. That's why I knew my account wasn't overdrawn."

"It could be overdrawn at any moment, however, if you know what I mean."

"No, I don't know what you mean. How can our account be overdrawn if I haven't overdrawn it?"

"Well, the bank owns all of the accounts, technically, and we wouldn't want any of them in poor stead."

"You don't own our money, either technically or any other way."

"Well, maybe *technically* was the wrong word. But things happen, accounts get mixed up, money mislaid, etc., etc."

"You listen to me Gaylan Morray. You mislay any of our money and there'll be hell to pay," Phoebe pronounced, rising from her seat.

"Lower your voice, Mrs. Higgins," he demanded, with insolence. "I was merely reminding you the bank is here for your convenience and we may not want to continue serving in that capacity for customers who are—difficult, uncooperative."

"Don't you think I'd use another bank if there was

one? It would be tempting to drive all the way to Herston or Dirkville for our banking needs if I could be certain your fingers weren't in those pies as well. It's that acre of land again, isn't it? I told you I'll sign those papers only the day hell freezes over and that is my final word. Now, are we through here? I have work to do."

"That's your final word, is it?"

"My final word and the last time I'll discuss it with you. We know you're responsible for the incidents at our farm and there better not be any more. And, you meddle with our accounts in any way and you'll find yourself slapped with a lawsuit faster than you can scream *sheriff.*"

"You've made your choice."

"Made my choice—what does that mean?" Phoebe asked, the needle on her concern meter suddenly moving toward the danger zone.

"Only that you've made your choice—not to sell," he quickly added, with a jerk of his head.

Striding through the lobby, Phoebe looked toward Vincent DeMar, who immediately bent his head and started counting bills. He seemed an innocent enough man but, since he'd been the one to call her, she had to wonder at his involvement.

Before going home Phoebe stopped at the feed mill for some supplies. It was a hot autumn day so she parked in the shade at the side of the mill then walked around to the front. A man pulled up alongside the curb next to her in a blue sedan. The cotton shirt he wore had become sheer with sweat in the overheated car, the fabric pressed against his chest hairs. He wore dark glasses tinted green that concealed his eyes and were perched on his thin nose like a bird on a wire. A baseball cap crowned his head, leaving large ears as his only defining feature.

"Excuse me, Ma'am. Can you tell me how to get to Elm Street? I guess I'm lost," he casually stated, looking her over as though tallying her flaws.

You'd have to be brain dead to get lost in Between,

Phoebe's thoughts responded. "Just turn left at the next corner, go down a block and take a right. That's Elm Street," she politely managed.

"Thanks," the stranger intoned, driving slowly away.

Phoebe thought the man looked familiar but, distracted by her mission, gave it no further thought. Inside the feed mill she purchased some bales of straw for the garden, arranged for Curtis to pick them up the next day, picked out a new rake, and went berserk in the flower bulb section.

After loading her parcels into the car, she drove down Main Street toward Digbert Road. The car the stranger drove was parked in front of the Sunset Bar and Grill, nowhere near Elm Street. Phoebe looked at the license tag, observing that it was not from Dirk County. Deciding the man had found whatever he was looking for, and was having a brew or sandwich before leaving town, she turned right and drove on home.

The kids were back from school and Curtis was out in the field when she arrived. The opportunity to discuss the situation at the bank didn't occur until after supper, when the kids were in bed and she and Curtis were sitting on the front porch together. As she related the details, Curtis tried to calm her but to no avail. While minimizing her concerns, his were growing exponentially. By the time they went to bed, after much debate, it was mutually decided, however naively, that something needed to be done about the threats from Morray and it was time to pay a visit to an attorney.

The next morning, after the kids had caught the bus to school, Phoebe collected her thoughts. Baking was meditative so she mixed up a batch of peanut butter cookies and was just pulling the last sheet full from the oven, when Curtis returned from chores, announcing he was ready to clean up and get ready to go to town.

Archie Litchfield, not known for his rectitude, was a large man, eclipsing everything else in his presence. Phoebe and Curtis didn't know him personally and had never seen him before but, as the only lawyer's name they'd heard, had arranged an appointment. He didn't bother to greet them as they were shown into his dark and dusky office by an ancient receptionist. The office décor included two dingy plastic plants covered with dust in orange pots cringing in the far corners of the room. One of the plants still had sparkly Christmas garland strung around it. Brown and gold sculptured carpet covered the floor and languid orange drapes hung tentatively at the small window.

Without looking up, Litchfield motioned to the two wooden side chairs positioned in front of his desk with a wave of his arm. When the couple stayed standing, staring at his tonsured head, he raised it enough to get a moiled look at them and Phoebe impulsively stepped back in surprise. Litchfield's large curved nose drooped down to meet pouting lips and flapping jowls, like he suffered from Bell's palsy.

"What can I do fer ya?" he asked, with a lazy tongue, not bothering to shake the hand Curtis extended toward him.

"We've been having some difficult..."

"Leave it alone—that's my advice," he mumbled, in an irascible tone.

"But, you..."

"I said, leave it alone," Litchfield intoned, standing to face them squarely but completely overlooking them. He was taller than his density looked seated. His suit fit him like tights on a weight lifter. Nonchalantly extending his arms out to the side, he stretched then sat back down with a thud, the compromised chair loudly creaking.

"How can you advise us when you don't even know what the difficulties are?"

"I think he knows very well what the difficulties are," Phoebe cut in. "We're wasting our time here, Curtis."

"I'd take the lady's counsel. Here's some free advice

for ya. Mind yer own damn business and be happy things have been going so well," he admonished, abstracting his attention.

Burying his manatee nose in the paperwork on his desk, he dismissively waved his hand toward the door—audience over. It was clear Litchfield was just another player on Morray's team of moral ambivalents.

"Not only the sheriff but the lawyers, judge, mayor, and half, if not all, of the town, are in Morray's palm," Phoebe complained, as they drove home.

"I guess I should have tried harder to get our point across with Litchfield but he didn't even pretend to care. I believe he's right though—we'd better let sleeping dogs lie," Curtis said, gesturing toward Max, asleep on the seat. "It's apparent that no one is going to side with us. Let's just get the crops in and go on about our business as usual."

"Unfortunately, I don't know what else we can do," Phoebe conceded. "With the harvest in, once the winter wheat is planted, we'll be in good shape for next spring and can rest a bit—keep a closer eye on things, be ready if anything else happens. I worry about the kids, though."

"Morray wouldn't harm the children, would he?" blurted Curtis, fending off evil thoughts swirling through his head.

"I wouldn't put anything past him. You can't sell that land to him, even if you might want to, Curtis. You need my signature."

"I know. Anyway, I don't want to sell either. I haven't entirely given up on the idea of an office building on that acre some day."

When they got home Virginia Small's green Ford station wagon was in the driveway and she was sitting on the porch, her three small children running about the yard and manhandling the new batch of kittens. Max jumped down from the truck and joined the chase. The Smalls lived about three miles away, on the road leading to Herston.

Virginia's oldest child was the same age as Phoebe's youngest and they'd met at a P.T.A. meeting. Despite their difference in age, the two women had become close friends. Curtis and Phoebe, and Virginia and her husband, Kenneth, sometimes socialized. The Smalls didn't farm but otherwise had much in common with Curtis and Phoebe—primarily their commitment to family and a meaningful way of life in the country. Virginia's cousin, Ted Whartley, was a state policeman and Phoebe briefly entertained the idea of asking her to see if he'd investigate their situation but was reluctant to drag anyone else into their personal affairs, convinced there was nothing to be done at the state or any other level.

"Hi Phoebe—Curtis," Virginia called, as they got out of the car.

"Hi, Virginia. What brings you over here today?"

"I picked up Rachael at school—and planned on bringing Jenny as well but she'd already gotten on the bus. I thought the kids might like to see the kittens—and I've missed you—haven't seen you for a few weeks, Phoebe."

"Well, since you only want to visit Phoebe, I'll get busy with chores," Curtis teased.

"I've missed you too, Curtis," Virginia conceded.

Curtis left to change his clothes then feed the livestock. Virginia seemed reluctant to go in the house but Phoebe coaxed her with the offer of a cup of tea. The children were busy playing in the yard as the women sat at the kitchen table. It was apparent this was not a typical visit. Virginia was visibly agitated.

"Is there anything wrong, Virginia?" Phoebe asked, pouring the tea.

Before she could answer, the door flew open and all the kids, including Virginia's, burst into the kitchen. Phoebe handed around a plate of the peanut butter cookies she'd made that morning then poured lemonade for everyone.

"Bart, Judd and Lily, go do your homework please, so Virginia and I can visit. Jenny, run upstairs and change your clothes before you go play with Rachael and the other kids." Once the kids were gone from the room, Phoebe sat down across from Virginia. "Well?"

"I can't talk here. Come outside with me for a minute."

"Why can't you talk here?"

"Come outside with me," Virginia repeated, more earnestly.

Phoebe had never seen Virginia, a calm, placid woman, so upset. She led the way to the back door. When they were outside, Virginia took Phoebe's elbow and led them farther away from the house toward the hog pens, apparently deemed a more preferable site for conversation, notwithstanding the smell.

"You need to be careful, Phoebe. Things are going on you don't know anything about—things that affect you."

"What kinds of things?"

"Things—that's all. Tomorrow morning, at ten o'clock, I want you to drive to Bishop's Woods—you know, that woods north of our house. I'll meet you there—at the entrance sign. Don't tell anyone you're coming, not even Curtis—promise?"

"What are you talking about? What's going on?"

Virginia didn't immediately answer as Rachael and Jenny ran past them toward the stable, presumably to see Tess.

"I can't tell you right now."

"But, I don't know if..."

"Just come—and don't tell a soul."

"All right—but why all the mystery?"

"Just promise me you'll come. You have to."

"All right, I'll be there. Geez, Virginia! You're scaring the hell out of me. Hey, there, you kids get away from that hog pen," Phoebe yelled, as Virginia's two youngest kids jumped off the fence and scattered.

"They're just looking at the big hogs," Virginia quietly defended.

"That's fine but what if one or both of them fell in?"

"The hogs wouldn't hurt them, surely?"

"Oh, wouldn't they? They probably wouldn't attack but they're so huge they could easily crush a child—and if knocked senseless, the hogs would move right in. They're well-fed but they'd eat anything if hungry enough—they're carnivorous—and can be quite malicious."

"Oh, oh, my God!" Virginia stammered, rounding up her two children. "I had no idea hogs were like that."

Jenny and Rachael came from the stable, intending to go into the house to play but Virginia had other plans.

"I'm sorry, Phoebe, but we need to go—it's not the hogs. Jenny, maybe you can come over to play with Rachael this weekend. You'll see each other at school tomorrow. See you in the morning, Phoebe," she concluded, urging her kids toward the car.

"What's going on in the morning?" Curtis asked, coming up behind Phoebe.

"Oh, I'm going to meet—I mean go over to Virginia's for coffee about ten. Is there anything you need me for here about that time?"

"No, I'm sure I'll manage. You need to see friends more often. And I know Virginia is a good friend. Is anything the matter? You seem upset."

"No, I'm fine."

"Can I go over to Rachael's this weekend, Mommy?" Jenny queried.

"We'll see. It might have to wait for another weekend."

"When, Mommy?"

"Soon, Jenny, soon. Why don't we go do some reading together before I start supper?"

"Nice diversion," Curtis whispered in her ear. "That wouldn't work on me, you know," he added, softly pinching her behind.

Phoebe was up well before dawn the next morning. It was her favorite part of the day. Sipping tea in peace and quiet, deep in thought, she watched in anticipation as the darkness subsided, the light slowly revealing first the outlines of the trees then their entirety. Life often seemed uncertain, a mystery, and she clung to moments she knew could be counted on, like the sun coming up each day. As the birds began chirping their morning greetings, she wondered what Virginia wanted, what she had to tell her, fear gurgling within.

"You're up awfully early," Curtis stated, interrupting her interlude.

"I have a lot to get done before I'll be able to go over to Virginia's guilt-free."

"You do too much. Sometimes I wish I'd chosen an easier life—for your sake."

"Have I ever complained?"

"Never. See you at breakfast," he declared, stooping to kiss her cheek.

Phoebe was able to enjoy a second cup of tea, and assure herself another day had arrived, before the kids converged on the kitchen, rattling lunch boxes and banging the refrigerator door. While she was busy making her family breakfast, the phone rang.

"You're coming aren't you?"

"Yes, Virginia, I'll be there," Phoebe answered, hanging up the phone.

"Was that Virginia?" asked Curtis, coming through the back door. He washed his hands at the kitchen sink, questioning her as he turned to the table. "You'll see her in a couple of hours. What's the urgency?"

"No urgency. She was just reminding me to bring my peanut butter cookie recipe," Phoebe lied. "She's furnishing some of the treats for the Halloween party at school."

With the kids off to school and Curtis back out in the fields, she took her shower then climbed into the car. The drive to Bishop's Woods would only take about fifteen minutes, time enough to allow her to speculate on every conceivable reason for the meeting. The one revealed would not be among them. She turned onto the road leading to the woods and soon saw the sign. When she stopped, confused at not finding Virginia, her friend ran up to the car and climbed into the passenger's seat.

"Goodness, Virginia. You scared me."

"Drive up the road farther, Phoebe."

"That's enough now, Virginia. I'm not moving another inch until you tell me what's going on."

"Please, Phoebe. Just drive on a little farther. It will all come to light in a few minutes."

"Have you arranged to have me murdered by someone? You don't work for Gaylan Morray do you, only masquerading as my friend?"

"Phoebe, for heaven's sake," Virginia reprimanded, as Phoebe shifted out of park and slowly drove forward.

"Stop here," Virginia suddenly commanded.

Phoebe stopped the car and, at Virginia's insistence, got out. Virginia took her arm and they'd walked into the woods about thirty feet when a man stepped from behind a large tree.

"Good lord, who are you? You about gave me a heart attack," Phoebe accused, glaring at the bald man in green tinted sunglasses.

"This is my cousin, Ted Whartley. You met him a couple of years ago when he stopped over at the house while you were there. He's an undercover agent for the state police," Virginia explained, as Phoebe stared past him at the blue sedan parked in the woods. "He has overheard and knows about things that greatly concern you— Curtis as well, of course, but especially you."

Phoebe turned her attention to Ted, recognizing him as the man that had stopped her to ask directions in front of the feed mill. She waited for him to start talking, concern growing, clueless as to what he might possibly say. The whole situation was too surreal for words. As with most

people in the presence of the police, her mind quickly
sorted through her recent behavior with scrutiny.

"You stopped me to ask directions in front of the mill
in Between one day, didn't you?"

"Yes. I didn't really need directions. I noticed someone following you and feared you might be in some danger, so I intervened in case they had ill intentions."

"Who was following me?"

"Gaylan Morray's two sons. I don't know what they
were up to but it looked like no good, as usual."

"You know them?"

"Let's just say I know of them."

"What were you doing in Between?"

"What I tell you must be held in strict confidence. Virginia says I can trust you."

"Yes, you can."

"I've been working undercover in Dirk County for
over two years now. I don't believe anyone knows who I
am or why I'm around. They certainly don't know that
I'm Virginia's cousin. If anyone asks, I tell them I'm an
insurance agent from south of here and have a great aunt
near Dirkville that I visit from time to time, hoping it
might then seem logical I'd be going through Between
now and then. Very few have asked my name and I never
offer it—not my real name anyway."

"Get to the point, Ted. What has any of this to do with
me? What is your undercover investigation about?"

"There are things going on in Between and Dirk
County that you know nothing about—and didn't need to
know anything about. I would have left it at that if not for
a conversation I overheard."

"What things?"

"The state police are interested in drug dealings that
are going on in the county, centered in Between. We now
know for sure who's involved and soon a sting operation
will be set up by the feds. Our investigations have revealed the problem to be widespread—most of the movers

and shakers of the county implicated."

"Illegal drugs are being sold here?"

It was common knowledge wife swapping was prevalent in Between. At private gatherings, car keys were tossed into a hat early in the evening then drawn at random at the close of the party to determine who the partners for the night were to be. Unwilling players were not welcomed back. Phoebe had heard about it, as well as rumors of other outlandish behavior in town, but had never suspected anything like drug dealing.

"Not only sold. We have evidence that a sophisticated system has been set up for bringing drugs into the county, usually under cover of darkness but often in broad daylight, and either via the French River or, in some cases, by the truckload. It's even suspected the train that stops here every Tuesday is carrying drugs. The drugs are then repackaged and sold in cities all over the state—and in other states. The FBI is going to be involved as soon as my investigation is completed, but the chief agent wants all the evidence collected before bringing them into it so there are no screw-ups."

"I can hardly believe it. Who is the head of it all? Never mind, I don't want to know."

"But that's the point. You do want to know. The ring leaders are the same group of men associated with the bank. It includes Morray, of course, but also the judge, lawyers, city officials, businessmen and the sheriff—even several of the state police are implicated. Hewes drugstore serves as the clearing house. The bank holds the trump card, riding herd and getting everyone who owes money, even if they don't want to cooperate, to do as they wish."

Phoebe could only stand, dumb-founded and staring.

"One more thing. We know Morray has repeatedly tried to buy that acre of land you own out on the highway and will stop at nothing to get it. You may wonder why he wants it so badly."

"Yes, I've often wondered. There's isn't anything special about that land."

"Oh, but there is. No one is supposed to know this yet but somehow word leaked out and Morray caught wind of it. The state is planning to run an interstate highway adjacent to that land within the next few years. The value will skyrocket. Morray has surreptitiously managed to *acquire* most of the land out there, except for the piece right in the middle which would provide access to all the others."

"Ours."

"That's right. Every hotel and restaurant chain imaginable will be vying for prime land adjacent to the interchange once news of the interstate breaks. How Morray found out is only speculation but he's apparently known about the plan for some time. You're in his way, Phoebe, and you'd better get out."

"So, you're saying to sell that acre to him?"

"Up until a couple of weeks ago I would have told you to hang onto that land and not sell it under any circumstance because of its potential value in years to come. But, what I overheard has changed my advice to you."

"Tell her, for God's sake, Ted," Virginia chimed in.

"I was at the Cozy Café a couple of weeks ago and overheard Morray and his two sons talking to Fred Morrison, the prosecuting attorney. Because I came in the back door they didn't see me sit in the booth behind them. They talked quietly but I overheard most of their conversation. Morrison was talking about some legal matters that had to do with a holding company, congratulating Morray on taking care of some urgent situation. Then Morray started talking about this farm couple outside of town. It wasn't until he used the name *Curtis* that I realized he was talking about you two."

"Well, what did he say about us?" Phoebe asked with urgency.

"That farm accidents happen all the time so no one would think anything of it if Curtis was found out in the back forty under the wheels of his tractor, crushed to death. They all laughed then."

"Are you serious? Do they plan to murder Curtis?"

"I don't think it's a solid plan, as such, only outlining possibilities, but it bears caution. You should talk with Curtis about it but I wanted most to warn you because of what else was said. Morray said it wouldn't take much to settle that matter but said they didn't know what to do about you because they never knew which way you'd jump."

"Oh, my God!"

"I tell you all this as warning. You and Curtis might have to leave Dirk County."

"We can't just leave. How can we walk away from our farm?"

"Morray would buy your farm in a heartbeat."

"I'd sell to the devil before I'd let him have it."

"Just be careful. Morray enjoys a challenge. It's that kind of obstinacy that he loves to get his teeth into and he always wins in the end."

"I've got to go. I've got to talk to Curtis about all of this. Thanks, Ted—Virginia," Phoebe said, hugging them both. "I'll not tell a soul about this, I swear—and Virginia, we'll never talk of it again."

She wanted to tell Ted about other things that had happened to them, to their farm, wondering if he knew of a connection but suddenly her only concern was for Curtis. Running to her car, she drove home at record speed. Once home she climbed onto the Allis-Chalmers that sat up by the house and drove to the fields, fearing something may already have happened to Curtis. He was no where to be found. Driving back to the house, she located him in the barn, attempting to repair his combine. Realizing it was where she would have looked first had she not been in such a panic, she ran to his side.

"Curtis!"

"Where were you going on the ATV in such a hurry?"

"We have to talk."

"Not now, Phoebe. This damn combine is broken down and I can't imagine what happened to it. I think it's the crankshaft. It worked just fine yester..."

"We're talking right now," Phoebe commanded, grabbing the wrench from Curtis' hand.

"What's come over you?"

"I just had a meeting with Ted Whartley, Virginia's cousin, the state cop."

"Seeing someone behind my back, are you?"

"This is serious, Curtis. Ted has been working under-cover in Dirk County for the last two years and had some very interesting things to tell me."

"You know I hate gossip, Phoebe. I really don't want to hear any of it. We have enough trouble keeping track of ourselves without getting into other people's business."

"This is not just gossip."

When Phoebe began relating what Ted had told her about the drug-selling ring, Curtis swore disbelief. When she told him about the proposed interstate highway and how their land would increase in value, he was more willing to listen. By the time she got to the part about what Ted had overheard at the Cozy Café, Curtis had come to the indisputable conclusion that it was the truth and they were in danger.

"We can weather this, somehow, and not sell that land. Maybe, some day, we'll sell it but not to Gaylan Morray—ever," Phoebe vowed.

CHAPTER THREE

Not long after this proclamation, occurrences too glaring to ignore began eroding her resolve. It was certain they were being watched, and probably from the woods, but could never catch anyone there. It was impossible to keep an eye on every corner of the farm. They purposely left the barn and house unattended, pretending to leave to see who might show up but nothing ever happened at those times. It was always when they were away or off guard that something went wrong. They knew it could only be Gaylan Morray behind their difficulties but, also, that he would never dirty his hands with direct involvement. And, while his sons probably carried out the mischief, someone else, someone much smarter, had to be in charge of subterfuge.

Pete Irving, Jesse's hired man was an early candidate given his frequent presence, often seen in the woods, hovering around the farm or aimlessly walking down Digbert Road. Curtis talked with Jesse about Pete, wondering if he could be trusted. Jesse told him that, though a complete dullard, Pete hadn't a sneaky bone in his body. After their conversation Curtis was only too glad to cross him off the culprits list.

Phoebe and Curtis briefly suspected Gaylan Morray's stepsister, Helen Weils. Far exceeding the normal bounds of frugality, she lived in a dilapidated mansion slowly being digested by nature across Digbert Road. Unlike her step-brother and half-sister, she was tall and meatless—turned sideways, she'd disappear. Her hoary hair draped over her head like rimed grass. She spoke pontifically, a bony finger thrust outward toward the target of her words. Unasked, she professed not to be afraid of anyone except God and sometimes her son, Harley. While proclaiming to be a Christian her piety had been the downfall of the family. In the winter of her years she found herself alone and bitter, her wealth of little comfort.

To most in town she was known as Hell on Wheels. She was born in Claverton, a tiny riparian village that had never grown, farther south on French River in the next county. It had flooded out every spring since settlement. The residents, referred to as river rats, waited for the flood to subside each year, scooped the mud from their houses, and moved back in to await the next catastrophe. Twenty years earlier, when the one hundred year flood swelled French River far beyond its banks, the town was wiped out. The more recalcitrant souls rebuilt their homes on the flats. The rest never missed a beat, moving trade, commerce and domicile to the top of the bluff overlooking the river and continuing as though nothing unusual had occurred.

Helen used to tell anyone who would listen that she was Claverton aristocracy, of the Claverton Smithers. It was a claim that never got a toehold in her husband, who dared to rebut her statement with a Diaspora lesson. "Everyone got off the same damn boat together at Claverton a hundred and fifty years ago, scattering to the far corners of the country. Get over it." While refusing to sanction the blue blood entitlement Helen advanced, he, and half the town, held tight to their own manufactured pedigrees.

Bertram P. Weils, or Bert as he was known, was a veteran of W.W.II.—an obtuse man who had somehow struggled his way up the military ladder to become a Lt. Colonel in the Army. According to him, Fort Weils, in the eastern part of the state, was named after his great, great grandfather, supposedly a hero general in the Spanish American War. Never mind that the fort was built and named long before he was born. However briefly he served with honor, Lt. Ernest T. Weils was in the cavalry, fighting Indians farther north before deserting and acquiring a dishonorable discharge. While the fort was, in fact, named after a man named Weils, it was Cyrus Weils, not Ernest T., and no relation.

Bert was a rotund, bald-headed man of more than average height, his beady eyes, dark brown. Before retiring,
he was a successful insurance salesman and did quite well
for his family, however short of approval was his wife.
Though continually dreary at home, around others he was
congenial, outgoing, personable. Phoebe felt sorry for Mr.
Weils who was pecked at, verbally abused, and ordered
around by Helen twenty-four hours a day. She admonished him with a critical comment or chastisement if he
didn't comply and often when he did. While he was on the
phone she kept up a running narrative in the background,
completing his sentences, correcting him, micromanaging
the conversation.

Bert occasionally wandered over to the Higgins farm
on the excuse of looking for their dog. Phoebe saw it as an
excuse to get away from Helen. McGee, a spoiled black
Scottish terrier and his only true friend, ran loose most of
the time. Every morning, Bert's car would appear in the
Higgins' driveway about seven. He'd open the car door
and McGee would exit, waddle to the back door, bark
twice then sit and wait for it to open. Phoebe would let
Max out and wave to Bert. The dogs followed Curtis
around or ran and romped in the woods and fields most of
the morning. At noon, Bert would be waiting with the car
to take McGee home. Assuming he feared McGee crossing the road, Phoebe once offered to escort him but Bert
had a curt response. "McGee prefers to be driven."

Bertram's arthritis caused him to curl up in his later
years. He was stooped, leaning far over forward when he
walked; his painful knees and hips attempting to keep
pace with shuffling feet. His gnarled hands had grown
useless by the time he died, unable even to accomplish the
tying of his shoe laces. This made his means of death
somewhat peculiar. He hung himself in the barn; a tight
slipknot in the noose. While he still swung from a rope,
the sheriff excused the huge bump on the back of his head
as being from the fall when being cut down; investigation

over. Shortly after his untimely death, McGee also died.

When Phoebe went with Max to offer condolences, Helen barred her at the door from entering her gloomy living quarters. Looking past her, through the screen door, Phoebe noticed a picture in the front hallway depicting Jesus hanging pitifully on the cross, draped in black; a bevy of angels that looked like bats fluttering around his lifeless body. Helen pushed the screen door open, nearly scraping Phoebe from the porch then, without speaking, gestured toward two ratty wicker rockers. Phoebe didn't dare be seated without the certainty that it was intended for her to do so; waiting with forced politeness until Helen was seated, before lowering herself into the second chair.

The few words Helen volunteered were in depreciation of others. Her embellished irritations were all inclusive; her children, Phoebe's children, townspeople and most particularly McGee and Mr. Weils. Speaking ill of the dead didn't concern her. While listening, with however much difficulty, to Helen's expiating pronouncements, Phoebe noticed a pair of binoculars sitting on the table next to her. It was creepy realizing her family was probably the target of their use. A notorious snoop, Helen most likely kept track of their comings and goings from the porch when the weather was decent but it was probably just idle curiosity. There was no doubt she possessed a mind devious enough for spying, but who would she pass the information to? It was general knowledge that she and Morray didn't get along; hadn't spoken in years. And, she was mean enough to be guilty of most anything loathsome but, older than dirt, her lack of physical prowess proved her innocence. Besides, as an aged woman facing her eminent demise, her entire declining energy was focused on regret; as with any mother who ate her children.

Her daughter, Madeline, had walked out the front door at sixteen, slamming it behind her; never heard from again. Her son, Harley Weils, who owned the gas station in town, was a disappointment too difficult to bear. He appeared to hate his mother and rarely came to see her; doing so only in an attempt to secure his inheritance, not from any sense of duty or family loyalty and certainly not love. When he was younger, Helen had constantly bragged about his intelligence, mistaking guile for keenness of mind. She always assumed he'd make something of himself after graduating from high school. When he went into the service then married his high school sweetheart, far beneath his station in life, she despaired. The marriage didn't last and there were no *issue* from the union; a blessing for whatever poor souls might have been her grandchildren.

Max sniffed around the house and porch for a while, before sitting at the bottom of the steps. It was clear he missed McGee but animals have an understanding of death humans often lack. Helen never looked at Phoebe the entire time they sat on the porch; barely acknowledging her as she attempted sincere condolences, responding in monosyllables only. When possible to do so without offending, she excused herself and led Max down the long driveway. He trotted way ahead of her, eager to get back to his master.

Curtis was an expert with machinery. There wasn't anything he couldn't fix, and so he soon had the combine up and running again, looking forward to the harvest. But it never stayed fixed for long; always down again within days with a part broken or, in one case, missing altogether. The ample supply of spare parts he kept around for fixing machinery began to shrink as he dipped into it to make necessary repairs. When he tried to get parts in town, he was told there weren't any, forcing him to go outside the county and traveling great distances for anything needed. There was no doubt his machinery was being sabotaged but how and by whom? He penned the dog out by the barns in the hope he'd bark and warn them of intruders but Max couldn't stand to be away from him. Though Curtis tied him up, the dog broke his lead then dug under, jumped over or otherwise found his way out of the pen and back to the house each time. It was probably just as well. He never knew a stranger.

Curtis turned for help to his uncle who still lived nearby. Ernest, quite elderly and clearly not up to the task of tirelessly working alongside him, lent moral and mechanical support. Together, they managed to keep the combine operational long enough to harvest a couple hundred bushels of corn before the predicted change in weather. Following a prolonged, severe thunderstorm and rain that lasted for days, Curtis watched, helpless to do anything, as the stalks of his remaining corn crop broke then bowed to the muddy ground. Expenses were mounting. It began to appear as though their only hope for an income until spring, depended on the sale of their feeder cattle and hogs. Well fed and nurtured toward market for nearly nine months, they were sure to bring top dollar.

Since the tractor still worked sporadically, when the weather cleared, Curtis turned his attention to getting the wheat crop sown. Though resources were dwindling, he managed to get enough money together for seed. Since the planter was motor-less, it would be hard to cripple. It was the tractor that most concerned him. Planting was slow, as the lame machine chugged along pulling the planter behind. Halfway through the first day, it had to be retired for repairs. He finally got it running by the end of the day but, too late to do more planting.

Over the next several days, they got the wheat crop in; the futility of it keenly understood. Without money from the sale of the corn crop, there wouldn't be any for a new combine, so there would be no way to cut it in the spring. If the tractor failed, which it was most likely to do, they would have no way of hauling the wheat to storage even if they did manage to get it cut with a borrowed machine. And, if they got much rain before it could be cut, like the corn crop it would mold where it stood.

Totally at the mercy of the weather, farming was always a crap shoot at best but, under Morray's guiding hand, the odds had been skewed. Still, Curtis persevered, pleading with neighboring farmers for assistance, offering everything but his children as compensation, but no one would loan him the necessary equipment. He even offered to use their machines only late at night when they would otherwise be idle. Everyone was sympathetic, concerned, but none would help.

"I'd be tempted to help ya if I didn't know it would put me in trouble with Morray," Jesse Tate told Curtis one afternoon, following a particularly ardent plea. "I've finally been able to slip below his notice and I can't do nothin' to change that. I'd rather be dirt poor than have money the way he's got it, any day a the week. If Morray's behind this, and I'm sure he is, there's more trouble to come. You can take that to the bank—sorry! Somebody really oughta to do something about that son-of-a- bitch."

Curtis' cousin, Warren, who the kids called uncle, was a turkey farmer several counties away. He would also liked to have helped but distance prevented him from loaning his equipment and he had his own crops to harvest with no time to spare. He called frequently to see how things were going but that was the best he could do. Exercising his only remaining option for getting enough money together to see the family through the winter, Curtis checked the farmer's stock report to see what the going rate was for hogs and cattle then called around the area to get quotes for selling them.

Gaylan Morray was one jump ahead of him, however. No matter where Curtis tried, the prices quoted for buying their livestock were so low it wasn't worth the bother. He checked stockyards great distances away and prices were fair but the livestock that survived the long trip wouldn't bring enough profit beyond gas money to make it worthwhile. He was at wits end with no apparent options left to him. There was enough stored corn and hay for the cattle and hogs for a couple of months but it would not last the winter. Late September, he and Bart jury-rigged the fencing, turning the feeder cattle and hogs loose in the corn field to feed on the downed crop. Curtis prayed for late snow so he could keep the livestock feeding from the field as long as possible, saving their stored grain for the dead of winter, and turned his attention to plowing. With fifty acres left to plow, the tractor joined the casualty list.

Thankful at least for the proceeds from Phoebe's garden, they butchered a couple of hogs and a steer. The meat and potato suppers the family was used to were replaced with casseroles and pasta dishes—anything that would stretch their budget and meat supply. A couple of hogs were secretly sold to friends in the next county and Curtis strong-armed his cousin, Warren, into buying ten head of cattle, but it was not enough income to make ends meet for long. The hardest part of their struggle was trying to keep all that was happening from the children.

"It's going to be a slim Christmas," Phoebe announced at breakfast one morning, before the kids went off to school.

"We don't mind," returned Jenny, assuming she represented the thinking of the entire family. "We'll just pretend we're poor, like Little Orphan Annie."

"Just because Annie was an orphan doesn't mean she was poor," Judd corrected.

"Well, she was—and so am I," Jenny defended.

"We're not poor, we're just temporarily out of funds," Phoebe amended.

Phoebe was the one who minded most. None of the children complained or made an issue of her announcement. She had always made the holiday very special, the only time she overindulged the children, and it hurt. Throwing her creativity into high gear, she dug out her stash of fabric and made flannel shirts for the boys and Curtis, nightgowns for the girls. Rummaging through her cache of saved treasures, she found something special for each of the children and wrapped it up. Focusing on baked goods, she made all their personal favorites to have on hand for the holidays.

Just before Christmas they got an unexpected reprieve of sorts. Curtis' uncle, Earnest, died and the small inheritance received allowed them a modest Christmas but, more importantly, promised to see them through. Snow came relatively late, the end of December, and even then it didn't cover the ground so Curtis kept the livestock, still loose in the cornfields, fed for a little longer. They faced the new year with high hopes the worst was behind them, relying on spring's perennial nature for renewal.

The weather was fierce in January, the ground covered with snow. Early in the month they had to turn to their stored grain to feed the livestock. By the end of February they were already running low on feed, speculating as to what might happen if the livestock feed ran out before winter's end. If not dead, the scrawny beasts would be worthless commodities. When spring came they could buy soy bean and corn seed on credit at the feed mill and Curtis clung to that promise. Even when reality set in, and he realized that without a tractor to pull the planter or a combine to harvest the crops, there was no point to it, he remained optimistic, firmly believing that something would happen to allow them to get their feet back on the ground once the weather warmed.

His natural tendency to look on the bright side of things was misplaced. In early March, after arranging a clandestine borrowing of someone's tractor from an adjacent county, he showed up at Farmer's United Cooperative to buy his crop seed and was told his credit was no longer any good. Without credit, the staple of farmers, there would be no seed and no seed meant no crops. To numb the sense of loss felt within, he considered stopping at Between's only bar for a drink. He had engaged in the usual beer drinking in college but had given it up following a hiatal hernia attack. If that hadn't set him straight, marrying Phoebe would have. Her father had been an alcoholic. She was a tolerant woman in most respects but the one thing she would never abide was a drinker. A vision of the disappointed look on her face if he caved in to his desire and ordered a brew kept him steering the truck past the bar.

Once home, he told Phoebe only that he'd had difficulties getting the seed, silently indicating it was something to be talked about later, out of ear shot of the kids. Supper was uncomfortably quiet. After the kids were all in bed, he and Phoebe talked far into the night. There was no point in hashing over all Gaylan Morray had set in motion. Their position was insuperable and they both knew it.

"The wisest thing to know when cornered is that you are," Curtis expounded, in conclusion. "The question is whether or not to try and save the farm or walk away, starting over somewhere else."

"We can't walk away, Curtis," Phoebe argued. "We've worked too hard to get this farm running efficiently. Besides, this is our home. What else would we do? I'd have to go back to teaching and you to selling insurance. Is that what you want?"

"No, of course not, but I don't see a lot of options here."

"Not only will we have to start over doing things we don't want to do, Morray will have won if we give up."

"Maybe that's not so bad either," Curtis dejectedly offered.

"It's not going to happen!" Phoebe affirmed.

Finding themselves with no other turns to take, they eventually agreed on the only course of action available to them, sensibly concluding that Curtis, the more even tempered of the two, should go alone to the bank. Unable to sleep on their reluctant decision, they sat together at the kitchen table most of the night licking their wounds. Early the next morning Curtis was dressed and ready to go by the time the kids were up. Phoebe had breakfast on the table at the usual time, trying her best to forge daily routines.

"You look nice, Dad," Judd commented, as they sat down at the table. "Hot date?"

"Yeah, I'll say," Curtis returned, winking at Phoebe.

When the kids were off to school, Phoebe and Curtis sat silently at the table, sipping tea, the stodgy state of their affairs weighing heavily on them. When the hall clock struck nine, Curtis stood up, a set to his jaw. After giving Phoebe a prolonged kiss, he got in the truck and drove into town. Walking into the bank, he prayed some more feasible solution might occur to him. *How about some divine intervention?* he implored the heavens. Vincent DeMar glanced at him from his small office as Curtis strode across the lobby, then buried his head in his work. Seeing Curtis, Morray rose from his desk, meeting him at the door to his office. With Curtis inside, he gestured toward a seat in front of his desk then closed the door.

"We've had many problems at the farm, as you know," Curtis began.

"Have you now?" Morray questioned, in contrived innocence.

Knowing full well Gaylan Morray was completely aware of the problems, his flippant question creating heat in his throat, Curtis took a moment to gain control of his emotions then itemized the incidences that had occurred.

"I'm sorry to hear you've had so many—difficulties," Morray inserted.

"As you also know, we've reached a point where, with no where else to turn, we have no choice but to come to you for help."

"What makes you think I can or will help you?"

"You can and will help us," Curtis spurt, at the end of his patience. "You haven't gone to all the trouble of ruining us for no reason. What is it that you want?"

"Want from you? What could I possibly want from you?"

"If you're gonna play more of your goddamn games, I'm out of here," Curtis swore, rising from his assigned chair and heading for the door.

"Well, just a minute there," Morray hummed, from behind the desk. "Maybe..."

"I repeat. What do you want?" Curtis demanded, hovering over Morray.

"You know full well what I want," Morray growled. "Now sit down."

Curtis knew his height was intimidating to Morray, so continued to stand until the effect was complete. The supposedly impromptu offer and conditions that followed made him keenly aware of how often, and for how long, Morray had rehearsed the answer he would give once his evil plans had come to fruition. It made their surrender even less palatable.

"If you'll mortgage your farm to the bank, I'll set up an automatic revolving credit program for you at Farmers United Co-op. That way you can get all the seed you want and get your crops in on time to begin recovering from your farming—*misfortunes*. The money from the mortgage should help you update your equipment and machinery—or allow you to buy new—and will enable you to make repairs to outbuildings, buy feed for your livestock until harvest time, etc., etc. For more operating expense assets, I suggest you sell that acre of land out on the highway."

"I don't suppose you know of anyone who wants to buy it? I'm on to you Morray. I know about the plans to put an interstate highway through there. How you found out I'll never know but word is out. Now we know why you're so interested in that piece of land. I bought that land from my uncle and it has meaning to us over and above its value."

"You can't let emotions rule your decisions. It's not business-like."

"The mortgage is something Phoebe and I have discussed and agreed upon. That's what I came here to talk to you about," Curtis continued, ignoring Morray's demeaning reprimand. "I'm so tired of the hassles you've put us through you might even get me to sign the sale papers if that would end all this, but I doubt you'll get any ink off Phoebe."

"Your wife would do well to do as she's told. I'd hate to see anything happen to those children of hers—yours."

"You touch one hair on the head of any of our children and I'll kill you, Morray," Curtis rasped into his face, rising to lean over the desk far enough to count his nose hairs.

"Now, now, there's no need to get hostile," Morray squirmed, visibly daunted for a second or two. "Why—don't you sit down—and we'll discuss this like two gentlemen."

"TWO gentlemen?"

"Just talk with your wife and we'll see if we can come up with some kind of reasonable deal on that land. And—the mortgage is yours for the asking."

"You won't give the mortgage without that acre, will you?"

"No."

"I'll talk with Phoebe but I wouldn't count on getting what you want, Morray."

"Oh, I'll get what I want. There's no doubt about that."

Curtis left the bank feeling violated, raped. He sat in the truck, his head resting on the steering wheel for some time, then started it up and slowly drove out of the bank lot. Going down Main Street, his mind in turmoil, he wished only to turn off the seditious thoughts reeling through his mind. Passing the Sunset Bar and Grill he hesitated, peering through the large showcase windows to see if anyone was inside. The bar appeared to be empty. He drove around the block then parked the truck in the back, sitting for several minutes before turning off the engine.

Succumbing to temptation, he got out, walked to the front door of the bar and went in.

It smelled of stale cigarette smoke and spilled beer. Wilson Pedigrue, the owner, stood behind the bar emptying ashtray, the play by play of a ball game in the background. He nodded to Curtis as he sat at the bar but no words were exchanged. There was no one else around. After a couple of minutes, Curtis ordered a whiskey, gulping it down to calm frayed nerves. Wilson brought the bottle, suggesting another drink, but Curtis refused. He tossed a couple of dollars onto the bar then, swallowing his anger, drove home, chewing on breath mints, to face Phoebe.

"I can't sign, Curtis. And—anyway, you know he'll never give us what that acre is actually worth. How can you even think of signing? Do I smell whiskey?"

"We have no alternative," Curtis answered quickly, in hopes of distracting her from closer scrutiny. "Unless you want to give up on farming, move somewhere else and start over, we need to have the machinery and seed to plant and harvest our crops. I've given it a great deal of thought and I think, all things considered, given who we're dealing with, we're lucky to still have some cattle and hogs—and our house."

"I've agreed to a mortgage on the farm but that's all. And that mortgage will not include the house," Phoebe warned. "We may eventually lose the farm but Gaylan Morray will not put our children out of their home. As for that acre, that's our insurance, Curtis, our nest egg for the future—and I refuse to sign it away."

"Then all we can do is fold up, pack up and move away," Curtis replied, moving toward the door. "He won't give the mortgage without that acre so unless you concede, we're done. I'd be interested in hearing your contingency plan for that. When you come to your senses, I'll be in the barn."

Phoebe moped around for three days, thinking about

all that had happened. She and Curtis barely spoke and slept in separate spaces, civil only when the children were around. She couldn't stand it when they fought. It eventually occurred to her that even if they lost everything, they had to protect their relationship and the family at all costs. Carefully weighing their choices, she ultimately saw the dismal reality of their situation, concluding that Curtis was right—there weren't any options left. Her main concern was that if she continued to defy Morray, her children might also be in jeopardy.

"Curtis," she called to him from the kitchen once the children were packed off to school. "Could you come here, please?"

After breakfast Curtis had gone to the office to tend the accounts—what accounts there were left to tend. Since she wasn't speaking to him, concern immediately grew for her well being when she called to him. He dropped the pen onto the ledger and returned to the kitchen. Phoebe was standing in the middle of the room, crying.

"What is it, Phoebe?" he coaxed, walking toward her.

"It goes against every fiber in me but I'll sign whatever papers you think I should," she blubbered. "I absolutely hate that man."

Curtis took her into his arms to console her—to console himself.

"I'll make the call to Morray while you get dressed."

"Can you get him to exclude the house?"

"I'll try," Curtis pledged, presenting an optimistic front. Realistically, there was no way for the house to be excluded but, as he reached for the phone, an idea surfaced.

Phoebe went to take a shower while Curtis made the call. It was a conversation she'd just as soon not hear. Dressed and ready to go, she went down to the kitchen.

"The dirty deed is done," he announced, as she entered the room.

"The house is not a part of the mortgage?"

"No."

"How did you convince him?"

"I'd rather not say. Let's go get this over with."

If Phoebe could have signed away their land and gotten the mortgage without laying eyes on Gaylan Morray, it would have made her task easier. Knowing her presence was necessary to complete the paperwork, she steeled herself for the trip to town.

"Have a seat, Mr. and Mrs. Higgins," Morray croaked from his desk chair, as his two sons leered at Curtis and Phoebe from the far corner of the office. "I hear you want to sell that acre you own out on the highway."

"You know very well we don't want to sell—you leave us no choice," Phoebe thrust.

"I think you'll need to find a way to keep your wife in check, Mr. Higgins. Her attitude is most unbecoming."

"Let's cut the crap," Curtis blurted. "Where's the paperwork?"

"These papers are for the mortgage on your farm. I've reluctantly agreed not to include the house—ah—as requested, since you've already had so much—you know—misfortune. I'm doing you a great charity here, don't you know. The seventy-five thousand dollars should get you going again—well on your way to buying seed and getting your crops in."

"That farm is worth far more than seventy-five thousand dollars even without the house," Curtis asserted.

"In today's market, if we—you—were to sell it, I don't think you'd get much more for it. It's a generous offer that I suggest you take. In the fall, if all goes well, if the growing season is favorable, we can see about adding to that if you wish. Now, as for the acre out on the highway, please sign here. I'm giving you five thousand dollars for that land which is much more than its worth."

"You know very well that land will be worth ten times that when news of the highway is more widespread," Curtis protested.

"That's the price I'm offering. Take it or leave it," Morray said, shrugging his sloped, narrow shoulders. "By the way, where did you hear about the new highway?"

"Word has a way of spreading, Mr. Morray, especially in a small town. Someone overheard one of your sons talking about it. Owen, I think," Phoebe inserted, as Owen emitted a pneumatic wheeze and went slack-jawed. "You'd do well to put a muzzle on that boy; both of your boys. Give me those sale papers to sign. You're not happy unless you're screwing someone out of something are you? You'll burn in hell for your dealings some day. Of that I'm sure."

Curtis and Phoebe signed the papers and left Morray's office. Vincent avoided eye contact and ducked into the back room as they crossed the lobby. Walking toward the front door, they could hear Morray lecturing his sons.

"Morons for sons, that's what I've got. You two better do as you're told and keep your mouths shut or I'll shut them for you—permanently."

"Is that a self-satisfied grin I see spreading across your face, Phoebe? That was quite a coup."

"We have to find satisfaction where we can," Phoebe said, pushing the door open. "Do you think Vincent has anything to do with all this? He always looks so guilty."

"I seriously doubt it from what I've heard of him but Morray is his stepfather, so he must be involved at some level?"

After going to the feed store, they stopped at the gas station. Harley Weils, the owner, was a diminutive, pragmatic man. He always wore baggy khakis and a blue work shirt—probably a throw back to his military days in uniform. If, as his mother claimed, he was intelligent, it wasn't obvious in conversation. He had steely blue eyes that focused in opposite directions, making it difficult to know who or what he was looking at. For years he'd gone on junkets to Las Vegas, until he was caught counting cards and told never to return. With a somewhat aggressive demeanor, he seemed always cool toward them and today was no exception. He arrived at the station as they pulled in. His red Chevy truck, usually spotless, was covered with road dust. Curtis waved to him but he did not respond, driving his truck past them into the garage and closing the door.

His employee, Jeremy, had an effulgent personality and was as congenial as ever. Though a bachelor, he was by far not the most eligible—the antithesis of debonair, with a wide-eyed look, red hair, usually a couple of day's beard growth on his scruffy chin and intermittent, yellow teeth. He spoke in a patois that was, at times, difficult to understand but his words were always quietly kind. He usually had grease up to his elbows, and looked like he'd slept in his navy blue mechanic's jumpsuit for several nights running. The monogram on his torn uniform pocket read *Jerem*, the *y* having come unraveled on a day long ago. People had taken to calling him Germ but he took it with good humor, only clarifying that he was not German but of "Scotch anstry." Harley ordered him around like a lackey but he never made a fuss, taking whatever life shoved his way with a relaxed countenance.

Phoebe sat in the truck with the window rolled down. Jeremy came out of the station, wiped his greasy hands on a red cloth grabbed from his back pocket then proceeded to pump their gas. Curtis took the squeegee and began washing the windshield as they chatted. Watching people coming and going from the shops along Main Street, she observed that their lives seemed to flow smoothly on while hers was caught in the vice-like grip of the vilest man she'd ever known. *Maybe they're caught too*, she mused, *forced to go through daily life with a brave facade*. She didn't know how they'd get through all this but they'd find a way, of that she was certain. What worried her most was that, with their acre gone, they now had no hedge—one slip, one failed crop, one bad growing season, and the farm, except for the house, would belong to

Gaylan Morray and his cronies and they'd have nothing. She consoled herself with the knowledge that both she and Curtis were strong, capable people who would fight to the finish.

A young man drove his green Cadillac Eldorado convertible into the gas station and stopped at the far pump. Leaving his car, he walked toward Curtis in deep strides, swinging his arms and legs as though hinged from the waist. From his impeccable dress and shiny new car, it was obvious he was someone who'd been grazing in the tall grass.

"Nice truck there fella," he proclaimed, nodding at Curtis. "Fill her up when you're done here," he ordered, addressing Jeremy.

"Thanks," Curtis replied, noting how tall the man was and the plates on his car.

The Texan's dark hair was slicked back under a white ten gallon hat, his eyes hidden behind reflective smoke-colored-lens sunglasses. His light blue chambray shirt was a good fit except for the cuffs of the sleeves which over-hung arms too short for his frame, nearly covering his hands. Silver nail head brads lined the pockets and collar of his shirt, matching the embossed silver buckle of his saddle tan belt. Tight Levis stretched down long legs, revealing only the pointed toes of his expensive, heeled alligator boots.

"You can't wear out a Ford, I always say. Name's Dixon—Herbert Dixon. I'm from near El Paso—Texas," the man said, offering his hand.

Curtis shook his hand, momentarily wondering how a cowboy with such soft hands and obvious money might earn a living. "Hello, name's Curtis Higgins."

"You live around here I take it."

"Yes, we farm out west of town a few miles. You're a long way from Texas. You just passing through?"

"Yeah, had to get gas. Just closed a cattle deal. I bought seven hundred head—paid cash."

Sitting out in front of the gas station with his chair tipped back against the building was Swifty McClaire, a wastrel and bounder—the town's, one of the town's, drunks. He was completely non-penitential regarding his chosen lifestyle, even bragged about his expertise in avoiding the typical drudgery of the working class. He looked and acted like a ferret with furtive eyes, jet black hair, a pin head and ears that were sure to keep him from entering narrow passageways. Intoxicated, he could be seen lying in most any gutter, if not in the town's bar. People often referred to him as Shifty, watching him weave in and out of businesses, moving around town with stealth. Semi-sober, his only other face, he hung out at Harley's gas station. Perking up at the Texan's disclosure, he tipped the chair upright, rose to gain his balance then, in a noticeably serpentine fashion, moved closer, intently listening to the two men talking.

"That's a lot of beef," Curtis commented.

"Yeah, I'll say. It'll cost a fortune to ship 'em back to Texas. By rail, don't ya know—that's the safest way. Not the cheapest by far—but the safest."

"Heading home now, back to Texas, are you?" Swifty questioned in sloppy locution, joining the conversation uninvited.

"Yeah. It's been a long trip. I should be home in a couple of days if I drive long hours each day. That Caddie'll get me there just fine."

"Nice chatting with you," Curtis commented, placing the squeegee back in the bucket. "Have a safe trip home."

He paid Jeremy for the gas. Jeremy stuffed the bills in his pocket then hurried off to fill the Texan's car.

"I like your silver belt buckle," Swifty offered.

"Oh, thanks. Got it in Puerto Rico. I travel all over the world—been to Singapore, Thailand, Beijing, Australia, you name it—but there's no place like home," he offered, clicking his boot heels together to draw attention to them—a gesture not lost on Swifty.

"How you gonna take care of all them cattle you just bought if yer traveling all over the place?" Swifty questioned.

"I don't have nothin to do with the cattle once they're bought. I just buy and sell 'em. I usually come up north to get cattle because they're a hardier stock of animal. Those long horns are good cattle but I like the northern breeds. I know my cattle for sure. I'm originally from the Midwest an' I know good cattle when I see 'em. Cost is no problem an' no matter how many I buy, I've got people to take care of 'em and land to put 'em on. I've got a huge spread there in Texas and a bunkhouse full of ranch hands."

"Oh, yeah?" Swifty chirped, with exaggerated interest.

"Your Caddie's all gassed up," Jeremy announced to the Texan, rejoining the trio.

Dixon only gave him a nod, took out a wad of bills from his vest pocket and handed him a twenty. "Keep the change. There's plenty more where that came from."

"You say you got a large ranch in Texas," Swifty pressed.

"Right-oh. It takes me two days to drive across my land," the Texan bragged.

"We heda ole truck like 'at once," Jeremy chimed in.

Concealing his laugh with difficulty, Curtis got back behind the wheel of his pickup. The Texan soon got into his car and left. Swifty and Harley were huddled together near the station's garage as Jeremy wandered around to the passenger side to say hello to Phoebe.

"Jeremy, I see your dog had puppies again. How many this time?" she queried, glancing over at the squirming pile of fur lying on a blanket beside the door of the station.

"Only four—las time she hed six. She gits herself a litter ever year."

"Are German Shepherds known to have large litters?"

"Well, largr'n four, anyhows."

"How old are the puppies now?

"Only two month ole thiz week."

"Nice dogs. I heard you've been out of town."

"Yeah, first time ever left Between. My youngr brothr zin the miltry near Warshingtin Deecee an he flew me up to see 'im. I don like flying non but it uz good to see Lincoln's tome an the white houz—and Bryan, corse."

"Got any other travel plans, Jeremy?"

"No. I'd like a go ta Hawaiya somday but it aint …."

"Jeremy, quit yakking with the customers and get over there and pump gas for that other fella," Harley ordered, as another car pulled into the station. No one noticed that Swifty had left the premises. "And, get these damn dogs outta here."

"See you later, Jeremy. You take good care of those pups, and especially the mother," Phoebe called after him.

"Theys good dawgs—the best watchdawgs there is," Jeremy threw over his shoulder.

"Unlike another dog we know," Curtis joked, gesturing toward the back of the truck where Max, drooling, stood enthusiastically wagging his tail.

"Wouldn't it be nice to have the kind of money that Texan has to throw around?" Phoebe commented, as they rode home.

"That Texan has a big mouth. I hope it doesn't get him into trouble."

Phoebe and Curtis didn't hear about it for months, being on the distant end of the gossip chain, but word had it Swifty was seen driving around town the next week in a brand new car and flashing a wad of bills. Speculation ranged from his getting a job—a notion quickly dismissed for its absurdity—to the loosening of the tight grip his mother held on her accounts and a rare spurt of generosity. A deeper enigma, far more difficult to explain away, were the alligator boots, opaque sunglasses and shiny belt buckle he sported, except to those who knew, and they weren't talking about the ill-fated Texan.

CHAPTER FOUR

The usually intrepid Phoebe became a spent force, as sullen as the late March skies. Gaylan Morray's threats had resurrected a graveyard of insecurities in her. Keeping a sharp eye on her children, she hovered over them to the point of distraction, managing every aspect of their lives. They found it suffocating but knew that complaining would be futile. Their mother was fair and loving but resolute and, changing her mind once set, about as easy as moving the Empire State Building. She kept them busy obeying orders, setting rigorous schedules to satisfy her perception of control. Ardently throwing herself into the children's school activities, she became home room parent for Jenny's class, baking cupcakes and organizing parties and events, volunteered as ticket taker at the high school games and wrestling meets, chaperoned at their dances. The kids' worst fear was that any day she might start riding the bus with them to school.

Unfortunately, Curtis' usual optimism did not serve him. His steady mind grew increasingly erratic, turning within to attempt balance. There he found blame for not being able to stand up to Gaylan Morray to keep their farm out of debt and regret over selling the acre of land out by the highway. Attempting to anesthetize mounting inner conflicts, he started drinking. At first it was only a drink in the evening, reason enough for Phoebe to turn away from him each night in bed. As winter drew to a close, he began surreptitiously hiding booze in the barn, taking nips throughout the day. Phoebe, smelling booze on his breath but unable able to locate his supply, lectured him with well-structured arguments for abstinence, the thrust being *where will it all lead*? On trips to town Curtis became a regular at the Sunset Bar and Grill then stopped at the liquor store on the way home, each time convinced it was for the last time.

After being a patron of the Sunset Bar and Grill for

some time, Wilson no longer let him pay for drinks. Usually there was someone else in the bar to assign credit for the single drink he had each time. If not, Wilson said it was on the house. While this generosity seemed incidental, always preoccupied, his mind in a swirl, Curtis never questioned the practice. In time he discovered that his liquor store bill was also being paid. Thinking efficient Phoebe, though disapproving, had taken care of it, naiveté overpowered logic.

As if their troubles with Morray weren't enough for concern, Judd started having difficulties at school. His grades slipped and his sanguine nature shifted to melancholy. When Phoebe questioned his teachers, they could not explain the change. Speaking with the principal, however, she discovered that Judd's honesty had been called into question when money was found missing from his treasurer's account at the bank. Despite great effort on her part to get Judd to talk about it, he wouldn't, saying only that he didn't take the money and didn't know what happened to it. Phoebe believed him and, recalling her conversation with Morray when he indicated that something could happen to their accounts, suspected foul play. Concerned for Judd, she put aside her suspicions to focus on supporting him, including giving him the money to make up the treasury account discrepancy.

Purple and gold wild flowers lined the ditches on Digbert Road and yellow daffodils then red tulips emerged in the beds around the house. Spring kept the Higgins family extremely busy as the school year wound down. The kids counted on summer for some relief from their overbearing mother. Curtis and Phoebe occasionally forgot the financial cloud looming over them but not for long. They learned from neighboring farmers the length and breadth of Morray's reach. Hardly any in the rural community had escaped drastic consequences in their dealings with him, and they were consoled in not being the only subjects of his dominion.

Though he continued to drink, Curtis was never drunk. He worked hard during the day. Taking only an occasional nip, and usually too exhausted to lift more than a single glass most evenings, he'd managed to convince himself his habit was indiscernible.

The mortgage loan money, as well as cash from the sale of the acre, allowed them to continue farming. It paid for a used combine, corn picker, and tractor, and the planter and hay wagon sported new tires. Taking advantage of their revolving credit from the Farmers United Co-op, they obtained seed. New calves bellowed from the south pasture and a horde of tiny pink piglets lined up piggyback to nurse from their enormous mothers in the hog pen. Doc Shepherd came out to vaccinate the new arrivals. One very large sow farrowed late, but Doc came back, as promised. Though he and Curtis exchanged frequent sidelong glances, nothing was said of his earlier refusal to help them.

The newly thawed ground invited plowing and Curtis did not disappoint. Scores of starlings circled as he plowed, poking through the upturned soil to retrieve worms. When the fields lay in neat furrows, he began disking in preparation for planting.

Phoebe spent much of her time worrying about the children. Unanswered questions regarding tensions between their parents and their mother's acute protectiveness, had opened small schisms in the family. Arguments and discipline problems that had never existed before began surfacing. Sibling rivalry was on the increase and spats frequent. Only Jenny remained sheltered from the storm.

Judd cultivated the garden plot at his mother's insistence, but sputtering louder than usual and exhibiting rebellion about nearly everything asked of him. The experiences at school had changed him and not for the better. He'd become quite argumentative, developing what could only be described as an attitude, and spending a great deal of time alone in the room he shared with his brother.

The evening before Memorial Day the family attended Lily's baccalaureate service and graduation. With a perfect high school record, she had ascended to the top of her class and, as valedictorian, gave the commencement speech. Even more than her high school awards, her parents were pleased with her desire to attend college. Despite some unexplained difficulties she detected at home, Lily seemed content to spend the summer with her family, but an earlier ambivalence about leaving home had morphed into a desire to get on with her own life.

At the close of the last day of school, Jenny and Lily took the bus home. Bart had driven the truck. He and Judd were to pick up fertilizer at the feed mill, on credit, to combine with the corn for planting. The owner, Jules Gotsie, gave them a hard time, at first refusing to let them take the fertilizer. Bart used the phone to call his dad then put Gotsie on the line to be convinced. It wasn't until Gotsie made another call, in the privacy of his office, that he finally relented and let the boys take the fertilizer.

Bart was embarrassed, demanding, but not getting answers from his dad as to why their credit was suddenly an issue. He scrutinized his parents' every move, asking questions and criticizing the way they were handling things. Insisting they were keeping things from him, and doubting their explanations, he grew insulted at their lack of trust.

Despite familial difficulties, everyone pitched in to help. Over the first weeks of summer vacation favorable weather prevailed and the boys helped their dad get all the corn planted. Judd reluctantly helped his mother and Lily plant the garden. When the corn was up, Curtis got the co-op, on credit, to spread nitrogen over the sprouted crop. By the time they got the soy beans planted, the wheat crop Curtis had sown the previous fall was ready for harvesting. A bounty of wheat was cut and stored for feed and two truckloads taken to the elevator to be sold. The hogs were well fed, their offspring gaining in weight. Calves, born in the spring, were moved up near the barn to join the feeder cattle and, except for their virgin mammary glands, the heifers, kept in a separate part of the pasture, were starting to look like mature cows. The corn was knee -high and looked healthy. The smoothness of operations easily lulled the Higgins family back into innocence for a time, exactly as Morray knew it would.

The Sunset Bar and Grill was a hang out for locals, especially businessmen, usually, but not necessarily, after hours. It wasn't much of a bar, truthfully, and the food mediocre at best, but large windows faced the main street of the downtown and one could sit and easily observe the town's affairs—at least those that were above board. While the farming community knew of Gaylan Morray's tactics, except for how his dealings directly affected them, most people in town seemed unaware of his closed system of avarice. His victims didn't speak of their duping, due to social embarrassment or fear of reprisals, consequently it rarely occurred to them that they had not been singled out for misery.

The bar was a favorite town rumor mill. If there was no news to dispense, the patrons made it up. It was where the rumor had started that Ted Whartley was an undercover cop for the state and had leaked the information about the new interstate highway to Gaylan Morray. However untrue most of their lies were, Ted's name became assigned to all unexplained occurrences in town.

It wasn't known where Ted got his information, or to what extent he knew of the town's behind the scenes dealings but in April the town druggist, Doug Hewes, had been brought up on charges related to dispensing illegal drugs. He was placed in jail pending a federal trial. Though Ted still worked undercover, seen around town occasionally, the news began circulating that he had assisted with the investigation and was, in fact, responsible for the arrest of Doug Hewes. The day before the trial,

June twelfth, Ted was found face down in French River with a knife through his back. "An obvious suicide," the sheriff declared.

Depressed over the news about Ted, Gaylan Morray's vice grip on his farm, and the general state of his affairs, Curtis started drinking more heavily. On his visits to the Sunset Bar and Grill, Roxanne, the local bar maid and town slut began flaunting herself—an obvious attempt at luring him into an affair even he recognized.

"You kin trusme," Roxanne slurred at Curtis, leaning over his bar stool so her cleavage would be hard to miss. "Whaz the truble, Curtis, honey?"

"Leave me alone, will you?"

"You think yer too good for me, is at it? I'm fine stuff."

"Yeah, you've got a lot of class, Roxanne," Curtis sarcastically commented.

"Hell, I got class I ain't even used yet," Roxanne shot back.

When every ploy known to her had been unsuccessful in getting his attention, she remained undaunted. While Curtis sat on a bar stool at the end of the bar, she called Phoebe to tell her of their affair. Phoebe knew better than to believe her but Roxanne's call succeeded in raising concerns Curtis might be spiraling out of control.

"I trust you, Curtis, but I'm tired of the calls, the innuendos about your behavior in town and all the other gossip being spread around. We have to keep our wits about us at all times. One slip and Morray will have us," Phoebe cautioned one night, as they got into bed. "You have got to quit drinking, if for no other reason than your health. You know you're not supposed to drink," she concluded, turning to face away from him.

But Curtis continued to drink until another hiatal hernia attack nearly landed him in the hospital. He'd been told years earlier to alter his diet, particularly eliminating alcohol and coffee, and had quit both, cold turkey. At some level, he knew reintroducing drink into his diet was a risk for which he would probably pay. Bedridden, and forced to listen to Phoebe's diatribes on the subject of alcohol, provided more incentive for quitting than any physical discomfort. Their arguments would eventually bring the truth to light, as he finally erupted in defense.

"If you're so hell bent against my having an occasional drink, why do you always pay the bill at the liquor store? I think they call that *enabling*," he thrust.

"I would never pay your liquor store bill—didn't even know you had a liquor store bill. Apparently, you're drinking more than I've suspected."

"What about my tab at the Sunset Bar and Grill with Wilson?" Curtis queried, denied suspicions suddenly coming sharply into focus.

"Never! What's going on?"

"Someone is paying for my liquor."

"Someone wants you drunk. That Morray is up to no good again. I was stupid enough to think our troubles were behind us. I might have known that selling him that acre was not the end of things. It's not enough he has the mortgage on our farm, he wants it outright. How could you be so blind, giving him the advantage over us by turning to drink?" Phoebe chastised. "Are you forgetting what Ted told me about the possibility of Morray having you murdered?"

"Maybe it's not him that's sponsoring my drink," Curtis argued.

"Yes, and maybe the sun won't come up in the morning. Curtis, I beg of you—quit drinking. Either of us being less than one hundred percent means the farm is not run efficiently and puts all of us in jeopardy. We can't give Morray the slightest excuse to shut us down, bankrupt us, and drive us out."

When she saw only a glazed look in Curtis' eyes, she turned and walked out of the room. She did not go to bed that night until she heard his thick breathing and knew he was asleep. Very early in the morning she got up and, sitting at the kitchen table with a cup of tea, made a vow. "I won't have it," she proclaimed aloud.

Two days later, after a good night's sleep, Curtis decided he'd recovered enough to get up and get dressed. Phoebe was already downstairs. It was still very early when he walked into the kitchen intending to tell her he felt well enough to do some chores—until he saw her face. He'd seen that look only once before—the day their third child, Annie had died just days after being born. He would rather have been drawn and quartered than see it again, but there it was.

"Trust me—you'll lose more than the farm if you don't quit drinking, Curtis. I'll leave you," she pronounced in a firm voice before he could speak.

While she waited for her words to take effect, Curtis sat down at the table and hung his head. He knew when he was defeated, but even more so, when he was wrong. The dire nature of his drinking suddenly struck him full force. The opportunity to talk further lapsed as Lily came into the kitchen. Judd and Bart soon followed. The fact that something was wrong could not be hidden—the tension in the air between their parents palpable. When breakfast was over the boys left for the barn, but Bart's backward glance made Phoebe's heart sink. Jenny straggled in last, as usual, to find the serving plates empty. She was about to whine her loss when Lily produced a plate from the oven with bacon, eggs, and toast. She had anticipated her sister's tardiness and prepared a plate for her, putting it in the oven to stay warm.

"Thanks," Phoebe said, patting her on the arm in recognition of her thoughtfulness. Lily sat with Jenny in uncomfortable silence while she ate. "Have Lily brush your hair a little before you go feed Tess, Jenny," Phoebe called, as the girls also fled the kitchen. When they had their privacy again, Curtis went to Phoebe.

"I'll quit this minute, Phoebe, I promise," Curtis

vowed, taking the resisting Phoebe into his arms.

"That's the problem—I'm not sure you can," she pronounced in a hurt voice, freeing herself from his embrace.

Much to her amazement, Curtis did quit drinking. That same morning he smashed the bottle kept in the barn and, to her knowledge, never had another drop. She was at first suspicious, unable to believe he could so easily quit. Watching him closely over the next couple of weeks, she could see no evidence of his drinking. She recalled how disciplined he had always been. If he gained a few pounds, he'd announce he was going to lose ten and in a week they'd melted off. Once his hiatal hernia was diagnosed he'd quit drinking beer which hadn't been too difficult but, even though he'd been a caffeine addict for years, he quit coffee that very day never to drink it again. Slowly, but cautiously, observing his disciplined abstinence, her anxiety diminished and she became comfortably satisfied that at least that concern was behind them.

On the Fourth of July the Higgins family attended the local festivities. The parade included every locatable wheeled or motorized conveyance, along with anything on four legs. There were modest, if not horrible, floats strung out between mediocre bands, animals pulling carts, doll buggies, children on bikes and tricycles decorated with crepe paper, roller skaters, flag bearers, acrobats, gymnasts and dance troops, tractors, motorcycles, politicians in convertibles, the tiny toy cars of the Shriners and lastly, the horses, pooping as they went. It was quintessential small town America and everyone enjoyed it, cheering their approval. The parade moved so slowly, and was so disjointed, that after each entry there was time to get a soda or ice cream and be back to your place in time to catch the next one. Clowns walked or rode unicycles, throwing candy, gum and balloons as the crowd rushed to catch them or retrieve them from sidewalks and gutters. The penultimate entry was a tractor pulling a manure spreader, in which sat a real bride and groom, fresh from the altar.

Jenny rode Tess in the parade, just ahead of the larger horses, wearing her cowboy boots and proudly sitting on her new saddle. Lily walked alongside to keep her company so her parents could be spectators for once. Bart, who would like to have driven the tractor accompanied by Judd, became upset when Curtis insisted, without explanation, that they keep a low profile and stay out of the parade.

Following the parade there was a community picnic then softball game. In the evening boring local politicians spoke over loud speakers to deaf ears and the community band played, their sour notes barely audible over the buzz of the crowd. When it grew dark fireworks capped the day. Though modest, they elicited the requisite oohs and aahs. There were much larger firework displays in Dirkville and Herston but it was considered disloyal to attend either affair.

Over the summer Judd appeared to be putting his blemished reputation aside and his mood improved somewhat. He and Bart helped their dad make repairs to the outbuildings. The well pumps were checked for any defects or wear and were found to be in good order. The fencing was secured, mended where the barbed wire had broken or was sagging. Some boards on the granary that had come loose were refastened. The crops were growing like weeds, requiring additional cultivating and spraying. The promise of the bounty they would harvest kept the boys and Curtis inspired and productive. Phoebe supervised the garden, getting help from Lily, and Jenny when she could be lured away from Tess. Phoebe remained determined to be room mother for Jenny in the fall but otherwise gradually backed off her earlier dictums, running the household less like a polity. Playing around with a soap recipe occupied her meager spare time.

Things were going so well that late July Curtis took his family on a brief vacation. It would go a long way toward healing familial conflicts and stresses. There was a lake four hours north of Between, just over the state line, on which Warren, Curtis' cousin, had a small cabin he allowed them to use. Ryan, a friend of Warren's, visiting from Boulder, agreed to stay at the farm and feed the hogs, take care of Tess and Max for a few days, and keep an eye on things, making their respite possible. Before planting, the barnyard had been refenced to again enclose the feeder cattle and hogs. Curtis carefully instructed Ryan in the proper mix of feed, advising him to make sure the livestock had fresh running water. Because the brood cattle were free-ranging, they needed little care and would be fine for a few days. To Judd's relief, Phoebe said the weeds in the garden would keep for a long weekend.

"You can stay home to keep up with the weeds while we go, if you'd like, Judd," she teased, as they made vacation preparations.

"That's all right," Judd managed, thinking her serious. "I need a break."

"When are we going, Mommy?" Jenny urgently questioned.

"Soon, Jenny, soon."

Late afternoon, the day before they were to leave, Curtis heard a truck in the woods and went to investigate. A pickup truck was just heading out of the far side but he couldn't get a clear look at it because the sun was directly in his eyes. Nothing strange or untoward had occurred lately, so he had no reason to be overly suspicious, but grew concerned about being away from the farm for an extended period. He finally concluded that he was just punchy. Friday evening the family packed the car to head north. The sad look on Max's face the next morning, staring at them from the back stoop as Curtis backed the car up, was more than they could bear.

"Why can't he come along?" Judd asked, as his dad steered the car onto the long driveway.

"There's barely enough room in the car for all of us. Where would we put a dog?"

"He's not a dog, he's Max," Jenny offered, as they all laughed.

"Dad—Bart, Lily and I are in the backseat," Judd interjected. "If we take a vote, and agree to fit him in, can Max come along?"

"Please, Daddy," Jenny pleaded, in the beguiling tone that always worked.

"Max can sit on Judd's lap," Bart suggested. "Let's take a vote."

"Don't bother," Curtis relented, stopping the car.

He knew when he was whipped. Slowly backing up, he parked, got out, and whistled. Max, whose expressive canine eyes had registered hope the moment he saw the car backing up, came running and leaped into Curtis' arms, nearly knocking him to the ground.

"We'll be taking Max with us after all, Ryan," Curtis informed their caretaker, who had come out to see what was going on.

Bart opened the back door. Judd patted his thigh, calling to Max and he jumped right into the middle of the kids.

"I want to sit with Max," Jenny whined.

"That's a good idea," Phoebe said. "Why don't you come sit up here, Lily?"

"Gladly," Lily commented, squeezing past the dog and out of the back seat.

She slid into the passenger seat beside her mother, who had scooted over to be next to her husband. Looking in the rear view mirror, Curtis saw a completely content dog, panting and licking the faces of Jenny and Judd.

"Now are we ready to go?" Curtis teased.

For three days the family fished, swam, grilled out, and had some leisurely time in the sun. Curtis borrowed a boat from the man in the neighboring cabin so he could teach the kids how to water ski. He was an experienced skier but Phoebe wouldn't try it. She didn't know how to swim, consequently she hated the water. Lily got up the first time and soon the boys also became prolific skiers. When Max wasn't on the boat with Curtis or in the water, he sat with Jenny on the beach. Watching Jenny build sand castles, Phoebe sat by the shore, between tranquil gazes reading another page of the novel she'd brought along. When rain threatened they moved to the cabin. With no sign of lightening, the rest of the family stayed on the lake. While Jenny colored and played with paper dolls on the porch, Phoebe sat in the rocker, perfectly content to be idle.

A public campground was situated right across the road from their cabin, and Phoebe watched as campers built fires, pitched tents or leveled their RVs, loading and unloading gear from various cars, trucks and trailers. It became obvious as she watched that several of the campers belonged to the same family and were setting up for a reunion. A sign that read *The Kent Family* was fastened over the middle camper. Two of the family members were quite old and she presumed them to be the matriarch and patriarch of this extensive family. Judging by the way Grandpa Kent shuffled his feet, his bent back and shaking hands, Phoebe recognized the signs of Parkinson's disease. Curtis' father had suffered from the disease. She began thinking of her own family—parents long gone, a brother who barely knew she existed. It made her sad as she continued to watch.

One of the men, apparently the owner of the trailer, created a shelter from the threatening rain by suspending a long tarp from the camper to poles stuck into the ground about ten feet away. Another man managed the grilling of meat, while two others moved picnic tables under the canopy. Several young children ran and played in the grass around the consolidated camp as the women, presumably their mothers, produced various dishes from coolers then scurried around to set up a buffet. Grandma and Grandpa Kent sat in lawn chairs, observing their brood with approval.

Lunch began ceremoniously, with the clanging of a triangle. Just as plates were loaded and everyone began being seated, an intermittent sprinkle escalated into a modest rainfall. A flurry of activity ensued as everyone sought shelter under the canopy. Crowded together, with the elder Kents seated in the middle across from each other, they commenced eating. A plurality of flies joined them under the tarp, frantically buzzing around ears, dive-bombing into food and sitting on drink containers. As rapidly as whooshed away, they landed nearby, especially annoying to Grandpa Kent who kept violently shooing them away from his bottle of beer. The inevitable finally occurred. He forcefully swiped away a fly with his shaking hand and his beer bottle went flying across the picnic table, hitting Grandma Kent in the head. It took several minutes to restore order to the scene. Though bleeding, she was not seriously hurt but, at the first ray of sunshine, the Kent family, sans Grandpa, scattered.

Phoebe had been missing her parents while first observing the Kent family. But, as she continued watching, she was able to find one positive element related to her parents' premature deaths. *At least I don't have to watch them grow old and infirm, gradually losing their grip on life.* She thought about her dad's alcoholism, wondering how her mother had coped. Assuming there were difficult times, she mentally thanked her for managing to shield her and her brother from the worst of it. They had been aware of his drinking, but not the extent to which it affected all their lives. It had been the hardest on her brother, who grew up lacking a proper role model. *No wonder he's had problems*, she deduced, for the first time excusing his distance and estrangement. Though never confirmed, she wondered if her dad's drinking had directly or indirectly caused the car accident that had killed her parents.

Curtis' parents had been model citizens—extraordinary, bucolic people who treated everyone with love and kindness, and raising their only child in their likeness. She knew it was what had most drawn her to Curtis. Though she found him handsome, she knew most women would not. That was fine with her because it meant she had him all to herself without fear of trespassing, except by the likes of Roxanne Temple. Unlike her dad, his was a very good role model for a family man, a loving father and husband. When his dad died, he'd been devastated. Having his mother move in with them had helped, but also greatly complicated their lives. In time, they had all adjusted to her presence and she'd managed to fit herself into their lifestyle without complaint. In fact, she had been an asset, helping to care for Jenny when she was a toddler. What Phoebe remembered most about her was her unerring generosity, positive outlook on life, and ability to face each day anew.

The rain finally disgorged Curtis and the older children from the lake. They arrived at the cabin claiming starvation and suggesting a drive into town for pizza. Jenny, usually the last one ready, loved pizza and was the first one out the door. Since they could eat outside, Max came along and sat beside them, begging for hand outs. After pizza, they went to the local ice cream shop for cones. The only damper on the evening, was the knowledge they'd be leaving the next morning. They were glorious days together that would be remembered, and provide strength, for the days ahead.

Arriving home on Monday afternoon, they were relieved to find everything in apparent order. Ryan reported that nothing out of the ordinary had occurred. Of course, he had no idea of what a typical farm day was like, but at least the house still stood, as did the barn and other outbuildings. The truck and three-wheel ATV were parked where Curtis had put them and the only change Curtis could detect was that the corn had grown visibly taller.

The next day, before anyone else was up, he counted the cattle and hogs near the barn then got on the ATV and drove to the south pasture to count the brood cattle. He then inspected the machinery, starting the tractor and combine, and found nothing wrong or missing. Surveying the back acreage and fields, however, he found tire tracks everywhere. Unwilling to worry Phoebe, he decided not to mention the tracks to her when he returned to the house for breakfast.

Gaylan Morray had counted on the horrible growing season for farming predicted by the Farmer's Almanac and National Weather Service. It was one explanation for his rare fit of compassion in excluding the house from the mortgage—certain it would not be an obstacle in expunging the Higgins family from their farm. The hot, dry weather forecast would have insured a much diminished crop of corn and soybeans. Without any overage of crops to sell for operating expenses or to pay for seed and nitrogen, the farm could not be maintained for long. Sure the mortgage would then fall into default with foreclosure to follow, he had assumed easy pickings. When the summer weather instead proved to be ideal for farming, the harvest promising to overfill all storage containers with bumper crops, he was forced to fall back on a contingency plan of action.

Despite Curtis' abstinence, gossip about his drinking persisted in town, his reputation impugned. Phoebe picked up bits and pieces while on errands. When anyone mentioned it to her, she vehemently denied the rumors, but the more she repudiated them, the more they stuck. Someone even suggested she commit Curtis to rehabilitation. When she told Curtis the rumors he persuaded her to ignore them and anyone who spread them.

Curtis' earlier suspicions that someone was snooping around the farm were confirmed two weeks later when he heard a truck leaving the woods. Investigating, he found fresh tire tracks near the barn. Keeping a watchful eye, he maintained his busy schedule, still unwilling to alarm Phoebe. A second cutting of hay was made and, if the weather held as predicted, a third would follow. The soy beans were ready for harvest by early August and the boys helped get the crop in. Mortgage payments were always made on time, though the amount was exorbitant. Curtis hoped the bountiful harvest would allow them to pay down part of the mortgage, as well as their bills of credit.

For the most part Phoebe and Curtis no longer discussed the acre out on the highway but cringing when they read in the local paper of another planned business or development. With word out that the highway was a done deal, spats over land ownership grew intense but, always, Gaylan Morray managed to seal the deal. He sold several acres to a prominent hotel chain then three more to fast food franchisers. Soon another national chain claimed ownership of some of his land then a major discount store made plans to move in. He persuaded the town manager to build a frontage road, then another street adjacent to one of his properties, the one that had belonged to Phoebe and Curtis. It gave him access to nearly every lot out by the proposed interchange.

The FBI and state police investigation of the drug case came to a dead halt without the testimony of Ted Whartley. Doug Hewes was released from jail and claimed impunity—another travesty of justice accomplished. The state police continued to investigate Ted Whartley's death throughout the summer. The sheriff, who had been first on the scene, was suspected of tampering with evidence but nothing could be proven, his conclusion as to C.O.D. upheld. Thanks to Ted's undercover work on the drug case other questionable affairs of the town were brought to light. The FBI probe extended to the bank and Gaylan Morray, resulting in the closing down of the holding company but, surprisingly, no other consequences. Without witnesses willing to come forward and testify, there was a limit to what the Federals could do. The investigation eventually dried up, tabled for lack of evidence, with no indictments. Undercover work continued, however, in the hope someone would eventually step forward and implicate the guilty.

Virginia knew who'd done her cousin in, as did Phoebe and Curtis but nothing was said, even to each other. Virginia and Kenneth sold their house in the country and moved to the next county. Phoebe rarely saw Virginia after that and avoided the subject when they met. She knew Phoebe or Curtis had never revealed Ted's undercover position but someone had, making her suspicious of nearly everyone. Phoebe envied Virginia and Ken their ability to just pull up roots and leave, suspecting it was what they should do instead of rail against Morray.

The nefarious Gaylan Morray was the poster child for greed. A snap shot of him might resemble that of Scrooge McDuck, rolling in his money and tossing money bags into the air. With no interests or hobbies, one could only wonder what he wanted with so much money. Edith spent lavishly but couldn't have put a dent in their resources. Besides, she had her own funds, thanks to her father. Morray drove a Jaguar, had a nice house but was otherwise not conspicuously consumptive. Money was power, though, and he knew it well. The only conclusion to be drawn, was that he maneuvered people, their properties, livelihoods and destinies purely for sport.

CHAPTER FIVE

Often, on sojourns into town, Phoebe stopped to see her friend Agnes who lived on Crawford Street. There were only two houses on the street, Agnes' and her neighbor, Nicholas Strathmore. Nicholas was originally from England and why and how he'd landed in Dirk County, much less Between, strained the mind. He drove to Dirkville each day for work. No one knew what he did there and no one asked, his mystique left to conjecture. Agnes was shunned by the town's people for being odd, an *artist,* when, in fact, she was probably the most normal among them. It seemed only appropriate that the two town outcasts live side-by-side on the same street, slightly away from the rest of the town. Agnes kept to herself, painting, sculpting, and occasionally driving to Lynchford to take her work to a gallery. No one locally had any interest in or knowledge of her work.

"Hi, Agnes," Phoebe greeted, when Agnes answered her knock. "I hope you don't mind my stopping by to see you unannounced?"

"Absolutely not, come on in," Agnes answered, holding the door open wide, a paint rag in her hand.

Agnes was a slight woman in her mid-forties. It always surprised Phoebe to hear such a deep voice coming from so petite a person. Her long auburn hair was pulled back into a loose ponytail at the base of her neck, with wisps of hair straggling down over pierced ears looped in sterling silver. Agnes had married young, divorced, and raised two children alone. They now lived in California and, like their mother, were artists. Her ex-husband came to visit occasionally, often enough to keep the local gossip pot stirred. Agnes' most outstanding feature was her dark gray eyes, their unfathomable depth a fountainhead of kindness.

"What have you been up to?"

"What I'm most always up to, I guess," Agnes responded, shrugging her shoulders.

"Can I see your latest work?"

"Sure. Come along to my studio."

Agnes's studio was just off the kitchen. It was a bright room filled, as was the rest of the house, with art work hung on every wall. Most were by Agnes, others were gifts from fellow artists in other parts of the country, along with several works by her children.

"Oh, I really like this new one you're working on," Phoebe trilled, crossing the room to stand in front of a large easel holding a canvas.

"I'm glad you like it. I'm not done of course. Can you tell what it is?" asked Agnes, always uncertain her abstract paintings would appeal to anyone.

"It looks like a woman holding a small child to me. What is it supposed to be?"

"A woman holding a small child."

"It's really quite amazing, Agnes. Of course, I like all your work," Phoebe added, gazing around the room.

"Do you have time for a cup of tea?"

"Sure do. Got any of that exotic stuff from China?"

"I think so. Let me get the kettle going. Look around all you want. I'll be in the kitchen. Lemon bar with your tea?"

"You bet!"

Phoebe had always wanted to be an artist or writer. She'd drawn constantly as a child but had never seriously followed through as an adult. Agnes had encouraged her to start drawing again, even offering to give her lessons, but her first love was writing—with no spare time, a creative endeavor more easily put aside.

"I don't have any cream," Agnes offered, as Phoebe wandered into the kitchen, eyeing the paintings hanging there.

"That's all right. I quit having cream in my tea anyway. I've decided I'm not British—besides its Chinese tea. Your neighbor is a rather odd sort, even for Between, isn't he?" she commented, looking out the window toward

Strathmore's house.

"Yeah, peculiar, you might say—a real novelty around this town," Agnes caustically responded. "Is he out there?"

"He's pulling weeds in the garden—I think."

"He's nice enough but we both keep to ourselves. He's been over a few times."

"Have you ever learned what he does for a living in Dirkville?" Phoebe asked, continuing to stare out the window.

"No. He's never offered. If I ask him then he might want to know something about me and we're both too private for that exchange. He's a cross dresser, you know."

"That explains the dress," Phoebe said, finally moving away from the window and sitting down at the kitchen table.

"You ought to get a good look at his toenails. They're painted bright red."

"No—thanks!"

"Two days ago he was mowing the lawn in a bikini. I'm pretty liberal but it was way over the top even for me—I had to pull my shades."

"Well, at least I've been spared that scene," Phoebe laughed. "These lemon bars are sensational."

"Thanks. You look good, Phoebe. Is everything going better since you sold that acre to Morray?"

"There don't seem to be any new problems but you have to wonder what he's up to when things are quiet."

"He's a bad one, that's for sure. And his sons should be slapped twice a day just on principle. Clyde, it's told, is the ringleader, Owen his stooge, if a stooge can have a stooge. Thinking for both of them must be exhausting. You have to wonder what their mother thinks of them. She actually seems rather nice. You're not the only ones Morray's put the screws to but most people, at least in town, don't seem to be aware of his collective damage."

"I know that. His reputation is more widely circulated

among the farmers. Given some of the stories I've heard, in many ways we've gotten off easy. Morray also holds the mortgage on our farm now, however, so we're always walking around on egg shells waiting for the other shoe to fall."

"I think you're mixing your metaphors, Phoebe."

"You know what I mean, Agnes," Phoebe returned, laughing.

"Yes, I know what you mean. I've lived in this town for eight years and am still shocked sometimes when I occasionally get wind of what's going on. As evil as Morray appears to be, I understand he's milk-and-water where his wife is concerned."

"Do you really think so?"

"That's what I've heard. She owns majority stock in the bank. Otherwise, I doubt he'd stay with her. There's no love lost between them."

"Do you know anything about her son, Vincent?"

"Not really. He's a very quiet sort of man. His father was well-respected and he's well-liked, despite his association with the bank and Morray."

"So you don't think he's in on the plots Morray devises or could be responsible for carrying them out?"

"I doubt it but you never know. Why, do you suspect him?"

"Only by association. He is vice president. On a different note, why on earth do you stay here, Agnes? I'd sure miss you but wouldn't it be better for you to live in the city with more open-minded people—and closer to the galleries?"

"I've never liked the city, except for the privacy—and since everyone here ignores me, I have that here—and a country setting surrounded by nature. It's very inspiring and the theme of most of my artwork—as I expect it is for most artists and writers. You ought to write about your experiences with Gaylan Morray."

"No one would believe it."

"It doesn't matter because you'd make it fiction anyway, wouldn't you?"

"Yes, I suppose so. Maybe some day when I have more time. Meanwhile, I'm keeping a journal."

"Good for you. With all the gossip floating around this town and the great abundance of characters, you could turn your journal entries into a juicy novel."

"Too juicy, maybe," Phoebe responded. "I have managed to write a couple of short stories but not about recent events. One is called *Going Postal*, about my experience working at a post office branch while in college. The other is *Coming to my Census*, documenting my census taking several years ago."

"Great titles! Hyperbole, I take it. Would you let me read them?"

"That's a scary thought. I never intended for anyone to read them. Say, how are your kids? Don't you miss them horribly?"

"They're doing well. Do I miss them? Sometimes. To loosely quote Oscar Wilde, 'I'm so miserable without them, it's almost like they're here.'"

"You're a trip, Agnes. Gotta go. I still need to get to the grocery store and feed mill." It suddenly occurred to Phoebe she'd always gone to Agnes' for tea, and that her friend had never been to her house. "You ought to come out to visit me sometime—no formal invitation needed."

"I'd like to, but you're always so busy."

"Not too busy for a friend. By the way, I'm taking a little trip to see my great aunt. She's my only living relative, besides my brother, who, judging by the lack of communication, might not be."

"Really? You still haven't heard a word from him?"

"No—not for years now."

"That's really a shame. I hope he's all right. Where does your aunt live?"

"In the northern part of the state. In a town called Monpree. I haven't seen her for years either—not since my parents died."

"When do you leave?"

"Next week. I'll take Jenny with me."

Knowing the books she'd borrowed would be long overdue by the time she got back from her trip, Phoebe stopped at the library after leaving Agnes. The librarian, Miss Winters, was a tall, dusty, plebian woman long past middle age with pince-nez glasses resting on a narrow hooked nose. She was a blight, spreading germs of bitterness wherever she went. Phoebe remembered her having a biological sounding first name, but couldn't recall what it was and her name tag read only *Miss Winters*. It was Phoebe's conviction that her personality was as icy as her name, as cold as the granite from which the library was constructed. Perfunctorily receiving the books offered, Miss Winters said nothing, returning her attention to the important work of filing index cards.

Miss Winters lived on the south end of town in a big, white, neglected house. Rumor had it she lived in only one room and had no running water. Her parents had owned the house and she'd taken care of them in their elder years, bypassing, it was said, any and all proposals of marriage or deflowering. When they died ownership of the house came to her. Children appeared to be her arch enemies. If a child accidentally hit their ball into her yard, straying onto her turf to retrieve it, she flew out of the house, broom in hand, to dispatch the trespasser. Since she walked to and from the library, the children of the neighborhood began referring to the broom as her only means of transportation and her, as Witch Winters. At Halloween her house was dark and foreboding, a deterrent to even the boldest trick-or-treater.

Trip preparations kept Phoebe busy for days. Though reluctant to leave her responsibilities, she knew this to be her last chance to visit her aunt who was failing in health. Packing the suitcases she thought about her brother, wishing she could visit him instead—a moot point, she concluded, since she didn't know where he was or how to get in touch with him. He had never invited her to come and see him nor for years indicated any interest in visiting. It made her sad but she didn't know what if anything could be done about it. Several years ago, before she'd lost track of his whereabouts, she had made several overtures toward him that had been rebuffed. The proverbial ball was in his court and she suspected that it was where it would stay.

Mid-August Curtis helped Phoebe load the car and she and Jenny headed north. The drive would take about five hours. Knowing it was going to be a long trip Jenny immediately lay down in the backseat and went to sleep, leaving Phoebe alone with her thoughts. Staring at the highway, an expanse of fields extending in all directions, she saw only an occasional farmhouse and scattered recumbent cows, passing through small rural towns without taking note of them as her active mind sorted. She thought about Morray for a time then her elderly aunt, wondering how to bridge the gap that had opened up between them. Phoebe's mother had two sisters, one older, another younger. She'd never gotten close to the younger aunt, who for years had lived in Europe, but Aunt Roseanne had been special to her when she was a child. Since the death of her parents, an involuntary estrangement had existed. They'd kept in touch but only by mail or phone. Roseanne had never married or had children. When her younger sister, also childless and unmarried, recently died, Roseanne made Phoebe executor of her will.

Seeing the city limits sign for Monpree, Phoebe was astounded to find herself at their destination. She woke up Jenny, prompting her to brush her hair. Monpree was a small town and it wasn't difficult to find Hickory Street. She knew the address and found it easily. As they drove into the driveway her aunt came out onto the porch to greet them, heavily leaning on a walker, her edematous ankles evidence of congestive heart failure.

Roseanne was spinster tall, probably the keeper of the genes from which Phoebe had gotten her height. Phoebe had once thought her aunt's equine features and florid complexion, while not converging into anything resembling beauty, had given her an air of dignity, almost royalty—her erect posture like that of a staked scarecrow out in the garden. It surprised Phoebe to see how diminished and frail she'd become. At ninety-six, shoulders that once held her strength had become fragile and sloped. Her snow white hair was pulled back into a chignon, a prominent widow's peak at her forehead, her bitter, unsmiling eyes emerging from sunken sockets.

Enjoying a cup of tea together, their reunion started out pleasantly but Roseanne soon began the catechism she was famous for, prying into all aspects of Phoebe's life. Phoebe grew defensive, explaining things she had no intention of discussing. Thankfully, Roseanne tired mid-afternoon and went to her bedroom for a nap. That's when Phoebe decided she would simply abide her aunt's behavior, be as kind and personable as she could be, and wrap up their visit at the earliest possible moment. Jenny declared boredom as they sat on the porch together. In a rare reprimand of her baby, Phoebe told her their visit was important and that she didn't want to hear any complaining.

The gardener arrived, tipped his tattered straw hat in greeting and began trimming the spirea bushes at the front of the house with reverence, an absorbed expression on his brown face. Since he was obviously Hispanic, and Phoebe knew her aunt to be prejudiced against all cultures sans those of her New England heritage, it surprised her. Carlos was the husband of Roseanne's housekeeper, Consuelo. When the bushes were trimmed Carlos started mowing the lawn, until a steady rain began falling. Phoebe and Jenny moved indoors just as Aunt Roseanne emerged from her bedroom.

Their visit was enjoyable in some ways but also quite depressing. Roseanne spoke in aphorisms. Phoebe had

never noticed before her aunt's mordant personality, a self
-righteous religious zealot, like her neighbor, Helen Weils.
Her impenitent pronouncements were punctuated with
outdated, politically incorrect terms to describe Coloreds,
Homos, and Retards, among others. It was hard to hear.
Phoebe wasn't extremely liberal but had learned tolerance,
and her kids had taught her the more acceptable terms for
various segments of the population.

While they were there Aunt Roseanne insisted they go
to church, then to the cemetery where her sister was buried. "I'll be joining her soon," she pronounced in her
dreariest tone, as they stood staring at the tombstone. It
took all the patience Phoebe could muster to abide their
visit. But, knowing she was her aunt's only relative bol-
stered her and, between lectures and tirades, they managed
to visit Roseanne's attorney to get all necessary papers
signed.

Four days after their arrival, Phoebe bid farewell to
her aunt with a gentle hug, promising to keep in touch.
Carlos put their suitcases in the car, as Consuelo pressed a
box lunch into Phoebe's hands. As the miles ticked on and
Jenny chattered away, Phoebe's thoughts turned to her
brother, Harry. As children they'd been very close, drift-
ing apart late in high school as their choices in friends began to differ. Attending colleges at opposite ends of the
country had driven them further from each other. When
their parents died something in Harry had collapsed. The
strong, confident brother she'd adored growing up disappeared, replaced by a confused, aimless vagabond she no
longer knew. Two hours into the trip Phoebe pulled the
car into a wayside park and they ate the lunch Consuelo
had packed for them. After stopping for gas they were on
the road again. Jenny soon crawled into the backseat and
slept for the remainder of the trip.

Curtis came out to greet them when they drove into
the driveway. Jenny told her dad all about the trip, as her
parents engagingly smiled. Jenny's innocence kept their

spirits high regardless of what else was going on in their lives. The older kids, out in the barn tending their calf, Margaret, came running upon hearing their Mom and Jenny were back. After hugs from her siblings, Jenny ran to the stable with Judd, who had been caretaker of Tess in her absence. Bart returned to his chores and Lily went to the garden, as Phoebe and Curtis walked arm in arm to the house. Though in serious debt, they still had their farm— and each other.

"Did everything go all right while I was away?" Phoebe questioned.

"Yes, I would say so. Judd, and especially Bart, seem to have settled down a bit, asking fewer questions and showing more cooperation. Lily is Lily—great as always. They've all managed to pamper Margaret from calf to heifer. It's good to see Judd involved with another animal. He still talks about Prudence, though."

"He probably always will. That was quite a blow for someone so young."

"It's been eerily quiet at the farm. I hope that's a good thing."

"I think our troubles are behind us, Curtis. If we can just keep things going long enough to get a little cushion, we'll be all right."

"I hope you're right. That corn grows so fast you can practically watch it. I should be able to start harvesting early."

Lily had cleaned up the kitchen and it virtually shone. The beds were made, laundry done, a nice pot roast in the oven filled the air with its savory aroma, and a fresh plum pie sat on the counter.

"It's good to be home," Phoebe sighed.

When Lily returned from the garden with fresh greens her mother was generous in praise of all her efforts. Talk at supper was about the trip, Aunt Roseanne, and how things had gone on the farm. The plum pie was sensational. After supper the family sat on the porch talking until bedtime, glad to be together again.

Early September, just after school started, was fair time. Lily won first prize for her latest pie recipe: Banana-Praline Cream Fluff. The decision of the judges was unanimous. She and Judd also won a blue ribbon for Margaret. Judd, missing Prudence, still avoided the hog barns but otherwise had a good time. Jenny enjoyed the fair but her attention was focused on the upcoming 4-H Horse and Pony Show. Talk around the barns at the fairgrounds was of the excellent growing season, abundant crops, and general well-being of the farms in the region. Phoebe entered her new soap in a Homemakers Contest and, although she didn't win, was repeatedly asked for the recipe.

"I don't know how you manage to fit soap-making into your busy schedule with all you have to do, Phoebe," Mrs. Curtain commented, looking over the display of soap on the table.

"Actually, I enjoy doing it, so I make sure it fits in," answered Phoebe.

"Well, I don't suppose your husband is much help these days... Zelma Hutchinson told me that he..."

"You can be sure of one thing, Mrs. Curtain. Never can you count on anything Zelma Hutchinson tells you. She makes things up with more energy than she does her face and I'll thank you not to repeat to me anything she has told you. Here's the recipe you asked for."

"No—thank you. I changed my mind. I have enough to do as it is," returned Mrs. Curtain, her eyes rapidly blinking in indignation.

Curtis, Bart, and Judd stayed late Friday night to watch the stock car races, while Max sat in the truck. Phoebe and the girls went on ahead to the farm in the car. Arriving late, and in the dark, there were a couple of tense moments. When Phoebe turned on the lights nothing appeared missing or disturbed but she couldn't dismiss the feeling that someone had been in the house. Had she known of Curtis' suspicions to add to her own she might have calculated differently. Still, something told her to exercise caution.

"Curtis, I think you should leave Max at home when we go out—like to the fair," she told Curtis the next morning.

"You know he likes to be with me, Phoebe."

"Yes, but it might be a good idea to have him watch the place—just in case someone is around that shouldn't be. He at least *looks* like a watchdog which might scare someone who doesn't know what a wimp he really is."

"He's proven time and again that he's no watchdog. Do you suspect someone has been here or is hanging around?"

"I can't put my finger on anything in particular, just an uneasy feeling."

"I'm sure, given all that's happened, you've become overly suspicious. With our mortgage and that acre in his greedy little hands I think Morray is well satisfied enough to leave us alone, so try not to worry."

It promised to be a beautiful fall. The trees in the woods alongside the farm were daubed in colors of red, orange and gold. The sun warmed the temperatures to a reasonable level during the day, and nights were crisp and cool. Lily went off to Lynchford, working in an insurance office and attending college, living with two other young gals in an apartment. Phoebe was sad to see her go but knew it was for Lily's benefit to be on her own. She would be coming home weekends to help with canning until the garden was fully spent.

Jenny couldn't have been more pleased than to be in second grade. An excellent reader, she enjoyed exploring the library's endless supply of books. At the open house, her teacher, Miss Hinstead, said she was an excellent student and a joy to have around but tended to talk about her pony, Tess, too much. Like her mother and Lily, she excelled in art, bringing home handfuls of pictures to tape onto the refrigerator. In the absence of Lily, she assisted her mother with the garden harvest and canning.

Bart started his senior year in high school and, although still not on the football team, managed to attend most games. He had done well in wrestling the year before and planned to go out for it again. Judd, a born politician, emboldened himself to put last year behind him and was again class treasurer, as well as being on student council and the debate team. Both boys did chores when they got home from school and in the morning, before leaving. Bart usually drove the truck or car to school, dependent on which vehicle was needed at home, often running errands for his dad after school. Since Lily was no longer home to ride the bus with Jenny, she rode with the boys in the morning then took the bus home afternoons.

Phoebe thought about her life quite a lot in the days after Lily left, wondering if she was the good mother she thought she was, wondering if, being always so busy, she allowed enough time for her children. Still, she wouldn't have traded her farm life with anyone else's. While she had lost her main helper, Jenny was becoming more able to assist. It was most likely she would become an actress or model, but Phoebe began training her in the methods and processes of the domestic side of farming. There was always an over-abundance of work but everyone pulled their weight, and the fact that she and Curtis were a great team made everything go easier.

With the help of the boys, Curtis got the winter wheat sown. Late summer rains and a long, hotter than average fall facilitated a third cutting of hay. Once baled and stored the additional crop insured their livestock would be well fed over the winter months. Curtis even got most of the plowing done before frost, satisfied in observing the long tidy fallow furrows awaiting spring planting. Since Judd was unwilling to work with the hogs, Curtis gave him responsibility for the cattle—feeding them, taking a head count, and making sure there was fresh water in the tank. Bart had helped with the hogs, mostly cleaning out the pens and watering them but, late fall, Curtis taught him how to mix the corn, soy meal, and minerals for their feed, turning their care over to him.

Thanksgiving was a small family gathering. Phoebe had invited Agnes to join them but she was going to the city to have dinner with friends. She also invited Helen Weils, from across the road, but she declined without reason. Lily made the pumpkin pies then prepared the yams, a green bean casserole, and mashed potatoes while Phoebe got the dressing made and the turkey stuffed. Mid-afternoon they sat down to a feast, thankful to be together—Phoebe and Curtis silently thankful for no further incidences.

Late afternoon, while the guys did chores, Phoebe, Jenny and Lily went for a walk down Digbert Road to ease swollen stomachs. They walked past the driveway to Helen Weils's house and on toward the Harker farm. A red pickup truck came barreling down the road, trailed by a cloud of dust. Phoebe recognized it as belonging to Harley Weils, Helen's son. Thinking she now understood why Helen had declined their offer for dinner, and how nice it was that she and her son were reconciled enough to spend a holiday together, she was surprised when the truck raced past her driveway then theirs. It never occurred to her to question what business Harley might have farther down Digbert Road.

The week after Thanksgiving Judd turned sixteen and Curtis took him into town to get his driver's license. After that he and Bart, not without arguments, took turns driving to school. Sometimes, in the evening after supper or on Saturday morning, Judd drove to debate team practice at the high school. Curtis and Phoebe never worried about him because he was so responsible but disallowed him from giving anyone else a ride until he'd had at least a year of experience in driving—certain he'd comply.

Christmas was conservative in terms of gifts but liberal with fussing. Phoebe went out of her way to make it festive and bright for everyone, especially with baking and candy making. In addition to divinity and fudge, she made dozens of their favorite cookies: pinwheels and chocolate chews. With her mother's assistance, Jenny threw herself into baking cookies. At the age of eight she was also ready to become more responsible for Tess' care, currying and combing her each morning, walking or riding her around the ring, and seeing to her feed and water. She even mucked out the stall most days.

Lily came home Christmas Eve to spend the weekend. She had matured in being on her own. Without saying too much about him, there were occasional references to her boyfriend, Keith. Involved with activities and farm chores, Lily hadn't seriously dated in high school. Her glow let Phoebe know that, even though she said they weren't yet serious, she was quite smitten. Lily was a very private person, like her father, and Phoebe knew when not to push for answers to the myriad of questions swimming in her mind.

"One of these weekends, when you plan to come home, why don't you bring him along?" Phoebe offered Christmas morning, as they made dinner preparations.

"We'll see," was all Lily replied.

"When are your exams?"

"Two weeks after Christmas break. The second semester begins toward the end of January. I can't wait to get going on my new classes."

"What subjects will you take?"

"Nutrition, home furnishings. I'll be glad when I'm done with organic chemistry."

"I'm sure you'll do well, Lily. You certainly seem to be doing nicely this semester," Phoebe assured.

During the cold winter months that followed, Curtis tended the machinery, kept the books, made out his seed list, kept their driveway plowed out, and secured their credit with Farmers United Co-op. With the boys taking over most of the winter farm chores, and Curtis' time spent more on management, things were running smoothly. Unaware of the dark shadow that had moved inexorably over their farm, they forgot about one of Murphy's unfailing Laws. *When things are going well, you've probably overlooked something.* With renewed enthusiasm Curtis anticipated spring, getting out in the fields and getting his hands dirty again. It promised to be a productive and lucrative year.

Phoebe appreciated the more relaxed pace of the winter months but, as usual, grew tired of canned and frozen vegetables and fruit, eager for the ground to thaw and itching to till the soil for another garden. By early-May she was ready to embed new seeds and enjoy fresh produce again. Rhubarb, always a harbinger of spring, promised fresh pies. Next, came asparagus, grown in the garden but also gathered wild along the roadsides. Phoebe loved spring and tried to relax into the full enjoyment of it but, try as she might, she couldn't get Gaylan Morray's derisive image off her mind for long. Nothing blatant happened but his drone sons seemed omnipresent when she went into town, covertly staring at her from across the street or a store window.

On her way to the grocery store mid-May she stopped at the feed store to buy garden seed then went to the dry cleaners. Stanley Worth, the owner, was behind the counter talking to a man sitting in a chair next to the door. It took a moment for Phoebe to recognize him.

"Good morning Mr. Fessle. I haven't seen you for quite a while—how are you today?" she questioned the older gentleman, who could always be counted on to give an oddly detailed accounting of things. Since he was known to be quite eccentric, she'd never thought much about it. She rarely bumped into him. When she did, he was most always pleasant, if not downright friendly, unlike most locals.

"Any day above ground is a good day. Some parts of me are great, others, not so much," said Mr. Fessle, ripping his polyester striped shirt open so exuberantly that he nearly tore the buttons off.

Phoebe found herself staring at a twenty inch scar that ran the length of his scrawny, wrinkled, gray-haired chest. The holes from the stitches were still red, verging on infectious in appearance.

"It IS a good morning. Got my scar here to prove it— could be dead you know, the only other alternative. Of course, I could also have died on the operating table. You just never know when your number's up."

"Glad you're doing so well," Phoebe managed, swallowing a giggle. "Nice to see you again. Here's my receipt for the dry cleaning, Stanley."

Phoebe paid for the cleaning then made a hasty retreat. At the grocery store she picked up the few items needed then went to checkout. Standing in line was Mrs. Sellerman, an old neighbor of Virginia's—a farming wife and renowned busy body.

"Your Lily is a lovely girl. How's she doing in college?" she questioned Phoebe. "What is she studying?"

"She's doing very well, thank you. She's studying home economics."

"That will certainly come in handy. Say, I heard you now have your mortgage with Morray like the rest of us. I don't know how he gets away with charging those kinds of interest rates, do you?" she fussed. "You'd think he was king or something and us farmers, mere serfs."

"I'd keep my voice down if I were you, Mrs. Sellerman," Trudy, the cashier advised, her eyes darting around the store.

Trudy had experienced a run in several years ago with Gaylan Morray that had left her and her husband bankrupt and, despite having two small children and a baby at home, she was forced to go back to work.

"There isn't anyone here that will report on me," Mrs. Sellerman argued. "There's only Phoebe and I know she'd never say anything. I'll tell you the truth, eight percent interest is killing us nice and slow. I don't know why we don't all just turn our land over to Morray and save ourselves the trouble."

Phoebe was shocked, turning instantly red in the face with anger. For nearly a year they had been paying ten percent interest on their mortgage. The going rate was around eight on residential mortgages but Morray had told them the rate for farm properties was higher. It never occurred to them that he was squeezing others less forcefully. She paid for her groceries, threw them in the car, and drove to the bank.

"May I ask why you've been charging us ten percent interest on our farm loan when the going rate is eight?" Phoebe thrust, barging into Morray's office.

"Lower your voice, Mrs. Higgins," he hissed, his startled eyes shifting to venomous.

"I'll not lower my voice. This is highway robbery, clear as water. We'd be better off borrowing money from the mob," she screamed over the voice in her head telling her to shut up.

"I'll thank you not to speak to me like that. I'm the president of this bank and should be treated with the appropriate respect."

"The appropriate respect paid to you would be the same as that shown any criminal. This is the last straw."

Morray ushered Phoebe to the front door with words too harsh and foul to repeat and an imprint of his thumb imbedded into her arm just below the elbow. Phoebe arrived at the farm with no recollection of how she'd gotten there. When she related the incident to Curtis, he was nearly as hard on her as Morray.

"The dead last thing we need to do is rile Morray and you've just managed to do that in spades," he scolded.

They had more than a few spats over the incident, arguing in front of the children and behind closed doors. Phoebe tried her best to keep her composure, a front of self-assurance that belied her insecurities, her facade crumbling, as common sense kicked in. Her error in judgment in going to see Morray was a major blunder, and she knew it well. Afraid Curtis would start drinking again, she decided to let her rebuttals slide. A contrite and heartfelt admission of guilt followed, warming the chilly atmosphere between them. Gradually, as the bruise on her arm turned from purple to yellow, their household eased back to normal—but not for long. The damage had been done.

School would end the last day of May and by then all danger of frost would be past. In anticipation of getting the corn and soy beans planted, and counting on the help of his boys for the summer, Curtis finished plowing the fields. He would then disc, preparing the soil for seed. Working in the warming sun felt good and he was happy to be back outdoors in nature. Theirs was prime farmland, not the rocky uneven acreage of farms farther south. It was a source of pride to him that his rows of corn were always the straightest in the county. The day before school was out he drove into town to pick up seed at the co-op. Phoebe and Curtis were a unified front again, the bond of their marriage intensified through their troubles. But, neither of them suspected for a moment the degree to which their unity would be tested in the days ahead.

CHAPTER SIX

When Bart and Judd showed up at the barn to start chores after school, their dad, usually there with a head start, was no where to be seen. They expected him to come any minute so simply launched into their work. Though the situation was somewhat out of the ordinary, there was no reason for alarm. Therefore, figuring their mother knew what was going on, they never took the time to go tell her of their dad's absence. They were just finishing chores, when they heard the bell rung for supper, the smell of boiled dinner wafting toward them as they made their way to the house.

"That really smells good, Mom," Bart commented, emerging with Judd through the mudroom door.

"I'm glad. You must be really hungry. It's all ready, so go get your hands washed up. Is Dad right behind you?"

"Where IS Dad?"

"What do you mean, where is Dad?" Phoebe questioned, freezing in her tracks.

"He didn't show up for chores," Judd responded, nervously rubbing his nose.

"Didn't show up—how can that be? He should have been back from town hours ago. Are you sure he's not in the pole barn or out in the field?"

"I looked for him. The tractor and planter are in the pole barn, and the ATV is parked by the house as usual so, unless he's on foot, he's not around."

"The truck is gone," Bart inserted. "So is Max."

"I hope nothing's happened to him. Boys, get this meal on the table. Jenny, you pour the milk. I'm going to call a few places and see if anyone has seen him."

Phoebe called several places Curtis might have stopped, including the Farmers United Co-op. He had never picked up the seed. Then, her preternaturally acute senses at full alert, she called some of his usual haunts, places where he was likely to run errands, but no one had seen him or Max. Wilson, at the Sunset Bar and Grill, said he hadn't seen him for months—news of some relief. She decided to drive his usual route to town to see if his truck had broken down or there'd been an accident. Shaking, she strode through the kitchen for the back door, Ted Whartley's warning prominent in her thoughts.

"I'll be back shortly. You kids go ahead and eat then clean up the kitchen, put the food away and get to your homework," she mechanically ordered.

"We don't have any homework. School is out tomorrow," Judd corrected.

"Well, do something else then," she snapped, immediately penitent for her tone. "Just find something to do—all right?"

"Where are you going?" asked Bart

"I'm going to drive into town to see if Dad is stuck somewhere and needs help."

"I'll come along," Bart offered.

"Me, too," added Judd.

"Judd, I'm sorry but someone needs to stay by the phone, and with Jenny. Bart and I will be back soon."

She tried not to notice the dejected look on Judd's face. It seemed like he was always being left out, no matter how hard she tried to compensate. She and Bart got into the car and slowly drove Digbert Road, looking each direction and into ditches, to see if they could find any sign of Curtis. Downtown, they visited every business, open or closed for the day. At the gas station Harley insisted they had not seen Curtis for days but she noticed that Jeremy, usually friendly and talkative, kept silent. They next went to the Cozy Café and the grocery store. No one had seen Curtis, Max or the truck. Reluctantly, they turned toward home, again going slow enough to detect anything out of the ordinary.

"Someone called," Judd offered, as they came into the house.

"Who was it?"

"He wouldn't say, just asked for you. When I said you weren't here he hung up."

"It was a man then."

"Yes. The voice sounded familiar but I couldn't place it."

"I knew that listening for the phone would be the best way you could help, Judd. Thank you for staying by the phone."

At ten Phoebe sent the children to bed then took up her vigil, hoping the caller would call back. She fell asleep in the chair with her head on the kitchen table, waking up around midnight when the phone finally rang.

"Miz Higgins?"

"Yes. Who is this?"

"You donno me but I jus wanna warn ya that thar's things goin on that ain't good for you or yorn family. Ya be carful—like where you dun go an the like, where the kids go—who's watching and like that."

"Who is this? Jeremy, is that you?" Click!

Unable to sleep, Phoebe paced the living room floor until dawn then, putting on a calm and collected front, walked into the kitchen to prepare breakfast. When the kids showed up, asking for their dad, she had blueberry pancakes with home made maple syrup and fresh farm sausages prepared for them.

"Did anyone call? Have you heard anything about Dad?" Bart queried.

"No news yet, but I'm sure he's fine, so don't worry. He must have needed to attend to something I'm not aware of. He'll be back sometime today, you can be sure."

"Where's Daddy?" Jenny whined, straggling into the kitchen. "Is he all right?"

"I'm sure he's fine."

"When will Daddy be home?"

"Soon, Jenny, soon."

"Has he ever not come home before—like when we

were too little to know?" Judd diplomatically asked, thinking of the time he'd smelled liquor on his dad's breath.

"No, Judd, your dad is dependable. Something unexpected has come up."

"Do you want me to stay home today, Mom," Bart offered. "Judd can collect my things from my locker."

"No, you go ahead. I need to make some calls then go to town. Your dad and Max will be just fine so none of you should worry. You'll have to take the bus, though. Enjoy your last day of school and Dad and I will see you this afternoon."

Hustling the children off to the bus, she managed to conceal her extreme alarm. Alone, concern and confusion turned to mounting anxiety. Curtis had never done anything like this in their entire married life. It was so unlike him that there could only be one possibility. He didn't come home because he couldn't. That meant that either he'd been murdered, had an accident or was in some way prevented from doing as he wished. She thought of all the things that had happened to them in the previous year, all that Gaylan Morray had perpetrated. If Curtis had been murdered she certainly knew who to blame. Pushing such thoughts aside, she mulled over other possibilities, unable to come up with a viable explanation for his absence. At a reasonable hour to expect the gas station to be open, she called Jeremy.

"Jeremy, this is Phoebe Higgins. I know you called last night—know you saw Curtis in town yesterday. Where is he?" There was silence on the other end for a time.

"Can I hep ya, Miz Ranchard," Jeremy said, loudly greeting a customer. "I cain't talk now," he huskily whispered. "I'll call ya back in bout a hav hour."

Usually quite stoic, Phoebe waited by the phone wringing her hands. Jeremy knew something, and suddenly she was afraid to find out what it was. With plenty of time for the tension to build, she jumped a foot when the phone finally rang an hour later.

"Ya cain't get me into it, Miz Higgins."

"Into what? What is going on?"

"I seen 'em take him 'way, was all."

"Take Curtis away?"

"Yeah."

"Who took him away?"

"I cain't talk, Miz Higgins."

"Jeremy, who took Curtis away and where did they take him? If you don't tell me on the phone, I'll come down to the station."

"No!" he screeched.

"Jeremy, I need your help!" Phoebe screamed into the phone.

"The sherff dun took him," he finally offered, after a very long pause.

"Where?"

"Call the Dirkvul Rehabitation place and...I be right there, Harley. Gotta go."

"The Dirkville Rehabilitation Center? Why did they take him there?"

"Don call me agin and for chrissaske don come down here. Iffin ya do I won talk with ya. Ida swears yer lying that I called ya."

"What about Max? Did you see..." Click went the receiver.

Phoebe felt like she was falling into an abyss. Off the phone she tried to figure out what turn of events had landed her husband in the Dirkville Rehabilitation Center, escorted by the sheriff. *He must have turned to drink again,* became her only rational conclusion. *If the sheriff's involved then Morray might be, too.* Remembering her encounter with him at the bank, the voice in her head cautioning her against agitating him, remorse came streaming back, multiplied, and she ran to the bathroom and threw up.

"I want to talk with the head supervisor," Phoebe demanded over the phone, once she'd composed herself enough to call the Dirkville Rehabilitation Center.

"He's busy right now. Can I help you?" the timid receptionist offered.

"You get him on the phone this instant—it's an emergency," Phoebe emphatically returned.

Placed on hold, she waited impatiently, in no mood for delays. Thoughts of burning down the town, starting with Gaylan Morray's house, circulated through her mind as serene elevator music played in the background.

"This is Sydney Parker. May I help you?"

"This is Phoebe Higgins. I'd like to talk with Curtis."

"I'm afraid that's not possible. But he'd like to see you. Can you come today?"

"I need some answers."

"Answers?"

"Why is he at the Rehabilitation Center in the first place?"

"Please, Mrs. Higgins. Don't be coy with me. You know very well why he's in here. Just please come, Mrs. Higgins. He is quite insistent. I have to warn you, he's rather upset with you, given all that's happened. Maybe you can calm him down a bit. We had to restrain him for a while."

"Restrain him? When did he get there?"

"They located him early yesterday afternoon but it was about four by the time the sheriff got him here. He's only just now sobered up, so it's the first chance he's had to figure things out. He wants to see you, pronto."

"Sobered up? He was drunk?"

"You know he was, Mrs. Higgins. You should not be at all surprised, given his problem. Will you come this afternoon—say around three?"

"I'm coming this instant. You'd better let me see him."

"I think we can arrange for you to see him in about an

hour. I must warn you, however that…"

Phoebe hung up the phone, cutting him off. She then left a note for the kids, telling them she'd be home later, that everything was all right and they should carry on as usual until she and their dad returned. All the way to the center she tried to imagine what had occurred, running through the rules of inquiry in her head. What sequence of events had led to Curtis being there? When could he leave? Where had they found him? Why was he again drunk and how much was she to blame for him landing there? No answers were forthcoming. Though she suspected Morray's hand in it, she couldn't be sure until she talked to Curtis. At Dirkville she drove up the long black-top driveway of the rehabilitation center and parked the car in a space designated for visitors.

"Thank you for coming, Mrs. Higgins," Sydney Parker ingratiated, intercepting her in the lobby.

Mr. Parker was a limp-looking man, short and spin-dly— someone that could easily be picked up with a thumb and index finger and moved out of the way.

"I must tell you that, although your husband had to be restrained at first, we've now removed the restraints. He was very upset, not violent, but exceedingly angry and agitated—with circumstances—but mostly, with you."

"How could he be upset with me? I didn't even know he was here?"

"Come now, Mrs. Higgins, you sure don't have to pre-tend with me."

"Pretend? What kind of nightmare time warp is this? I don't have any idea what you're talking about."

"You must," Parker quizzically offered. "Your signa-ture on the commitment form from the judge is clear as a bell. The sheriff said they'd checked your signature on the form against your account signature card on file at the bank and it was a match."

"The bank? What has the bank to do with any of this?"

"Nothing, only to verify your signature. We don't take

these things lightly."

The wheels were turning in Phoebe's head faster than a whirling dervish, suspicions falling into place like tokens into gaming machine slots. It didn't take long to figure out what had happened and who was behind it. She knew all about Gaylan Morray's cruelty, so should not have been surprised. The length and breadth of their predicament slowly spread across her mind as she fought back tears.

"How long is he in for?"

"Ninety days."

"Any possibility of getting the commitment overturned."

"Overturned? Why would you want your wishes overturned? You can't enable Curtis, you know. It's not in his best interest. Enabling him probably is what landed him here in the first place," Parker stated as counsel.

Don't placate me! It was enabling all right but not by me, Phoebe's mind spit in a visceral reaction. "Just answer the question. Can the commitment be overturned?"

"I doubt it. The papers were signed by Judge Wilcox. It's unlikely he'd sign another reversing his decision. Believe me, it's the best for all concerned. You..."

"Take me to Curtis," she demanded.

Following closely behind the weasel-like man, Phoebe mentally prepared herself for Curtis' wrath. She had seen it very seldom. It was not a pretty sight and something she would just as soon not face. Parker unlocked a door and ushered her into a stark and cold room, where she was surprised to find a composed Curtis get up from the bed and walk toward her. He was dressed all in white, the logo of the rehabilitation center stenciled above the pocket of the buttonless, V-neck, cotton short-sleeved shirt. In the baggy pants and shirt, he looked like a bunch of bones someone had neglected to assemble. Instead of the horrifically angry expression she expected to see on his face, one of total contrition greeted her.

"Phoebe, I…"

"Shush," Phoebe whispered, holding her index finger to her mouth.

"Thank you Sydney. Will you please get his clothes together for me to take home and launder and give us some privacy?"

"Are you sure? Will you be…"

"Leave us!"

Sydney Parker first grew rigid then red in the face, slowly backing from the room and closing the door behind him. It was no longer locked from the outside nor was there a lock on the inside so they would have to assume privacy.

"Curtis, I didn't do this, you must know that."

"I know."

"You know? Sydney said you were angry with me."

"Not you—circumstances—beyond my control. I know you would never do anything like this. I can't believe it took me so long to sort it all out—guess I was just too groggy and angry to think rationally."

"When did you start drinking again?"

"That's just it. I didn't. I stopped at the gas station before going to the co-op. I had just opened the door and stepped out when someone grabbed me from behind and put something over my nose and mouth. That's the last I remember. They must have poured whiskey on me because the staff here assumed I was drunk from the smell— and from my drugged behavior. It's told I wasn't very docile."

"Jeremy told me it was Sheriff Tagwell that grabbed you. Did you see him?"

"No, I didn't see anything. What happened to Max? Did he come home?"

"No. We haven't seen Max. You don't know where they took him?"

"No. Last I saw him he was in the back of the truck."

"Where's the truck?"

"I don't know that either. Try and find Max will you? He's used to being with me and would get really insecure on his own. It scares me to think what they might have done with him."

"We'll do our best to find him—and the truck—so don't worry."

"How long am I in here for? They wouldn't tell me."

"Ninety days."

"Ninety days. But that's just...."

"Yes, Curtis, just long enough to prevent us from planting the spring crops and tending them. If we can get the wheat cut we'll have some feed but, without the corn and soy bean harvest, there won't be any crops to sell—or with which to make the mortgage payment," she added, watching the full impact of her statement register on Curtis' face.

"He's really got us this time. I don't know what we'll do, Phoebe. I'm sorry."

"He doesn't have us yet, Curtis. I've still got a lot of fight in me and the kids are fresh troops. We'll find a way to manage it. You told me last winter that you'd gotten all the fields plowed. Bart and Judd are capable of disking and planting the corn and beans aren't they? And I'm no novice at farming, you know."

"I know but it's too much to manage for all of you. Jenny's so young, though willing I'm sure. Lily is at school. You have the house and children to look after. I'd ask my cousin to help but he has his own work to do, and besides, he's too far away. Spring is the worst time for anything like this to happen. There's so much work to be done on the farm and everything depends on getting the crops planted and getting the growing season off to a good start," Curtis expounded, pacing the room. "Sorry—you know this. I'm just thinking out loud," he added, stopping to face Phoebe. "I'm sure the timing is no accident, given who's probably responsible."

"Yeah, I wonder who that could be?"

"I should have known, when I saw all those tire tracks in the fields and around the barn, that our troubles weren't over."

"When was that?" Phoebe asked in a shocked tone.

"When we got back from vacation."

"Why didn't you say something? Maybe we could have done something."

"I didn't want to worry you—and what could we have done?"

"Never mind. We've both had clues. I should have told you I suspected someone had been in our house."

"When was that?"

"During the county fair."

"Why didn't you say anything?"

"Same reason you gave—I didn't want to worry you. I started to tell you when I suggested Max stay at home, but you convinced me I was worrying for nothing."

"Well, I know I should have confided in you, too, but I didn't see that they'd messed with anything—it never occurred to me that they were up to anything more than a reconnaissance snoop."

"Reconnaissance snoop? You should know they'd never stop with that. You had evidence, decipherable clues there'd been someone around. I only had suspicions. If you hadn't gained a reputation in town for drinking, none of this would have happened."

"Yes, and you should have known better than to storm into the bank and descend like the wrath of God on Gaylan Morray," Curtis blurted back. The minute he said it, he regretted it. "I'm sorry, Phoebe, this is no more your fault than mine."

"Let's just get on with things and forget about whose fault it is. There's enough blame to go around," she reasoned.

"Even if we could get the crops planted, what makes you think they'd stay planted, or that some other scheme to undo us wouldn't kick in?"

"Let's give it a try. If we fail then at least we'll know we gave it our all."

"We can start over if need be. It might be the best thing anyway."

"You quit talking like that. Don't discount us yet. I'll not let that bastard get us if it's the last thing I do on this earth."

"Don't YOU talk like that, Phoebe. I don't want to ever hear you talk like that. He's a bastard all right but not worth losing ourselves over. We'll—you'll give it a try is all. Unfortunately, there's nothing I can do from here but give moral support and advice when needed."

"I'd better get going so I can let the kids know what's ahead. I'd like to keep them out of this as much as possible, but I don't know to what extent we can. I hope to God someone isn't listening so they know what we plan. Sydney said you could have phone privileges in a few days. If you sense anything strange, or you think they know we're not giving up, make them let you use the phone and call me. Tomorrow I'll go to the co-op and get our seed on credit. Is that list for quantities you made out on your desk or do they know what is needed?"

"The list is on the desk, right under the ledger, but they know what's needed, as well. Just tell them the usual. I hope the co-op gives you a credit line."

"It's revolving, automatic, remember. A rare oversight by Morray, I'm sure. I'll let you know when we find Max—and the truck—and come and see you again first chance I get. You just try to get sober, all right?" she said, winking.

"You're something else, Phoebe," Curtis said, reaching for her. "If we pull this off it will be a miracle, but I'm glad you're willing to try. Please don't get upset if it doesn't work. We'll just start over. He might eventually get the farm, despite all your effort, but we can't let him break up our family or pull you and me apart."

"That's right. No matter what happens we have to remember that. It will all work out. I'll make sure of it," Phoebe whispered in his ear, as they parted.

Not knowing who else to turn to, and unwilling to involve the few people in town she knew to trust, when Phoebe got to Between she paid a visit to the parish priest. Father McClaine, wearing his alb, assumed she had come for confession and, when she indicated otherwise, he seemed disappointed. While she laid out her troubles to him, trying earnestly to remember all that had happened, all she suspected of Gaylan Morray, the priest eyed her with a lascivious look that opposed celibacy. *Scratch a priest, find a sinner.* She didn't attend church but two or three times a year so had little experience with Father McClaine or any other priest, but the way he leered made her wonder why priests were so exalted.

"Phoebe, I think you're exaggerating the situation a bit," he responded, after a long silence once she'd finished talking.

"Trust me, I'm not."

"Gaylan Morray isn't a member of my congregation, so I don't know him well, only know of him. If he'd done even half the things you accuse him of, he'd be in jail."

"You just don't get it, do you? He owns everybody around here. They're all scared of him so they do what he asks. There's no one at a higher level of law enforcement than the local absurdity that knows what he's up to because none of us will talk, for fear of losing our properties or worse. He's clever, I'll give him that. Of course he never does the dirty work himself. His sons, from some unknown planet, do most of it but you can be sure it's on his orders."

"I don't know what you want me to say, what you expect me to do?"

"Nothing, I guess. I just thought you might be the one person in town who didn't owe him money and therefore wasn't under his thumb."

"The church would never be under anyone's thumb,"

he spouted, haughtily.

"No, but that's probably because everyone is under the church's thumb."

"Now, Phoebe. I don't think that's a very Christian thing to say."

"That's true enough. Sorry to have bothered you with my worries. It's only the loss of our farm and break-up of my family that's threatened," she quipped, sailing out the door of his office.

Driving through town, she chastised herself for having such a short fuse, for turning to someone so unworldly for advice. She blamed herself for not suspecting problems last winter when everything was going so well, for not realizing that when things were quiet there was sure to be trouble lurking. Gaylan Morray was beyond redemption. He had successfully lured them into letting their guard down by allowing a period of calm. One thing she knew for sure, thicker skin would be required to endure. Steeling herself, she turned onto Digbert Road and headed home.

Corralling the kids into the kitchen, she tried her best to alleviate their concerns regarding their father and explain the latest turn of events. Her adroit mind calculated, weighed, and sorted as she spoke, providing information without unduly alarming them. Her main concern was their safety so she swore them to secrecy.

"I don't want any of you to go anywhere I don't know about and never alone—and NEVER speak of anything that happens on our farm or with our family to anyone, no matter how many questions they may fire at you. Do you understand?"

"What will happen to us, Mommy?" Jenny questioned.

"Nothing—I just want all of you to be careful and I don't want our business spread all over town. There are people in this community that do not want us to be here. It's nothing we've done, it's simply that this is prime land and they want it. But, we can't let them have it and I need

your help. We think they're the same people that are responsible for your father being in rehab for three months."

"Who are these people?" Bart questioned.

"We don't know—that's the problem. Whoever it is,
they apparently think that if they prevent your dad from
planting this season's crops, the farm will fail, we'll leave,
and they can have the land. But we're going to try to keep
everything going without him."

"How will we do that?" Bart asked.

"I haven't figured that out yet, but I will. Meanwhile,
please don't ask me a bunch of questions I can't answer.
I've told you all I know. We'll have to work very hard.
Will you all help with everything I ask of you?"

"Yes, Mom, we will," the kids sang in chorus.

"Me, too," Lily added, from the doorway.

"Lily, what are you doing home?"

"Bart called me and said Dad was missing. I thought I
should be here. School's out next week. I've arranged to
take my exams early, on Monday, so I'll have to go back
for the day. But I'm here for the weekend and can come
home after that to stay for as long as you need me."

"What about your job?"

"Mr. Bertram gave me a leave of absence until fall on
the promise I'd find him a reliable summer replacement."

"What do you want us to do, Mom?" Bart questioned.

Despite every attempt to prevent it, Phoebe started
crying. "You're the best kids in the world. I know we can
get through this if we stick together. Bart, you and Judd
will have to plant the crops. Lily, your help will be most
valuable in the garden, running the household, getting
meals and taking care of Jenny."

"I don't need to be taken care of," Jenny protested.

"I don't mean like babysitting," Phoebe amended.
"But, Lily will be telling you how you can best help. It's
like you'll be her assistant."

"Assistant Jenny," Jenny announced to the group. "I
like that."

"Where is the truck—and Max?" Judd burst.

"I don't know," Phoebe definitively answered.

"Sorry to ask, its' just that…"

"Judd, could you please check on the free ranging stock? Bart and I will go into town and try to find the truck and Max. Lily, after work in the garden, please sort out all those seed packets in the pantry, then you can get supper organized. Jenny, you do as Lily asks. You can really be a great help to Mommy—to us all. We can work on the garden tomorrow and get that going, before the other work demands our full attention. Meanwhile, we need to all be alert to anything unusual around here; anything out of place or anyone here that shouldn't be. If you suspect anything, let me know."

"I hate to bring this up," Judd started, "but Jenny and I are supposed to go to 4-H camp this summer. Does this mean we won't be able to go?"

"Jenny will still go but I'm afraid I'm going to have to ask you not to, Judd. You're a big boy now and I very much need you here."

"It's all right, Mom. 4-H camp is for kids, anyway."

"Is not," protested Jenny.

"It's important, of that I'm sure," Phoebe interjected, as Judd opened his mouth to argue, "but right now our situation is more important. We each need to do whatever is most helpful. Jenny can help best by attending 4-H camp and Judd, by being here."

Judd got on the three-wheeler and left for the south pasture. Lily and Jenny went to the garden. Phoebe watched with pride as her kids dispersed, going to their assigned chores. She knew they'd do their best but doubted they were old enough, strong enough, to be the help needed. Refusing to listen to the echoes of defeat in her head, she grew determined not to succumb to negative thinking.

"You must know who's causing all these troubles," Bart accused, once the others had left.

"Bart, please. We don't know," Phoebe lied to her son. "All we know is what I've told you."

"I think you do know."

"No, I don't and I'll thank you not to keep pressing me about it. You don't want to know anyway—I'm not sure I do. If there's something you need to know about we'll tell you. Otherwise, leave it alone."

His mother's tone made Bart realize she wouldn't divulge anything to him, but he couldn't let go of the suspicion she knew more than she was telling. When he looked down, refusing to look at her, Phoebe modified her tone.

"It's going to be hardest of all for you to not question what's going on and to simply do as I ask. One thing I can say to you, and ask you not to tell the others. I think we're being watched from the woods, so please be alert to anyone hanging around the back side of the barns. I'm relying on you most of all and I need your trust, all right?"

"What do you want me to do?" Bart answered, nodding his assent.

"We think the truck might be at the sheriff's office. If so, you'll need to drive it home while I go to the co-op."

"Why would the sheriff have the truck?"

"It's the only place I can think of where an abandoned truck might be. When you get the truck back home," Phoebe continued, before Bart had a chance to ask more, "you and Judd see about the livestock and make sure the disc and harrow are ready to hook up to the tractor. Dad got the plowing done last fall and the winter wheat was planted. Once the other fields have been disked, we'll plant so make sure the planter is functional."

On the outskirts of town they stopped at the animal shelter to see if Max might be there. No one had seen him. Patricia Mosely was the head of the modest shelter. It wasn't so much a shelter as cages in a vacant barn. A soft-hearted, lovely woman in her mid-fifties, she devoted all her time and effort to finding homes for stray animals. She wouldn't allow any to be euthanized, instead taking them home if they weren't adopted. Her growing menagerie consisted of a wide assortment of animals. She promised to keep an eye out for Max and notify them if he was found.

Next, Phoebe drove to the sheriff's office. They could see the truck parked in the lot behind the office. The sheriff wasn't in, only the deputy on duty. Phoebe had dealt with LaDu Mercer once before. It was a shame there was no cure for stupid. Striding toward him, she wondered if beer bellies were a prerequisite for law enforcement in Dirk County. The deputy's left eyelid sagged, never fully open. He had chubby short fingers that looked like the tips had been sawed off in childhood then healed over. His fingers, nails bitten down to the quick, held enough dirt to plant a garden, his shirt was filthy and his deputy's badge smeared and bent. One stained pant leg was down the other stuffed into his boot—new boots, as far as she could tell—a superlative touch to his otherwise slovenly appearance.

"What do ya want?" he asked, through chipped teeth, ambling toward her from his office and scratching his immense stomach.

"I want our truck that's parked behind this building."

"That truk was confizkate in a arrest so it blongs to the county now," he said, as officiously as he could emulate.

"My husband was never arrested so it has nothing to do with the situation."

"Well, the sheriff's not here and I ain't authrizd to giv it up ta ya."

"You'll give it up to me or I'll call the state police. They'll want to know what you're doing with my truck. That truck is registered to me, not Curtis. Here's a copy of the title. You'll find the original in the glove box. You have no right to MY truck."

"I need to call the sheriff."

"You do that."

As dull as he was, LaDu knew when he'd been had.

Turning slowly, he disappeared into the sheriff's office and shut the door. Phoebe and Bart couldn't hear what was being said over the CB but the look of disappointment on LaDu's face told them they'd won. Reemerging, he looked positively dejected.

"The sheriff ain't non too pleased but he sed to giv ya the truk," LaDu conceded, reluctantly handing Phoebe the keys.

"I'm sure he'd approve of your acquiescing to the law without state police intervention," Phoebe pronounced, purposefully using vocabulary beyond his reach. "Now, where's our dog, Max?"

"I don know nothin bout no dawg."

"He was in the back of the truck. Now where is he?"

Phoebe could tell by the blank, blanker, look on LaDu's face that he knew nothing about the situation beyond what the sheriff had chosen to relate to him.

"You tell the sheriff I expect our dog back pronto," Phoebe called over her shoulder, urging Bart toward the door.

"I'll mak shur of it," LaDu forcefully responded.

"That was really good, Mom," Bart said, as they got into the car.

"Not the most shining example of a mother, I'm afraid."

"I disagree," Bart said, patting her on the back.

Phoebe drove around to the back of the sheriff's office where the truck was tucked away in the corner.

"I was hoping Max might still be with the truck," Bart commented.

"So was I, actually. Take the truck straight home. Be on the lookout for Max on your way. He may just wander home on his own. Make sure everyone's busy. I'll be home shortly."

CHAPTER SEVEN

"What do you mean I can't have a line of credit?" Phoebe questioned Wilfred Burkhardt, the bird-like president of Farmers United Co-op. With a nose and mouth merging into a large beak, he looked like an ostrich. Long eyelashes and large vacuous eyes belied his intelligence. Even with hunched shoulders, he was taller than her. "We have a revolving line of credit that is automatic."

"Yes, but that account is in your husband's name, not yours."

"I'm half owner of that farm."

"I'm sorry but there's nothing I—we—can do," Burkhardt arrogantly opposed.

Phoebe stood silently for a minute, gathering her thoughts, knowing full well that without credit to buy seed they were dead in the water.

"Well, there's something I can do. I'm half owner, an equal partner in that farm. As an equal partner I have just as much right to that line of credit as Curtis and, if you don't give it to me, I'll sue you."

"Now, just a minute, Mrs. Higgins, let's not be hasty," Wilfred cautioned, his eyes going stony.

"You either extend to me that line of credit or I'm going to an attorney—and it won't be one of the clowns here in Dirk County."

"I tell you what we'll do, Mrs. Higgins," Wilfred began, in a condescending tone that made Phoebe bristle. "The board meets tonight and we'll discuss it then. I'll let you know in a few days what we've decided to do."

"You can discuss it all you want but the answer better be the one I'm looking for. Let me know by nine o'clock in the morning because after that I'll be headed for Lynchford to visit an attorney friend of mine," Phoebe said in parley, turning on her heels and striding from his office.

Shaking so hard she could hardly get in the car, Phoebe agonized over the woman she was becoming—the kind of woman that, when her bare feet hit the floorboards each morning, the devil was heard to say *Oh shit! She's awake.* She hardly knew herself, her threats idle posturing. She didn't know anyone in Lynchford, much less an attorney. In great need of a friend, she stopped over at Agnes' house before going home. Though reluctant to involve Agnes, she needed a reality check.

"Hello, Phoebe. How was your trip to see your aunt?" Agnes cheerfully greeted, before noting Phoebe's glum countenance. "What's wrong?"

"The trip was fine. I never realized how judgmental my aunt was though, always speaking critically of others, especially old people. She's ninety-six herself. I don't think I'll be seeing her again. She wasn't doing very well when we left."

"What is it about people when they age, like there's some kind of prize for outlasting their siblings or the old lady down the street? I ran into Mrs. Creighton who lives over on Ashton Street the other day. She's in her nineties and talking about all the old people around town. When I asked her how she was doing she said she was doing fine but quit buying green bananas. I thought that was pretty funny. Anyway, I'm glad you're back, but you seem upset."

"It was good to get home but we've had trouble since."

"I can't believe what you're telling me, Phoebe," Agnes offered, after hearing of the situation over tea. "It sounds like a chapter in a novel."

"Believe it! You don't by any chance know of a good attorney in Lynchford?"

"No, but I could call the gallery to see if they know of anyone."

"Thanks, but never mind. The fewer people involved in this the better. Anyway, it's very likely Morray's domain extends to that county as well. He seems to know, and be able to influence, nearly everyone in the region, probably even the state."

"What are you going to do?"

"The only thing we can do—try to keep the farm going as best we can."

"Is there anyone that can help?"

"No, we'll have to carry on by ourselves. Curtis' cousin would help if he could but has his own farm to run. He's a turkey farmer in Strivet County."

"That's quite a ways away, but you could at least ask him. He can't say worse than no. If there's ever anything I can do let me know. I'm good for some trouble if need be."

"I appreciate it but you'd do best to stay as far away from me or the farm as you can. Your moral support is enough. Thank you for offering, though."

"Just remember what I said. My offer stands," Agnes repeated, pouring more tea. "Say, I saw Doctor Huntley's wife today while I was downtown. I'd heard rumors about her but we'd never met before. She was made up like a French whore—orange hair and all—had a formal gown on under her long sweater. The black tennis shoes were haute couture. How long has she been in a wheel chair?"

"Ruwina, oh, about twelve or thirteen years, I should say. She was already paralyzed when we moved here."

"What happened? I heard Polio."

"No, nothing that conventional. According to local gossip she found out her husband was having an affair with Marion Hewes, the druggist's wife. She confronted him but he denied it. Several days later she was found at the bottom of the railroad bridge over Bullfrog Slough. Fortunately, there was no water in the slough at the time or she'd have drowned. Unfortunately, due to drought, the dry mud flat was hard as rock. She broke her back. Once she'd recovered enough to get around in that chair of hers, she let it be known far and wide that her husband had pushed her off the bridge. Now he's straddled with her constant care and the expense of caretakers."

"I'm surprised he didn't divorce her—or try to do her in again. Nothing worse than an affair that ends badly."

"The affair continues to this day but Ruwina was sharp enough to contact a relative who worked for the state with a confidential letter saying that if anything further happened to her, they should arrest Jim Huntley and Marion Hewes. Then she showed the letter to her husband and Mrs. Hewes. I guess the people involved have worked out an arrangement. Dr. Huntley and Marion have their affair, Doug Hewes pretends he doesn't know and Ruwina no longer cares."

"This town is something else. I've heard about wife swapping, so apparently adultery is not only blatant but acceptable. What about Paul Gunther? I heard he left town under peculiar circumstances, but not the details."

"Gunther, who used to own the manufacturing plant out on the road to Dirkville, small machine parts, had a long standing affair with the dentist's wife, Grace Flanning. It ended when Phyllis, Mrs. Gunther, found them in bed together and shot Grace."

"Killed her?"

"Afraid so, though no charges were ever filed. What a surprise! You can get away with murder in Dirk County, you know. She and Paul both claimed it was self-defense, though Grace's gun was never found—why a naked woman in bed with a naked man, not her husband, would think to arm herself, never questioned. Paul and Phyllis Gunther left town shortly after the incident, leaving his manufacturing plant to his partner, Ernest Hepling. It's suspected that he was the one who informed Phyllis of the affair to begin with, hoping for the outcome he got. Pete Flanning stayed for a while but word has it he never considered his wife's death much of a loss. He eventually sold his dentistry practice and moved."

"Unbelievable! I'm afraid to ask if there's more to know."

"I'm sure that barely scratches the surface but those

are two of the most widely circulated stories I've heard."

"Well—on a much brighter note—my neighbor, Nicholas Strathmore now has a partner, Hank, who lives with him. They seem quite happy together."

"Is his partner a cross dresser as well?"

"I don't think so. They seem like nice enough fellows, and afford me my privacy, so I don't ask questions."

"You've met Hank then?"

"Just once. Nicholas sent him over to see if I had any borax. Seems Hank is an amateur taxidermist. He collects road kill, strips the guts out then stuffs them. He uses borax to cure the insides—works in that shed behind their house.

"And I thought it was only the natives that were strange. You certainly don't need a television do you? There's enough going on right outside your window."

"Frankly, I try not to watch. I only hope his hobby doesn't expand to include humans, like Ed Gein's did. Gein wrote a book you know—called it *Gourmet.*"

"You're kidding!"

"Yes, I'm kidding. Honestly, Phoebe, I worry about you sometimes. It's a Wisconsin joke."

"Not really very funny though, is it? I should get going. Thanks for the tea—and the comic relief."

As Phoebe turned onto Digbert Road from Mulberry Street, Harley Weils turned in front of her and drove into his gas station. She waved but, as usual, he didn't. Continuing down Digbert Road, she headed home. Nearing their farm, she saw a white pickup truck parked at the end of her driveway. Turning past it and into the drive, she almost ran over Jesse Tate carrying something heavy in his arms. Immediately she could see that it was Max. Stopping the car, she got out to confront him.

"Where did you find him?"

"I was drivin down Digbert toward home when I saw somethin in the ditch. When I got out to see what it was, I seen it was Max. I was just carryin him to my truck so as I could take him to ya. He's dead—shot through the fore-head."

Phoebe let out what could only be described as a wail.

"This were no accident," Jesse offered. "Who would do such a thing?"

"I don't know but I don't want the kids to see," Phoebe said, composing herself. "Is there any way you could bury him at your place or in the woods?"

"Sure enough, I can. Just didn't know what you want-ed to do with 'im. Where's Curtis? Will he want to help? He's pretty attached to this here dog."

"No, he can't help right now. He's—out of town. Would you mind?"

Nodding, Jesse turned. "Tell Curtis I'm sorry and I'll let him know where the grave is so as he kin visit."

Phoebe watched as Jesse gently laid Max down in the back of his truck, then started it up and drove off. Practic-ing her best impression of a poker face, she continued down the driveway. Taking a deep breath, she entered the house. Thankfully the kids were busy with chores. Lily was at the stove frying chicken. She could tell her mother was upset, but said nothing. Their meal that evening was awkwardly quiet. Despite warnings, after supper the kids had questions.

"Bart said you didn't find Max in town," Jenny began. "Where is he? Is he in the rehabilitation center with Dad?"

"No, he's not with Dad. I don't know where Max is," Phoebe lied. "If he's able to, I'm sure he'll find his way home, but he may not be able to."

"Why not?" Jenny questioned.

"I don't know. I just don't know," Phoebe sighed.

"Come on, let's go watch the *Incredible Hulk*," Bart commanded, steering Jenny out of the kitchen and mo-tioning to Judd and Lily.

Phoebe said nothing but Bart could see gratitude regis-ter in her eyes. No one said a word as they left the kitchen. Once they were all asleep that night, Phoebe could have called Curtis but she procrastinated, unwilling to be the bearer of bad news. After having a good cry, she remembered Curtis' clothes she'd taken to the laundry room. Unfolding the wadded bundle, she found blood on the cuffs of his jeans, something Curtis had neglected to mention. *I'll talk with him about that...and other things, tomorrow*, she concluded, trying to erase the image of Max from her mind.

Sitting in a rocker on the front porch, thinking about their situation, tears ran down her cheeks and they weren't only for Max. Without seed there was no point in wasting time strategizing their next move. *Is this punishment for some sin I have no recollection of committing?* she questioned within, trying to come to grips with the fact that they were finished. Staring at the waning slit of moon rising over the treetops, however, a plan began to form in her mind. First she remembered Curtis talking about his attempts at borrowing equipment from neighboring farmers after the tractor broke down, even offering to use their machines at night when they weren't using them. Then she remembered Warren's words, offering assistance and Agnes, suggesting she call him. *That's it!* she thought, stopping the rocker. *That's what we'll do, how we'll get the planting done. It all hinges on Warren. I'll call him tomorrow.* Certain it was the solution she'd been seeking she began rocking again, finalizing plans in her head.

Gaylan Morray had them in a tight spot. She was happy it hadn't taken much to convince Curtis she had no part in the commitment—that her signature had been forged. Morray's scheming was epic but, having a marriage in name only, with no knowledge of what a real partnership looked like, he had underestimated the strength of a good union.

"Mom, I can't sleep. Can I join you?" Lily timidly asked from the doorway. "We don't have to talk and I won't ask any questions. I'd just like to sit with you. Bart gave me the low down on what's been happening. Sorry I wasn't here."

"You couldn't have known—and you're right, I don't want to talk about it. You're here now and that's all that matters. Thank you for coming home to help, Lily."

"I'll do whatever I can. Anyway, more practice in the kitchen might do me some good. If Dad's going to be gone three months, that's almost the whole…"

"That's right. Your father will be in the rehab center the entire growing season. We'll have to keep everything going until he gets home, hopefully in time for harvest. I don't know if we can do it but we have to try."

"We'll all try our best, Mom."

"I know you will. We'd better get some sleep. The work begins tomorrow."

Phoebe hugged Lily good night then checked on Jenny before going to bed. Lying awake, it never occurred to her that Warren wouldn't help, instead she thought about all the work the next few months entailed. Rather than dwell on Max, Curtis' predicament or the difficulties ahead, she straightened her back, rolled over and willed herself to sleep.

In the morning the kids had just gone to their chores when the phone rang.

"Mrs. Higgins," an effeminate voice pronounced. "This is Wilfred Burkhardt. The board met last night and we decided not to extend you a line of credit for buying seed, but if you have the cash, we'll sell you the seed needed. I hope you realize what a position you've put me in with—the board."

"Sorry, Mr. Burkhardt but I'm not particularly worried about *your situation*. As for the seed, tell Morray that hell will freeze over before I'll give him any business."

"Gay…Mr. Morray has nothing to do with this."

"No, I'm sure not," Phoebe replied with zealous sarcasm, as she hung up. It was the answer she'd expected, even a moot point given her plan, but still annoying.

Unused to begging, she was nervous as a cat when she

dialed the phone. Their entire future depended on Warren's willingness to help.

"Warren, this is Phoebe."

After explaining their situation, where Curtis was installed and the dire nature of their circumstance, she swallowed hard before continuing.

"I remember Curtis saying that you'd help if you could. Though you live some distance away and can't help with the actual work of farming, I've decided there is something you can do for us."

"What is it, Phoebe. I'll help if I can."

"Knowing you probably have a good credit standing at your co-op, could you see your way to buying seed for us. I know it's a terrible imposition but it's our last hope and we'll pay you back with interest."

"I think I still have some credit so it wouldn't be that much of a problem to extend it. I'll see what I can do and call you back later this morning."

"Thanks, Warren. I really appreciate it."

When Warren called two hours later he agreed to buy all the seed they needed on credit at the co-op in Strivet County and to deliver it part way to them. Phoebe retrieved the list from the office and gave Warren the order.

"I'd do more if I could, Phoebe," he apologized. "That drought around here last year hit me hard."

"I know, Warren. Don't worry about it. It's enough that you're getting the seed."

"Meet me at the Chesterton grain elevators tomorrow afternoon about three o'clock and I'll transfer the seed to your truck."

Phoebe never actually saw anyone lurking about the farm but there was no doubt they were being watched. A creepy feeling, much like dread, lay heavy on her stomach as she contemplated meeting Warren, strong enough to cause her to rethink the plan for getting the seed. She almost never drove the truck. Unwilling to do anything to raise suspicions, involve Warren or jeopardize their seed supply, she devised an alternate plan. If Bart left the farm in the truck, it would not be questioned since he often drove it into town, so she decided to give him the task, convinced she was not putting him in harm's way. When she asked Bart to meet Warren, he was more than willing to be the gopher. She also gave him instructions for unceremoniously parking the truck in the barn when he returned. Though curious as to why they were getting their seed from Warren and wondering at the secrecy, he knew not to ask.

Regardless of her resolve, Phoebe paced nervously in the driveway when Bart left late morning to meet Warren. She had simply told the other children that he had gone to pick up some seed. Doing her level best for it to appear like any other day, she put the girls and Judd to work weeding the garden then washed clothes, hanging them on the line in the early afternoon sunshine. Mid-afternoon Judd was sent to check on the cattle, Jenny to clean out Tess' stable. In the house, while Lily prepared their evening meal, Phoebe dusted and vacuumed. Late afternoon she walked the west perimeter of their farm, where the barns abutted the woods, to make sure that if anyone was there they'd slip away for fear of being found out before Bart returned with the seed.

Just as the western sky was suggesting dusk, Bart came home, parked the truck in the barn and closed the door, as instructed, then casually strolled to the house. The kids knew something was up but waited for Phoebe to explain. In virtual silence, the family ate the pork roast Lily had prepared. Later that evening, over fresh rhubarb pie a la mode, Phoebe laid out the general plan she'd formulated for keeping the farm operational then a more detailed one for the next couple of weeks.

"You'll simply have to trust me to know what's best this summer while Dad's gone. He can't help, except to give advice. My plan is that during the day we'll work in the garden, do the chores. Bart, you and Judd stay close to the barns and work on the machinery—polish the paint off if it comes to that, but stay nearby."

"We need to guard the machinery?" Judd asked. "Shouldn't we be using it to finish getting the fields ready for planting?"

"With you and Bart near the barns and shed, and the girls and I near the house, we can keep an eye on everything."

"Are we being watched?"

"I really don't know but we need to stay alert," Phoebe answered, glancing at Bart. "In case someone is, it's important for us to appear as normal as possible, like we're just managing, biding our time until your dad gets home. When its dark, the real work begins—in the fields."

"We're going to disc and plant at night?" Bart questioned, a concerned look on his young face.

"We probably have the most flat and level fields in Dirk County, boys. There are lights on the tractor and I don't see why we can't work the fields as well at night as during the day. Our fields abut those of other farmers in the area but I doubt they'll think anything of it, since they often work after dark themselves. We'll just be working longer after dark. Anyway, I know these people. They might become curious but they'll mind their own business.

"We'll be working all night, if necessary, but need to get the fields prepared and planted before anyone knows what we're doing. By the time the seedlings show, I'm hoping it will be too late for them to do anything about it. When everything is planted, we can concentrate on other things that need to be done."

"What will happen if they find out what we're doing, Mom?" Judd queried.

"I don't know. I can't even think about that right now. Are you with me?"

"I think it's a good plan, Mom," Bart stated.

Though the kids had many questions, especially about

Max, they accepted their mother's word that she didn't know more than she was telling. Max's demise was a secret from the kids Phoebe would take to her grave. Focusing attention on what they had to gain, not what had been lost, she massaged her children into compliance and they were more than happy to assist—their spirits lifting in recognition of their integral part.

Phoebe was up well before the sun the next morning, showered and with breakfast ready before anyone else stirred. When she rousted the children from their beds, they moved quickly, getting dressed and eating their breakfast with intention. Orders for the day delivered, she went with the boys to the barn. While they got busy unloading the bags of seed, she checked for intruders. The barn and outbuildings were situated away from the fields, more toward the house. It would be difficult for anyone to see the fields from a vantage point near the barns and woods, but she wanted to be sure. There were fresh tire tracks, so someone had been there recently, but there were no footprints near the barn indicating anyone had seen Bart arrive with the seed.

Since the chicaneries with Gaylan Morray had started nearly two years earlier, Phoebe had become hypersensitive, always vigilant and with her senses fully engaged. She was working in the garden late morning with Lily and Jenny when she heard the remote sound of a motor. Someone was driving a truck deep into the woods near the barns. Phoebe waited until she heard the motor killed, allowed time for the interlopers to position themselves, then went out to the barn, loudly announcing herself to her sons.

"Hi, boys. How's the work on the tractor going? Don't tamper with the motor, just keep it clean for when your father gets home," Phoebe began, as Judd looked at her in confusion.

"What's going...?" Judd began, turning to Bart for answers, as Phoebe interrupted.

"I know how well you boys take care of things, but it needs some grease, so don't clean it all off, all right? When its cleaned well, all we have to do is start it up once in a while to make sure it's in running condition when your dad gets back. I'm going back to the house. Lunch will be ready soon. This afternoon I want you boys to work in the barn, cleaning up some of that loose hay—and Jenny will need some help with Tess' stable."

"Sure thing, Mom," the boys haltingly responded.

Phoebe turned from them and left. Judd looked at Bart who shrugged his shoulders and suggested they get back to work. Ignoring the woods like she was void of suspicion, Phoebe walked toward the garden, calling out orders.

"Lily, please get lunch prepared. Jenny you can help me hoe," she said, taking the hoe from Lily and starting to chop at the weeds next to the row of lettuce.

Pausing moments later she heard the truck motor, first in the woods then turning onto Digbert Road and moving away from the farm. While eating lunch, the family talked about plans for the evening hours.

"After supper we'll start getting those fields disked."

"Do you think we can get much done tonight, Mom?" Bart questioned.

"Just do what you can. I'm not sure how long it's going to take. Go for as long as you can but don't get so tired you fall off the tractor—or disc funny. We need to have the fields ready to plant by next week, if possible."

Phoebe kept everyone busy the rest of the day. After supper, while Jenny and Lily did the dishes, she checked the perimeter then went with Bart and Judd to the barn. They had helped their dad but never handled the disking alone. Shouldering his responsibilities, Bart took control of the situation. Instead of lording it over his younger brother, as some boys might, he made sure Judd had things to be responsible for so he'd feel included.

At dusk they hitched the disc to the tractor then Bart

took the steering wheel. Judd sat beside him on the tire hood as lookout and to advise Bart as to adjustments in course. When it grew darker they turned on the lights. Under a sickle moon they disked back and forth across the field, continuing until hardly able to keep their eyes open. It was after one o'clock when they drove into the barn where Phoebe was waiting for them. They hadn't seen that she'd stood guard with a rifle while they worked in the field.

"I appreciate your effort but I'm not sure you need to work so long, boys. Pace yourselves. How did it go?"

"We got quite a bit done, Mom. You'll see tomorrow. But there's still a lot to do," Judd responded, jumping off the tractor.

"Do you suppose Lily has any of that pie left?" Bart asked, turning off the tractor and shifting himself down to eye level with his mother.

"I'm sure she does. You have a nice big slice and then I think you'd better shower and get to bed."

Most of the family was soon sound asleep. The farm was quiet but Phoebe sat up until nearly three o'clock to make sure everything was all right. In the morning, the boys found her asleep in the living room recliner. Her first thought for the day was of Max, the feeling of dread spreading across her belly as she searched for the right words to tell Curtis about his beloved dog.

"Mom, you've got to get a good night's sleep like the rest of us," Bart advised.

"I will. Didn't realize I was still here, though. You boys go get chores started will you. I'll get breakfast going."

About the time breakfast was ready Lily appeared and helped her mother set the table. The boys returned from the barn, reporting that the livestock was fed and watered and Tess' stall mucked out.

"Where's Jenny?" Judd asked Lily.

"She's on her summer schedule which means late getting up again every day," Lily responded.

"Let her sleep," Phoebe interjected. "We'll get her working soon enough."

"When does she go to 4-H camp?" Judd asked.

"The third week in July. Wish you were still going, too"

"No, not really. I like working with Bart. It's good to know I'm finally useful."

"You've always been helpful. It just wasn't necessarily in the way you thought it should be," Phoebe corrected, giving him a hug.

"What's the plan for the day—anything different than yesterday?" Bart queried.

"I thought we'd concentrate on the garden and wood cutting during the day. Bart, if you can hold down the fort here, I'd like to drive over to Dirkville to see Dad."

"Can do, Mom."

"Just keep busy. I'll only be gone a few hours."

"Say hello to Dad for me—us," Judd responded.

"He knows you all love him and I'm sure that helps him tolerate his confinement. We'll go over to see him one day soon. Lily, if Jenny isn't up in an hour you'll have to get her up. She can do the dishes and clean up the kitchen after she eats."

Just outside of Dirkville, Phoebe stopped at a traffic light behind a guy in a beat up old Ford Falcon that listed to the right. The light seemed particularly long so, to ward off impatience, she amused herself by reading the numerous bumper stickers on his car. *Darwin, The Road to Hell is Paved with Republicans, Just Say No to Sex with a Pro-Lifer, Dare to Keep Cops Off Donuts* and the one on the far right, *Jesus is a Liberal*. It seemed like a rather mixed bag of statements. When the light finally changed, the man drove off in a cloud of exhaust fumes, leaving her coughing—and wishing he'd spent his bumper sticker money on a catalytic converter.

Her smile quickly faded in mulling over how to tell

Curtis the bad news. She decided to start their conversation with the bumper stickers, keeping things light before she laid the bombshell on him. Used to freely speaking, choosing words felt cumbersome.

"Hi, Hon," Curtis cheerily greeted, when she was again ushered into his locked room.

"They still have you locked up?"

"Not all the time. Sometimes they lock it, and sometimes they don't. Of course, they always lock it at night. I have my classes and sessions most of the day so I'm busy and I wonder if they don't just lock it out of habit."

"Some habit. I'll see about keeping it unlocked during the day before I leave. I know for a fact that you can't be trusted at night."

"Phoebe! How's everyone holding up?"

"They're troopers, that's for sure. We're managing all right for now, I guess. You forgot to mention the blood, by the way."

"What blood?"

"On your legs. The cuffs of your jeans were bloody. Pull up your pant legs and let's have a look."

"It's nothing, Phoebe, really."

"Come on, pull them up—or I'll do it for you."

Curtis obediently pulled up his white pant legs. The wounds had scabbed over but clearly covered cuts in his ankles.

"They tied you up?"

"I'm not sure. When I woke up I had bandages on my ankles. I took them off so I'd heal faster. They don't hurt any more—probably just severe rope burns."

"That was too much blood for mere rope burns."

"Maybe they were chains. I don't know, Phoebe. I'm all right, really. Can we drop it? I want to hear about how things are going on the farm—how you're doing."

"There's not much to tell, really. We're managing, that's all," she offered, whispering that Warren had arranged for them to get seed and they were planning to plant it after dark the next week.

"Any sign of old Max?"

"I'm afraid the news about Max isn't good, Curtis," Phoebe began.

Relating the news to him she burst into tears. Curtis became immediately consoling, better able to swallow hard and accept Max's fate out of concern for his wife. Confined for three months, he'd have plenty of time to grieve alone.

"He wasn't much of a watchdog, really," Curtis managed, choked with emotion. "I'll miss him, that's for sure."

"The kids must never know what happened to him," she pronounced, as Curtis somberly nodded his agreement.

In their limited time remaining, Phoebe talked to him about how the kids were doing. Tip-toeing around subjects in case someone was listening made communication difficult, to say the least. Phoebe decided that if they ever got out of their current dilemma she and Curtis should learn to speak some obscure language for privacy's sake. An hour later she left.

Arriving home, Phoebe found Lily on the phone with Keith. She couldn't stop smiling, blushing when her mother winked at her. *It must be love*, Phoebe said to herself. That evening they followed the same routine. She checked the woods for intruders while the boys finished supper, then stood guard with the rifle at the barn while they disked. Around eleven o'clock, hearing the tractor approach, she hid the rifle. When the boys joined her they announced that the disking was about half done, and they would be able to begin planting the next week for sure. After a late snack everyone went to bed.

Over the next several days the sky was intermittently gloomy during the day but it didn't rain, so at night, under a waxing moon, the boys were able to get the disking done. Their nightly routine continued without incident and, by the time the moon was full the fields were ready for planting. Just before a beautiful soaking rain, they got all the seed planted. There was nothing more to do relative to the corn and soy beans, except wait for sprouts to emerge. The boys had worked hard, eager to see the manifestation of all their effort and innocent to whatever repercussions visible crops might set off. Their next project was to cut the wheat their dad had planted the previous fall. It proved a more difficult task to accomplish at night under a new moon, but they got the job done, letting it dry adequately before gathering it up. Usually some of the wheat was stored, the rest taken to the elevator to sell. But this year, at their mother's instructions, they put all the wheat in storage.

During the day Phoebe kept the kids busy with domestic or farming chores. They frequently asked about their dad and she assured them he was fine. When they asked about Max she continued her charade, telling them she didn't know what had happened to him but he'd probably found a good home or would have come back. With the wheat cut and stored they turned their attention to the hay, mowing and baling it. Phoebe worked right alongside the boys. Judd drove the tractor, pulling the wagon behind. Bart hefted the sixty-five pound bales up onto the wagon and Phoebe stacked them. Each time the hay wagon was full they drove to the barn to unload.

Lily managed the house, especially the kitchen, and she and Jenny worked in the garden, weeding, never complaining. Phoebe made sure that at least part of each day was pleasant, even playful. She and the kids played softball, badminton or croquet, watched Jenny ride Tess or just sat around talking. Despite continued tensions and unanswered questions, the kids enjoyed those summer days while waiting for their dad's return.

It didn't take long for the crops to appear. With adequate rain and plenty of sunshine, it was less than two weeks before the green corn and soy bean sprouts surfaced, lined up in perfect rows. The contrast between the black dirt and tiny green shoots was picturesque, creating a sense of intense satisfaction in the boys. The last week in June, on her morning rounds near the barns before the boys were up, Phoebe surprised Clyde, lurking in the woods.

"What is it you think you're doing spying on our property?" she thrust.

"It's not actually your property any more," Clyde blurted, his beady eyes darting left then right. As he spoke, Owen, looking like just another tree, strode anomalously from behind an oak to stand beside him.

Phoebe looked at Owen, foolishly expecting some kind of intelligible comment to originate from his mouth.

"Yeah, what he said," Owen slurred, shuffling his boots in the dirt.

"This isn't your property until we're through with it or can no longer run the farm. Is that clear? Now get the hell off our property and stay off."

Clyde and Owen stood motionless for a time, their defiance obvious. Owen seemed on the verge of speaking when Clyde jerked him by the arm, turning him then pushing him forward. Phoebe watched as they walked back into the woods, listening for car doors to slam, the motor start, and the truck move toward Digbert Road before following their footsteps to the barn. She couldn't be sure, but it didn't appear as though they could see much beyond the barns to the fields they'd so carefully tended. It was only later, in the middle of the night, that she realized the strap she'd noticed around Owen's neck when he stepped out from behind the tree was for binoculars.

She tossed and turned for hours. They had worked hard for weeks but something told her that the real battle was just beginning. She went over her plan, wondering if she'd overlooked or neglected anything. The corn and soy beans were planted, the machinery in good working order, the hay and wheat were cut and stored, the kids were doing all they could to help. Sliding into sleep, she told herself it was all she could do.

With the planting and haying done the boys didn't have to work at night. Relaxing into a more normal routine, they kept close to the machinery and barns during the day, except when taking turns checking the fields or cattle. At night they slept soundly, assuming their mother did as well. Had they ventured downstairs they would have found her pacing the floor or drinking tea in the kitchen—antennae out, ears cocked to trouble. She slept only in fits and starts and rarely in her bed. The responsibility of the farm resting squarely on her shoulders was taking its toll.

Unwilling to leave the farm without just cause, Phoebe sent Lily or Bart to town on errands to the grocery store or post office, reserving her trips only for visits to Curtis. She did her best to shield the children from all difficulties they didn't know of first hand. Therefore, she never shared with them her discovery of Owen and Clyde Morray spying on them, most likely discovering their planted fields.

"Bart, could you go into town to get these groceries?" she asked, handing him a list. "And stop at the post office and pick up some stamps, please. This should be enough money to cover everything. Just get a small book of stamps. I heard the post office is planning on raising their rates soon."

Bart washed his hands, put on a clean shirt and drove the truck to town, parking in front of the post office. Strolling through the double glass doors to the lobby, he found Mr. Stevens, the post master, sitting back in the corner at his desk as usual. Stevens rarely left his desk, except to go home for lunch, something he would have done well to occasionally skip. He was an institution in Between, a true, malingering bureaucrat. Since he wouldn't condescend to wait on customers, all sales at the counter fell to Seymour Dunwoody, the postal clerk. Of average height and build, with colicky red hair, a large nose, and lipless, Dunwoody looked like a cartoon character. People in town called him "Woody," a handle he accepted as a foreshortening of Dunwoody, when the intent was a reference to Woody Woodpecker. The stems of his frameless glasses, with lenses as thick as coke bottles, were wrapped tightly around his tiny ears as though holding his face to his head. He had only one speed—the white flakes on his shoulders more likely dead lice rather than dandruff. Because he moved so slowly, a nearly perpetual line of customers awaited his assistance, often exhibiting impatience.

Bart lined up behind two men as a woman he recognized as Mrs. Chisholm stepped to the counter for service. She had been his eighth grade history teacher and was known for her dyspeptic personality and strong opinions, voiced without the slightest hesitation to those who listened and especially those who didn't. Dorothy Chisholm was another actor in the cast of unusual Between characters. She was a homely woman, chunky and with questionable taste, the plaid skirt and floral blouse she was sporting a case in point. Bart was no expert but even he knew that anklets with heels was a fashion *faux pas*. The kids at school called her Mr. Chisholm, sniggering behind her back at her abundant facial hair which, it was obvious, she shaved—a procedural step in her toilette apparently abandoned in retirement. She looked like a bearded gnu.

"May I help you," Stanley Dunwoody innocently asked.

"I'd like some stamps," Mrs. Chisholm curtly responded.

"Liberty stamps all right?"

"What would be the use of that—none of us is free—God rules over us and liberty is just a meaningless concept because it is God we must surrender ourselves to," the malicious woman countered. "Do you have any commemorative stamps?"

Attempting to digest the outburst, Stanley suggested the baby animal series, reaching for the envelope.

Chisholm let out such a screech that he jumped a foot, jerking the envelope in his hand, the stamps sliding to the floor.

"I don't care about baby animals. Nobody seems to care about the safety and care of human babies, especially babies in the womb. It's disgusting! Do you believe I saw a billboard yesterday with a baby on it and a caption that read *Too bad they don't come with instructions.* Doesn't anybody read their Bible? Everything you need to know about raising a Christian child is in there."

Stanley struggled with composure while Bart, along with the others in line, squelched snickers. Though a placid man, Stanley appeared to be fighting back the urge to tell the old bag to remove her Bible thumping carcass from the post office. Inhaling deeply, he finally responded.

"What then might be your stamp choice today, Mrs. Chisholm?"

"Well, of course, you don't have any Christian stamps, I suppose."

"We have some stamps left over from Christmas depicting the Virgin Mary," he optimistically offered.

"The Virgin Mary!" she snorted. "That Catholic mumbo-jumbo. I walk with the Lord—and Jesus, his son, our Savior, who died on the cross for our sins."

Stanley stood silently staring at the woman. Clearly, she could not be appeased. It was too much for Bart. He forfeited his place in line and went to the grocery store, intending to stop later on his way home when, hopefully, Mrs. Chisholm would be elsewhere. After filling the brief list of items his mother had given him, he stopped again at the post office and found a much longer line but with fewer characters in it, and the wait went quickly. Stamps in hand, he headed for the truck, eager to get home and report his postal experience to his family.

At home he handed over the stamps and groceries to his mother who encouraged him to chores. With no time for telling stories, he left for the barn. Lily's boyfriend, Keith, had come out for a visit and tagged along to help. Phoebe had gotten to know him and Judd had shown him around the farm. Tall and lanky, with blond hair and azure blue eyes, he was not only good looking but considerate and fun—immediately given their stamp of approval. He was invited to stay for supper and accepted, seeing it as a chance to see if Lily was the good cook she claimed to be.

At supper Bart told them about the fiasco he'd witnessed at the post office with Mrs. Chisholm.

"Everyone at school says we're very lucky she retired a year ago and we didn't have to take her class," Judd offered.

"When she showed films," Bart began, "she always used a small pink rectangular eraser to slow down the reel after it shut off from rewinding. One day Tom Edgar put a huge eraser on the film cart while the lights were still out. When she reached for her usual eraser she instead found the giant one. She huffed and puffed, said we couldn't leave class until someone confessed, but when the bell rang we all just filed out."

"What I remember about her," said Lily, "is that she hissed *esses* through her bottom teeth when speaking, sending a spray of spit at anyone sitting in the first row. While she was talking, and spraying one day, Jim Burkit put up a tiny umbrella over his head."

The children all laughed. They continued talking about school then played *word square*. They were having such a good time, Phoebe decided to leave them to it, suggesting only that they make some ice cream. After checking things out at the barn she did up the dishes before joining her kids on the porch for some lemon ice cream. When Keith had left the kids reminisced about their days at the lake, water skiing and swimming, their memories bolstering them.

The garden was growing well and, with the ideal weather they were having, a bumper crop of produce was

promised. Besides keeping the household running smoothly, Lily supervised the gardening when Phoebe was busy.
Jenny helped with weeding and was given the responsibility of hauling them in her red wagon to the compost pile
east of the house. Otherwise she kept busy with Tess.

The old adage pertaining to corn, *knee-high by the
Fourth of July,* promised to be true. Standing in the nourishing morning rain, the boys, with their mother, surveyed
their handiwork. The corn would be ready the end of August when, presumably, Curtis would be home. Early August they would be able to harvest soy beans, though they
weren't sure what they'd do with them.

It rained for several days in a row before slowly clearing. Since the kids had been cooped up in the house so
long, Phoebe decided to take them to the fireworks display
in Dirkville the evening of the Fourth. Before going they
stopped to see Curtis. The children had been rehearsed as
to what they could and couldn't say to their dad so it was
a somewhat awkward visitation, but Curtis hadn't seen his
children for a month and it was a happy reunion.

At the park in Dirkville, Phoebe treated the kids to
snow cones while they waited for the fireworks to begin.
She noted an inexplicably restless feeling the entire evening, assigning it to her general unease since Curtis had
been locked up. The kids thoroughly enjoyed the pyro-
technic display and it made Phoebe's heart sing to see
them having a lark. She insisted they leave immediately
after the fireworks, however, and they arrived home very
tired around eleven o'clock. Jenny had fallen asleep in the
car. When Phoebe carried her upstairs to bed she thought
she saw flashes of light out near the fields, dismissing it as
fireworks set off by the neighbors or heat lightning. Lily
and the boys went to their rooms. Phoebe sat in the living
room, sleeping only intermittently. Something told her all
was not well.

CHAPTER EIGHT

By early morning light Phoebe mounted the ATV, bracing herself for what she might find when surveying the farm. Even she could not have envisioned the extent of the damage. There were truck tire tracks everywhere in the fields. The lights she'd seen the night before were the spotlights of bushwhackers. Dozens of rows of corn had been run down, their stalks pressed into the muddy soil. The soy bean crop was decimated.

The fencing on the west side of the farm was down, lying inward toward the cattle, as it had numerous times before, except this time the heifers got out. They were probably strewn all over the county but, for certain, were in the neighbors' cornfields. Thankful at least that she had followed her instincts and they hadn't lingered long after the fireworks, she made a promise to herself never to ignore her intuition again. Whatever had prompted her to leave the fireworks, their early arrival home had probably saved what was left of the corn crop.

Phoebe was back at the house before anyone else was up. She had breakfast ready and waiting when the kids straggled in. After breakfast and before chores, she explained, as best she could, the damage that had occurred. Judd and Bart were particularly upset since they'd done all the work. Phoebe kept her suspicions as to who was responsible close to the chest, engaging the assistance of her children while prompting them to keep family affairs private. But too much had happened. This time they wanted answers.

"Who is doing this?" Judd questioned.

"I don't know Judd," Phoebe answered, as her children stared at her, unbelieving. It was then she realized she would need to share with the others what she'd told Bart.

"What I do know is that someone knows when we're not here," she began, glancing at Bart. "From now on we never leave—not all at once, anyway."

"If we know someone is watching us, can't we go to the sheriff?" Lily asked.

"We've asked him for help but he won't do anything about it because he needs to catch someone red-handed, and he can't be out here all the time."

"How about if we try to catch them?" Judd offered.

"Absolutely not!" Phoebe blurted. "We've got problems for sure. We could even lose the farm in the long run. But I will not put you children in harm's way and that's final. Let your dad and I take care of this."

"How is Dad going to help?" Judd queried, his tone sarcastic.

"He will when he gets home. Meanwhile, we need to try and put things back together the best we can. Do your chores while I call Dad and then we'll get started rounding up the cows."

"What if...?" Judd began.

"Please!" Phoebe pleaded. "I know this is difficult and I wish I had answers for you. The only thing that could make things worse, is if you children become involved or talk of our difficulties to others, so I must ask you again to please trust your dad and me to handle the situation," she concluded. Once the children left for chores, she called Curtis.

"It all happened while we were at the fireworks. I'm sorry. We shouldn't have gone," Phoebe confessed, explaining the damage to Curtis.

"The kids can't work all the time," Curtis offered, after a long pause. "I'm glad you gave them a break. I guess that's it then."

"I'm not ready to throw in the towel yet. We'll do what we can but I can't promise it will be enough."

"You have to wonder what we're in for next, Phoebe. Please be careful."

"Everything will be all right. It has to be."

The heifers were eventually retrieved from various

fields of nearby farms. It took them two days to round them up. They found all but three rogues, actually two—one was found dead near the road, hit by a car or truck.

Sleep deprivation threatened as Phoebe continued her nightly watch. Bart, noticing his mother's ebbing energy, suggested naps during the day and, surprisingly, she complied. While she slept he kept an eye on things but, despite his best efforts, a repeat fencing incident occurred the end of the week—minor relative to previous damage but again involving Jesse Tate's corn crop and the heifers. This time he threatened to sue.

By explanation, Phoebe felt compelled to tell him about Curtis being in rehab and how he got there, assuring him they would make up the difference from their own crop in the fall. *Assuming we have any crop left,* she mumbled within.

"I'd heerd something about that but didn't want to believe it. I wondered why I ain't seen Curtis around lately. Do ya think theys the one that shot Max.?"

"I suspect so," Phoebe responded.

"I understand you've got problems with him away but you've got to keep them cows out of my fields," Jesse responded, as sympathetically as he could.

Once the cattle were rounded up it took two more days to repair the fencing. After inspecting the hog pen for damage and seeing the procines happily immersed in their muddy enclosures, Phoebe satisfied herself that at least they remained unharmed for the time being and, as long as the feed held out, were fattening for market.

The second week of July Jenny again entrusted the care of Tess to Judd and Phoebe took her into town to board the bus for 4-H camp. Before driving to school to meet the bus they stopped at the market. Phoebe parked the car in front and ran inside to get Jenny some juice and a candy bar for her trip. When she came out there was a commotion across the street in the town square. One of the local characters, a resident of the county home, was pacing back and forth in front of the bandstand, ranting and raving. Though his words were barely discernible, it was clear his theme was social injustice—what was wrong with the world, everyone in it, and advocating violence and anarchy as the only solutions. Jenny sat gaping, staring across the street, as Phoebe slid behind the steering wheel.

"Who is that man, Mommy?"

"That's Mr. Sharlotte, honey."

"I think Mr. Sharlotte has a mental health problem."

Try insane, Phoebe muttered within. "I think you may be right."

As Phoebe started the car and pulled away from the curb, she noticed Owen and Clyde leering at them from across the square. While Jenny continued to crane her neck, staring back at Eugene Sharlotte, Phoebe drove around the block and turned down the street leading to the school. She had put Jenny on the bus for camp two other times, but always with Judd. This time she saw Jenny as very vulnerable and alone but, unwilling to destroy her daughter's dream by making her stay home from camp, grew determined to give her an enthusiastic send off. Relying on Jenny being under the watchful eyes of several counselors, she swallowed her concerns and waved goodbye as the bus pulled away.

By the time she went to bed that night Phoebe had decided it probably didn't matter that the soy bean crop had been ruined, since it was unlikely they'd be able to sell the harvest anyway. As long as the cattle were healthy and fed, assuming they could keep them contained, she felt confident she and Curtis could find a way to get them to market somewhere when they were ready in the fall. They'd butcher several of the hogs for their own use then try to sell the others. Wondering if she was starting to sound like Scarlet, and thinking of Jenny, she drifted off to sleep.

In the morning after breakfast, she assigned chores

then took the ATV to check on the cattle, telling Judd she'd count them and asking him to work in the garden. It gave her a chance to look things over more thoroughly. After counting the brood cattle she surveyed the fields and fencing. Everything seemed to be in tact until she noticed that the water tank was nearly empty and the well pump wasn't working. *Pumps breakdown sometimes*, she rationalized. Without alerting the boys, who were busy in the barn, she drove back to the house and called Darrell Prescott. The hair on the back of her neck prickled as she waited for him to answer.

"We have a problem with our well pump, Darrell. Could you come out and see what's wrong with it?"

"I've got some other calls but should be there about three o'clock."

By four o'clock Darrell still hadn't arrived so Phoebe gave him another call.

"I won't be coming out, Mrs. Higgins," Darrell began in a monotone.

"Too busy, I guess. Can you come tomorrow morning? I think we can manage until then."

"No, I won't be coming then either. I won't be coming at all. I just can't," Darrell advised, before hanging up the phone.

Phoebe's feeling of *déjà vu* was like a punch in the gut. Darrell's unwillingness to fix the well pump erased all naiveté. She knew who to blame for tampering with the well, who had threatened Darrell if he came to repair the pump. She tried two other well and pump outfitters to be sure her suspicions were correct. The answer was always the same. No one would come to their farm. She could hardly blame them for being unwilling to risk possible repercussions but the cattle had to have water so she shifted her mind away from the problem to focus on a solution. Carrying water from the well up by the barns would require too much effort. Between a rock and a hard place, she paid a visit to Curtis, advising him of the situation and asking his advice.

"I don't know what you can do. You could refence the grazing area again to allow the brood cattle to come up to the well by the barn with the feeder cattle like we did before, but that's a lot of work. It will take a couple of days."

"What other options do we have?"

"None, I guess."

It was Sunday. When Phoebe got back to the farm she told Bart about the pump, soliciting his help. She made it seem like just an ordinary farm mishap, asking him to move the tank from the barn and fill it. The ease with which she told lies had become vaguely troubling and she fortified her belief in atonement.

While Bart saw to the water tank Phoebe wondered what calamity they'd have to face next, what forest fire would need to be stamped out. It made her punchy and irritable, say nothing of exhausted. They were running out of money. She had carefully watched all expenditures, certain Gaylan Morray's malevolent eyes watched their accounts even more closely. Though tightening their financial belt to the last hole, they were down to fourteen hundred dollars, barely enough for several weeks of groceries.

Despite difficulties, she remained determined to make it through the summer. With intensified effort she assisted the boys in moving the fencing, cautioning them to more closely watch the watering troughs, well, and machinery. While she kept an eye on the barn and house they sprayed the corn fields again. Staying close to the farm, the family only went to town for groceries and errands, and never together. When a couple of weeks passed without incident Phoebe managed to convince herself they'd experienced the worst and were coming around the last quarter mile turn.

With the weather so ideal for growing hay, another cutting was made, another batch of bales stacked neatly in the barn. The brood cattle grazed on grass during the summer months but it was reassuring to know they'd have enough feed for the winter. A third cutting of hay late August or early September seemed assured. Thoughts of a barn full of hay for the winter and a more abundant than usual corn crop, despite losses, invigorated her for a time. The hogs and feeder cattle were fattening and would be ready for market about the time Curtis got home at the end of the summer.

Sometimes, during the early morning hours when the kids were still asleep, or late afternoons when they were busy with chores, she'd go to the woods. Positioning herself near the dirt road that ran through the thick woods, she'd wait, trying to espy whoever might show up. Never did she catch anyone in the act, coming or going. Someone knew their whereabouts each minute of the day but remained invisible. She kept the rifle in the barn but felt defenseless in the house. To allay accumulating concerns, she located Curtis' shotgun in the basement, loaded it, and stashed it high on a pantry shelf.

The phone was ringing as she came back from the barn one morning. When she entered the kitchen Lily handed her the phone, saying it was a long distance call from Monpree. Phoebe knew immediately what the call signified. Aunt Roseanne had died. As executer of her will, she would need to make sure her aunt was properly buried and any remaining funds distributed according to her wishes. If there were no funds, she would be responsible for burial expenses and any unpaid bills. Wondering where she would find the money to carry out her promised duties, she took the phone from Lily.

"I can help with the disbursement of her property and belongings for you, if you wish," the attorney continued, after informing Phoebe of her aunt's death. "You don't need to come here. The items Roseanne wanted you to have are small and easy to ship, like her jewelry, photo albums, English tea service and some French linens. She wanted most of her furniture and household items, no loss there, to go to Consuelo and Carlos. There's not much else. The rest can go to the Salvation Army. Consuelo said she'd pack everything up."

"I'd appreciate that. Are there funds enough to take care of the burial and any outstanding bills?"

"Yes, I'll see to it. There's plenty of money. The will is very simple, really. She left everything to you."

"Everything?"

"Yes—about two hundred thousand dollars, including the house when it sells."

"Oh, my God."

"That's a tidy sum, all right. It will take a few months to put everything through probate but you should have part of your inheritance by October—all of it, if the house sells soon. I have some people interested."

It was with renewed optimism that Phoebe faced the remainder of the summer. In the fall Curtis would be back home and the money Aunt Roseanne had left her would put them well on their way to paying off the mortgage and getting back on their feet. With no further incidents arising that the kids knew of, they let their questions slide, much to Phoebe's relief. Though they still occasionally commented about poor Max, they eventually accepted that he was gone. The growing season was so advantageous that, by the end of July, Phoebe and Lily began harvesting, canning, and freezing their abundant cache of vegetables and fruit. Soon they had a pantry full of catsup, tomato juice, and tomato pieces. Most Mondays Phoebe made a fresh batch of bread then usually cookies or a cake to have as dessert during the week. She taught her home economics teacher presumptive to make bread and do other kitchen related farm chores, over and above those learned in the past.

While busy, she was continually present and watchful. Anxious about Jenny's return, she had intended to be the one to pick her up at the bus when it arrived from 4-H

Camp. After hearing a truck motor in the woods that morning, however, she decided to send Lily instead.

"Get the groceries first, Lily then pick up Jenny. That way you can get her back here right after the bus arrives. My arms won't wait much longer," Phoebe teased, concealing her concern about the truck. "The main thing at the grocery store is to pick up peaches for making pickles tomorrow."

Shortly after Lily left, Phoebe hurried out to the barn to investigate. Bart was busy piling hay bales.

"Where's Judd?" Phoebe questioned.

"He's checking on the cattle in the south pasture."

"I heard a motor. It sounded like it was in the woods but now I don't hear it. Did you hear anything?"

"No, it's been pretty quiet, except I had the tractor running for a while. Do you want me to go check?"

"No, let's just wait here a bit and listen. Maybe it was the tractor I heard. If it remains quiet, I'll go back to the house. Lily went to get Jenny. They should be home within the hour."

As she was saying this, she realized the vehicle she'd heard had turned onto, not off, Digbert Road. That meant that whoever was driving it, had managed to sneak up on them undetected and was leaving, not coming.

"I guess they've left. You didn't see anyone around?"

"No, but I've been busy. Sorry, Mom."

"It's all right. Maybe they were just seeing if we're here."

To stem growing concern, Phoebe got busy in the kitchen, anxiously awaiting Jenny's return. The only time Jenny was away from her mother was for camp each year, and it was a difficult time for them both. They had all worked hard but, in reflection, Phoebe realized the summer had emotionally been hardest on Jenny. Too young to understand what was going on, she knew only that her mother was constantly preoccupied, her dad, absent. She found a summer calendar in Jenny's room that she'd drawn, with each passing day marked off and a big circle around August 31st, the day her dad would be coming home. His absence was difficult for them all. At times Phoebe felt unable to ward off her anger toward him, even though she knew the situation they found themselves in wasn't his fault. What she finally figured out was that she was angry at him for not being there beside her—angry at being the sole person on whose shoulders their future sat.

It was taking Lily longer than reasonable to get groceries and pick up Jenny. Knowing the bus had come from some distance, and most anything could delay a busload of children, Phoebe tried not to worry. But, as the minutes stretched into another hour, she grew increasingly tense. She called the 4-H office, the school, and the camp but there was no answer. Then she called the grocery store. Lily had been and gone. She was just getting ready to call Virginia, whose daughter, Rachael, had also attended the camp, when she heard a car turn into their farm. Looking out the front window, her relief was immeasurable, as she watched their car come down the winding driveway. By the time she came out of the kitchen door, Lily had parked the car. Phoebe's heart froze when she saw only Lily get out.

"Where's Jenny?" she urgently inquired, rushing toward Lily.

"I don't know. I got there a little late because the cashier got a phone call just as I was checking out at the grocery store. Everyone had already gotten off the bus. Others were still picking up kids but I couldn't find Jenny."

"Couldn't find her? How can that be? Was she on the bus? Did she ride back to town with the other kids? Is she still at the camp?" Phoebe fired off, with an intensity that set Lily aback.

"I asked several mothers about Jenny. They said they'd seen her at camp and on the bus but, in the confusion of everyone getting off the bus and meeting, not since then. One of the mothers, Mrs. Templer, Cindy's mother, said she thought she'd seen Jenny get into a car with a woman."

The look of horror on her mother's face prompted Lily to continue.

"Do you want me to go back into town to look for her? Maybe Virginia picked her up with Rachael or she rode home with some other family and will be here soon."

"What other family? Something has happened to her, I just know it."

"I'm sorry, Mom. I didn't know what to do."

"It's all right, Lily. It's not your fault. You did right to come home to tell me. We'll find her."

By this time Bart and Judd had converged on the scene.

"Bart, get the truck. We need to go see where Jenny is," Phoebe ordered.

"What are we going...there's a car coming down the driveway," Lily announced, seeing an unfamiliar car come toward them.

"Maybe you're right, Lily," Phoebe acknowledged, turning to look and feeling an easing of the knot in her stomach. "Maybe someone else has brought her home."

They made way for the gray coupe slowly approaching. No one recognized the car at first. Soon enough, however, Phoebe could see that the driver was her friend, Agnes. When the car had come to a full stop the passenger door opened and Jenny ran to her mother's arms. Phoebe fought back tears as she stroked Jenny's blond head of hair and held her close. Responding to her mother's silent signals, Lily then grabbed Jenny's suitcase and prodded her sister toward the house with the promise of raspberry pie and ice cream—and news of Tess. The boys thought pie was a keen idea, as well, and followed her into the kitchen.

"Agnes, I..."

"I hope you don't mind—that you didn't worry too much about Jenny—but I just couldn't leave her there at the school. I was on my way to the library, passing the school, when I saw Clyde and Owen's truck parked near where the busses were arriving. I remembered all you'd told me about them. I don't know what they were up to but it looked like no good, so I stopped my car and watched them. When Jenny got off the bus, they approached her, and it appeared they were trying to persuade her to get into their truck. I got out of the car and ran to her. They fled to their truck and immediately sped away. Phoebe, I think they were going to kidnap Jenny."

"Oh, my God, now they're after my kids. Is Jenny all right? I mean, did they touch her? Did it look like she might go with them?"

"She was pretty matter-of-fact about it. I told her she was right not to go with them, and that I would take her home. Do you know what she told me?"

"I can't imagine."

"That you had told her not to go with anyone no matter what they offered to give her or said about her mom and dad—even if they told her you were hurt—and to kick and scream bloody murder if anyone tried to take her away."

"Atta, girl, Jenny."

"Then she held up her thumb and index finger about a quarter of an inch apart and said 'I was about this far from kicking and screaming'."

"Thank you, Agnes," Phoebe said, giving Agnes a hug. "I don't know how you got Jenny to go with you but I'm glad. You've seen her with me but she doesn't really know you."

"She resisted at first, so you have to give her credit for that, but then a woman came up and started asking me about you so I guess Jenny decided it was all right. I think her name was Virginia. On the way here I tried to reassure Jenny by talking about Tess and you, and she seemed calm. I told her she needed to come over and pick apples for Tess. Then I told her I had some Chinese tea for you.

She knew that was the kind you liked. She's a sharp little girl."

"I can't thank you enough, Agnes. Now, how about some raspberry pie ala mode and some of that exotic Chinese tea you brought?"

"The pie sounds great. Sorry, I didn't bring you any tea. That was just a ruse to convince Jenny I knew you."

"That ruse would work on me, too," Phoebe laughed, squeezing her friend's arm as they walked to the house. Given the circumstances, her laughter surprised her. "I've wanted you to come for a visit but I never thought it would be under such bizarre circumstances."

"I've been hearing rumors about Morray in town. He's even more evil than I thought. Yes, I know you've told me about him but I guess a part of me didn't want to believe it. This experience, in seeing first hand what he's capable of, has convinced me something needs to be done about that man."

"Yes, but what?" Phoebe returned, as they entered the kitchen and joined her family to enjoy some fresh pie.

"Did you like my friend, Agnes?" Phoebe questioned Jenny, as they climbed the stairs to the bath that evening.

"Yes, she's real nice."

"After you've had a nice bath, come downstairs for a glass of lemonade with us."

The family gathered in the kitchen for cool drinks. When Jenny came down the stairs it was as though royalty had entered the room. Everyone cheered and gave her hugs. Taking their glasses to the front porch, they sat for over an hour, patiently listening to a blow by blow account of Jenny's week at camp—how her friend Mitchell had fallen out of a tree and broke his arm, how a family of raccoons ate all their desserts one afternoon before supper. She was glad to be home and, fortunately, didn't seem to fully comprehend the danger she had been in before rescued by Agnes.

Phoebe debated for hours, through a sleepless night, as

to whether or not she should tell Curtis about the incident with Jenny. Eventually, afraid he'd explode in anger and jeopardize his ability to leave when scheduled, she decided against it, shouldering another calamity. Analyzing the situation, she realized the truck she'd heard leaving the woods was probably someone letting Owen and Clyde know that she was home so they could proceed with their plans. Even the phone call to the cashier at the grocery store might have been orchestrated to delay Lily from picking Jenny up. *I need to be more alert where the children are concerned*, she concluded. *Who is it that's involved in this and watching us so closely, anyway?*

The next morning when she called Curtis there was no mention of the events of the day before. When Curtis asked about Jenny's camp experience, Phoebe called her to the phone to talk with her dad and tell him all about it. He talked to Jenny for some time then with the other children. Finally, Phoebe got on the phone again. Curtis expressed a suspicion that something might be wrong but Phoebe disavowed any problems, assuring him they were all fine.

"So—Dad says he loves you, huh? Can you imagine that?" Phoebe said, cheerfully, when she hung up.

"Yes, I can," Jenny answered, with a gleeful smile.

On Saturday morning Phoebe was up early preparing a large breakfast for her family. Jenny actually made it down in time to eat with everyone else for a change. After breakfast she went immediately to the stable to see Tess and the boys went to their chores. Phoebe and Lily got busy in the kitchen, first cleaning up after breakfast then beginning the long, but worthy, process of making peach pickles. By lunch time they had fifteen quarts cooling in the pantry and the kitchen was filled with the smell of cinnamon and cloves.

After lunch Bart went to hook up the cultivator while Judd enjoyed a second helping of fruit salad. Phoebe went upstairs to strip the beds. She had already done Jenny's before her homecoming, but the boys sheets were due to be washed. She was picking up the pile of sheets to take downstairs to the laundry room when she heard a truck turn into their drive, bringing her to full alert.

"Who's that, I wonder," she exclaimed, dropping the sheets and rushing to the window.

Watching a light brown van wend its way down the driveway, she tried to think where she'd put the shotgun. She flew down the stairs, making a dramatic landing in the kitchen. Lily and Judd, who were just finishing up the lunch dishes, turned around upon hearing her, wondering what was going on.

"Someone's here," Phoebe yelled, as the children looked at her in alarm.

"What's wrong?" Lily asked. "Who is it?"

"Oh, for god's sake, never mind. It's Uncle Warren, your Dad's cousin," Phoebe answered, looking out the window. "I wonder what he's doing here. Judd, run to the barn and tell Bart to come as soon as he's finished there—help him if he needs it."

"Warren!" Phoebe called, pushing open the screen door and approaching the van pulling up near the house. "You just missed lunch."

"Hello, Phoebe. I already ate. How's everything going?" he asked, getting out of the van. He gave a hug then stepped back to take a look at her. "You look rode hard and put away wet."

"Thanks, Warren. I can always count on you for a compliment."

"I'm sorry. It's just that you've lost a lot of weight."

"What are you doing here, Warren?"

"Guilt, mostly. I've been feeling badly that there wasn't more that I could have done, especially early in the summer. Now I see that I've wasted that emotion. I've never seen healthier looking corn."

"Yes, what there is of it. That's thanks to the boys."

"Did they plant the soy bean seed I got?"

"Come on in and we'll talk. It's a long story."

Warren was taller and leaner than Curtis. He looked more like a cousin to Phoebe. His dark hair sat like a divot on top of his head, except for the long lock that kept falling forward into his eyes then combed back with his fingers. Sky blue eyes stared out from deep sockets intensifying a prominent nose. He had a broad mouth and high cheekbones that sat above convex cheeks, bordered by bushy sideburns. The white around his neck below the tan line betrayed his daily exposure to the sun. He looked like the sodbuster he was. In addition to raising crops, last year he'd marketed thirty-five thousand turkeys just before Thanksgiving at a dollar a head—or carcass, as it were.

"You remember Lily, Warren. Judd's gone to get Bart and Jenny is taking care of her pony."

"Nice to see you again, Lily."

"How about a piece of raspberry pie with ice cream—home made?" Lily inquired.

"I saw it sittin there. I can't pass that up."

Lily had baked the pie because Keith was coming to pick her up. They were going to a play at the outdoor amphitheater in Herston. After Lily served Warren a piece of pie, Phoebe suggested she go work in the garden so she and Warren could have a talk in private. She let him enjoy his pie before relating to him all happenings, even those Curtis didn't know about, requesting his confidence. He was very solicitous, clinging to his guilt in not being able to help more despite Phoebe's assurances they were all right.

"I went to see Curtis before coming here. They weren't going to let me see him but I insisted, threatened really."

"How did he seem to you?"

"He's got a far worse case of the guilts than me, I'm afraid. Physically he looks all right—a little thinner maybe. He's logically depressed and antsy to get back home."

"Thanks for going to see him. He really needs all our

support."

"I assured Curtis I'd do what I could now that the work at my farm has diminished for the season. There's not much I can do for the turkeys now that they're market ready, just keep them fed and from killing each other. I've already signed the contracts for their sale. My crops are nearly in, as well. It's been an amazing year for growing things."

"It's only three weeks now until Curtis gets out of rehab. We should be able to manage until then, Warren," Phoebe assured.

"If there's anything you need, let me know. I'll do what I can."

"We appreciate it. You never know. I may need to call on you and I'm glad for the offer."

"I'd better get going. Doris will wonder why I've been so long."

"Say hello to her for us."

"I'll do that."

"How's that new baby girl?"

"Yes, Maggie. She's growing so fast you can almost watch. After two boys, a girl seems really different but we love it. Doris couldn't be happier."

Warren got up and was heading for the door when Jenny came in from the stable.

"Who are you?" Jenny questioned.

"My goodness, girl, you've grown like a weed," Warren said. "You remember your dad's ole cousin, Uncle Warren, don't you?"

Jenny came timidly forward then ran to him once she'd made the connection. He swung her up in his arms and gave her a big hug. "You and your family will have to come over to see us one of these days, maybe around Thanksgiving time. We've got a bunch of new kittens."

"We've got kittens enough here," Jenny responded.

"Well," Warren laughed, "maybe Josh's new pony would make it worth the trip."

"Josh has a new pony? Is it as nice as Tess?"

"I doubt it but it's a good one. You might also be interested in meeting Maggie."

"Who's Maggie, your dog?"

"Don't you remember—our dog's name is Fergus? Maggie is our new baby girl."

"Can I see her, Mom, can I?"

"Soon, Jenny, soon."

"Gotta run," Warren said, setting Jenny back on the floor. He was heading out the door when the boys came up from the barn. There was only time for brief greetings and another hug for Phoebe, then Warren was out the driveway and heading home.

Keith came by just after supper and he and Lily left for the play. The boys were watching television in the living room. Listening to the continuing minutiae of Jenny's camp experience, Phoebe tucked her in bed late evening. She called good night to the boys then went to her room, closed the door, and had a good cry in private. You'd think she would be crying about their circumstance or missing Curtis, but what came up was her remembrance of her parents—how supportive they might be if they were still around. She guessed that seeing Warren, a relative if only by marriage, had set her mind whirling into the past, back to the time of her parents' deaths. As an adult orphan she'd felt very alone in realizing she would no longer be able to call her mother with questions, for advice or just to hear *I love you*. Still, it couldn't compare in devastation to the current emptiness she felt.

Her love for Curtis was as strong as ever but, without him, even surrounded by her children, she felt very alone. In a sense Curtis had died as well, at least temporarily. When she met him the year she practice taught, she had felt sanctified, so drawn to him that an immediate connection was fastened. They were different people then, even more different now, but had grown together. She nursed her loneliness for a time, wondering if she had the strength to hang on, soon putting her tears aside with the resolve to make it through the next three weeks. Hearing Lily come home, she got up to say good night. When Lily went upstairs, Phoebe called Curtis.

"Hi, Hon."

"Hi. It's so late. Is everything all right?"

"Yeah, just missing you."

"Are the kids all right?"

"They're working so hard, Curtis. I don't know if we can hold out until you get home. I'm afraid the boys will be so exhausted by the time school starts they won't be able to manage."

"You must be exhausted yourself. I can hear it in your voice. We knew it wouldn't be easy. Maybe it's time to count our losses and quit."

"No, we can't do that. I'm sorry. I don't mean to complain. It's just that...I don't know what to say."

"Phoebe, the majority of the work has already been accomplished. It's only three weeks now until I get out of here. Then I can help with the harvest and be a father and husband again. You can hold on that long, can't you?"

"Yes, I think so—if nothing else goes wrong. Warren stopped by here after he'd seen you. He said you were depressed."

"That shouldn't be a big news flash. I get depressed for myself, in here, unable to help, but mostly for you. I know this has been, is, a terrible burden on you and I can't stand it sometimes that I'm not there to help out. If we could hold onto each other it might be easier."

"I feel the same, Curtis. I guess what I feel more than anything else is loneliness."

"Soon, Phoebe, soon—it will all be behind us," Curtis said, as Phoebe laughed.

"I hope you're right. What if they don't let you out of there?"

"Let's not go there."

"Sorry. I've suggested that the kids go to the movies

Sunday night. They need a break from all this confusion and disruption."

"Will you be all right home alone?"

"Yes. Maybe I should bell one of the cats."

"That's not funny, Phoebe. Why don't you get yourself another dog?"

"I'll be fine."

"I'll try to call that evening to make sure you're doing okay. What time are the kids going to the movies?"

"They'll leave around six so why don't you try to call around eight."

Phoebe hung up the phone in a daze, looking for a way to mitigate their circumstances. She would need to find the strength to continue but with the endless stream of dire circumstances, she wondered what would be next, could she endure. She was no fool and knew it wouldn't be long before her strength was again tested.

After a restless night she was up very early, sitting on the porch with her cup of tea, hoping to experience the calming moments of another day dawning. She had no sooner sat down when she saw Jesse Tate coming down the driveway, leading Tess. Phoebe ran through the house and out the back door, meeting Jesse at the end of the driveway near the stable. Reacting to the look on her face, he pulled the pony toward him as a protective barrier, halting in his tracks.

"What, may I ask, are you doing with Jenny's pony?" she thrust toward him, before he could say anything.

"Well, it's the damndest thing," Jesse stammered. "Pete went to the woods this morning early and found Tess—tied to a tree up by the road—with no one around."

"That doesn't entirely explain what you're doing with her."

"Well, ain't it obvious? I'm puttin her back. I know where she belongs."

"Do you now?" Phoebe curtly replied.

"You don't think for one minute that I..."

"I don't know what to think anymore. We've had so much trouble around here that I suspect everyone, expecting something else bad to go wrong any minute, and am numb from worry. Thanks for returning Tess," Phoebe said, taking the pony's lead from his hand, pausing to pat it.

Jesse followed her to the stable and helped her put Tess in the stall. He'd known of the incidents with the fencing and about Curtis being in rehab but nothing of all the other circumstances befallen the Higgins family.

"Things are as bad as that, are they?"

"Afraid so."

For some reason she would later find irrational, if not dangerous, she began bearing her soul to Jesse. Maybe it was because, knowing his nature, she found it difficult to believe him capable of perpetrating the kinds of things to which they'd become victims. Something about his eyes made her trust him. It was a relief to get it off her chest, to talk with an adult besides Curtis or Agnes, someone who knew Morray's tortures well. After listening intently for some time, he scratched his head.

"You know, I've seen a red pickup around here quite often, come to think on it. I guess I thought it was Harley Weils come to collect firewood or something. His mother owns these woods, you know. I've heard a chain saw in the woods more than once."

"Did he ever say anything to you?"

"Well, no, I never got close to him or talked to him— just seen him from a distance like."

Unable to think of anything to say, Phoebe stood staring at Jesse, an uncomfortable silence between them.

"I know I ain't been any help and I'm sorry," Jesse offered finally. "I jest don't want to tangle with that bastard no more. If I was to help ya, he'd be on me like stink on—ah—a skunk."

"It's all right, Jesse, really. We know you'd help if you could. I'm just sorry about the cattle crushing some of your corn."

"If you'd like, I could have a look at the well pump and see if I can fix it."

"That would really be grand, Jesse."

"One of these days this'll all be over with and we can get back to normal."

"Promise? Thanks again for bringing Tess back—and for listening."

"No problem there, Phoebe. Tell Curtis I said hey and I'll see about that pump in the next day or two."

They walked from the stable together then Jesse turned into the woods and Phoebe went to the house. The kids had just gotten up and were gathering in the kitchen as she walked through the door with a smile plastered on her face.

"Is anything wrong, Mom?" Bart asked. "You're out and about early."

"No, just checking things over," Phoebe responded in a forced calm tone.

"Did I see Jesse Tate just now, leaving?"

"Yes, he came to borrow something."

Bart eyed her suspiciously but she deflected his stare, choosing to ignore it. The rest of the weekend was spent taking care of the usual chores. The kids, reading her well, knew something was wrong but couldn't get her to talk about it. Though nothing was said, it created a somber atmosphere. Phoebe thought a great deal about the incident with Tess—and Harley Weils—wondering if he could be the third party behind the incidents at their farm. She came to no immediate conclusions but determined to keep a watchful eye on him in the future. He was a sly one, she knew that much. He could very easily observe their comings and goings from his mother's porch or from the woods she owned.

While Lily tended the garden in the afternoon on Sunday, Phoebe fixed a nice supper for her family. Meals came almost entirely from the garden: lettuce, tomatoes, green onion, cucumbers, and squash. She prepared their favorite entrée that evening, fried chicken, attempting to belie her concerns and fears.

"Are you sure you're all right, Mother?" Bart inquired.

"Yes, I'm sorry to be so preoccupied. I guess I'm just upset—but I don't want to talk about it. It's nothing in particular," she lied, "just things—circumstances. I just wish your dad was here. I miss him."

"He'll be home soon," Bart consoled.

"You kids have been great but the ultimate responsibility falls to me and it gets to me sometimes. I'm sorry if I'm curt or distracted, and hope you understand."

At six o'clock the kids piled into the family sedan, with Bart as driver, and left for Herston to go to the movie theatre. Keith would meet them there. Phoebe watched until they were out of the driveway and the road dust had settled back down. The new batch of kittens sprawled at her feet as she attempted to get to the kitchen door. She stopped to pet a few of them then hustled them to their mother and went inside. Tired from another day of worry, she sat down in the recliner and was soon asleep. A ringing phone awakened her. Groggy from her nap, she wasn't sure how long it had been ringing, stumbling to the phone in the dark.

"Phoebe, are you all right?"

"Yes, Curtis, I'm fine. What time is it?"

"It's around nine. Sorry I couldn't call earlier like I said I would, but the orderly on duty is kind of uncooperative and I had to wait until the next shift, when the new guy came on board, to try again. It sure took you a long time to answer the phone."

"I guess I fell asleep in the chair."

"You need more rest."

"Curtis—about the other night. I'm sorry I burdened you with things. I know there's nothing you can do, how helpless you feel, so I don't need to whine."

"You were hardly whining—and who would blame

you if you were. It's good that you told me exactly how you felt. I know how hard this is on everyone. You have to have an outlet valve, someone to talk to."

"Speaking of outlet valves, I have a confession to make. I spilled the beans to Jesse Tate," Phoebe offered; evasive about how much she'd told him. "I don't know what got into me. I just looked into his eyes and started talking."

"What did he say?"

"He was surprisingly sympathetic, repeating that he would like to help but can't. The same excuses he gave you, I guess. I hope he doesn't repeat what I told him."

"He's a good guy, Phoebe. I think we can trust him not to gossip about us to anyone, especially Morray. He absolutely hates the man. Meanwhile, let's just focus on getting through this."

"Yeah. Try not to worry and I'll do the same."

"What movie are the kids seeing tonig... What's that crackling sound, Phoebe?"

"I don't know. The phone doesn't seem to be working well. We must have a poor connection. I'll call you back."

Hanging up the phone, Phoebe froze in seeing a shadowy figure moving outside the kitchen window, quickly crouching down beneath it to listen. Someone was outside near where the juncture box for the telephone was located. It took her a nanosecond to figure out they were trying to cut the line. *They must have been watching the house and saw the kids leave in the car*, she speculated. *With the house dark, they probably figured I had gone along and there was no one at home.* Without taking a moment to think about what to do next, she grabbed the shotgun from the pantry closet and opened the door.

"Whoever is out here, it's only fair to warn you that I'm holding a shotgun and if I see so much as a finger move, I'm firing."

First she heard a soft rustling sound then someone made a dash for the woods. She fired a shot, purposely over the head of the intruder but close enough to let them know she meant business. Standing in the dark, perfectly still, she heard a truck engine start, move away then fade into the distance. Inside, she turned on every light in the house before putting the gun back in the closet. Calling Curtis she was shaking so hard she could hardly manage to dial.

"It took you long enough to call back. Is everything all right?"

"Yes, everything's fine. I just got myself a glass of water and turned on some lights. The kids should be home soon and you can talk with them."

"That would be great. Are they doing all right?"

"Yes, I'd say so—working too hard but otherwise fine. Curtis, do you know anything about Harley Weils?"

"Not really, why?"

"I just wondered. Doesn't he drive a red pickup truck?"

"Yes, you know he does, why?"

"I've seen it around a lot lately that's all."

"Well, his mother lives right across the road from us—and she owns those woods next to our farm. It's only logical he'd be around."

"Yes, I guess you're right. It seems like I suspect everyone these days."

"Yes, and with good reason."

Phoebe and Curtis talked for nearly an hour about everything but what was foremost on her mind. Since there wasn't a thing he could do from where he was, it seemed pointless to burden him with details, even though she'd experienced quite a scare.

"Hold the line. I think the kids are here. You'll have to save the rest of your sweet talk for another time."

"Got enough lights on in here?" Judd questioned, barging through the back door.

"What's that about the lights?" Curtis questioned, once Bart was on the phone.

"Nothing. Everything is fine here," he stated, giving his mother the thumbs up with a questioning look.

When she returned the gesture in assurance he turned his attention to the conversation with his father, telling him all about the movie and how things were going at home. Phoebe half-listened, occupied instead with self-indulgent ruminations. When each of the children had talked with their dad she and Curtis said good night. He thought he detected some unease in her voice but decided not to question her about it. At times he suspected she was keeping the entirety of their affairs at home from him, but knew wild horses couldn't drag it out of her if she wasn't talking—and he had to admit that a small part of him, the cowardly part, didn't want to know.

Off the phone, Bart came to sit with his mother in the living room.

"Are you sure you're all right, Mom?"

"What do you mean?"

"The lights, Mom. Honestly, every light in the house is turned on."

"I'm fine. I just turned the lights on to feel safer because I was alone."

Just as she'd withheld other incidents, Phoebe refused to worry the children about the telephone or nighttime visitor. It seemed as though not a single aspect of their lives or property was safe from the truculence of Gaylan Morray.

In the morning she surveyed the phone lines while the kids were otherwise occupied. There was a slice on part of the wire but she'd stopped him before he could cut it through. She got some duct tape and wrapped it around the wires then put a padlock on the juncture box. The phone company might not like it but that was too bad. Her vixenish behavior, gradually seeping into her personality, was of less concern by the day. *Necessity is the mother of invention*, she excused. She needed a break. After making sure everything was secure at home, she went into town to buy a few groceries, leaving the kids in charge. Passing by the sheriff's office on her way to the market, she noticed a state police car parked out in front and, seeing her chance, took it.

"Sheriff, I'd like to report an attempted crime," she said, bursting into the dispatch office where the sheriff stood with the state policeman. It was not the state policeman suspected of being in cahoots with Tagwell.

"What crime is that," the sheriff returned in a placating tone.

"Someone tried to cut our phone line last night. You can spread the word that if anyone comes around our property again, uninvited, they'll get a load of buckshot in their rear or worse."

"Now, Mrs. Higgins, I wouldn't..."

"The first person I see on our property, daylight or night, gets shot. Trust me, I mean it. I've complained to you several times before. You won't do anything about it, so I will. You won't even come out to investigate. Isn't that your job?" Phoebe didn't wait for a response. She shot a threatening look at the state policeman, who was wearing a shocked expression, and exited the office as brusquely as she'd entered. Instead of going immediately to the market, she drove to Agnes' house.

"Agnes," Phoebe said, greeting her friend, "can I please use your phone?"

"Of course. Come on in. If it can wait a minute, let's have a cup of tea and talk."

Phoebe shared with Agnes all that had happened the last few weeks. Knowing Phoebe was usually very forthcoming and calm, not at all depressed or moody, Agnes could clearly see what all the stress was doing to her friend. The worst part seemed to be the burden of keeping things from Curtis and the children. Phoebe had no one else to talk to so she was happy to listen. After they'd talked a while, and had had a second cup of tea, Phoebe calmed a bit and told Agnes why she wanted to use the phone. Agnes agreed it was a good idea.

"Hi, Jeremy, it's Phoebe Higgins. Can you talk?"

"Jeremy," Harley yelled from across the garage. "I gotta run to the auto parts store. Take over will ya?"

"I'll do 'er," Jeremy called back.

After an uncomfortably long time, Jeremy finally answered.

"Yeah, wha is it Miz Higgins?" he asked, suspicious.

"Did your dog have another batch of puppies this year?"

"Yeah?"

"How old are they?"

"They's bout six month ole by now—hardly puppies—still playful, shur nuf."

"We've been having some trouble out at the farm and I need a good watchdog. Are any of them suitable?"

"Why da ya need nother watch dawg?"

"Max was murdered right after they took Curtis—shot through the forehead."

"Oh."

"I'd like to buy one of your dogs, Jeremy."

"They's two of em left. Ones a male—worthless but a butiful lukin dog. The other uns a bitch. Name's Ruby an she da tear the pants off anyun who'd came near her that shudn't. Sounds like she ud be perfect."

"How much do you want for her?"

"One hunred dallars."

"Can I pick her up or meet you somewhere to get her? I assume you don't want me to come to your house or the station—or be seen coming to the farm."

"We kin meet at Bullfrog Crick Bridge east a town. When daya wants to git her?"

"Today?"

"I'll meet ya thar after werk—bout eight-thirty."

"Judd will be with me and the children don't know about Max being shot, so please don't say anything, Jeremy. And, let's say Ruby came from the pound so you're not implicated."

Shur nuf, Miz Higgins."

Before Phoebe could say more, Jeremy hung up.

"It's all settled. We'll pick the dog up tonight. Thanks, Agnes. Sorry I can't stay longer but I have to cash a check at the grocery store then get home."

Before Phoebe could make it to the door, Agnes caught her shoulders, turned her around and looked her squarely in the face. "You'll get through this, Phoebe. And—if you need anything—anything—call me."

"Thanks, Agnes," Phoebe responded, hugging her friend.

At exactly eight-thirty, Phoebe and Judd were waiting in the truck at the Bullfrog Creek Bridge. By nine o'clock Jeremy still hadn't shown. Just as they were talking of leaving, they heard a truck coming down the gravel road. Jeremy seemed nervous and in a hurry as he got out of the truck, leaving the door open as one might if they expected to have to make a quick get away. He went to the back of the truck and lowered the tailgate. Judd and Phoebe stepped back as a fierce looking German shepherd lunged at them.

"I hope I ain't been follered. I hed a hell a time— sorry—heck a time gettin 'way from Harley. Then I hed to go home'n…go pick up Ruby. You brung a leash?"

"Yeah. She won't bite us will she?"

"No, she's frenly enuf iffen she knows ya—and since yur with me it should be a'right. I cain't stay so let's get this o'er with. C'mon Ruby, girl," he called out.

Ruby jumped out of the truck bed to stand next to Jeremy and he snapped on the leash Phoebe handed him. Judd led Ruby to the truck cab and opened the door. She jumped right up onto the bench seat and Judd slid in next to her.

"Here's the hundred dollars—and thank you, Jeremy. I brought cash so you wouldn't have to explain a check to anyone."

"Ya keep yer money," Jeremy pronounced, shutting the tailgate.

"But why—we had a deal?"

"We hedda deal but I thot on it hard an I don want ya to pay non. Shootin a dawg," he added in a whisper, "that's the worst I herd a. Make like it wuz my small war agin—things."

"Thank you so much, Jeremy," Phoebe offered, shaking his hand.

"Ya jus take good care a Ruby."

"We will, for sure," Phoebe answered.

Jeremy hopped into his truck, slammed the door shut and sped off, trailing dust. By the time Phoebe got into their truck, Judd and Ruby had already bonded. Ruby was licking his face and slapping her tail against the back of the seat.

"Look how nice she is, Mom. Do you think she'll really be a good watchdog?"

"We'll see," Phoebe noncommittally answered, starting the truck and grinding it into gear.

"Careful, Mom, that shoulder's soft—you almost drove over the embankment into the creek. It sure is high this year. Maybe Bart and me will have to go canoeing one of these days—with Ruby."

"Bart and I. There'll be plenty of time for that once your father gets home," Phoebe assured, easing the truck down the sloping road.

"When will he be coming home?" Judd inquired.

"In twelve days. It won't be any too soon for me—for any of us, I suspect."

All the kids immediately fell in love with Ruby. As far as any of them knew, she'd come from the pound, delivered by Jeremy. She was such a kind gentle dog that Phoebe had doubts about her being any kind of watchdog, until Jesse Tate stopped by to borrow a tool. Ruby started barking the minute his truck hit the driveway. She tried to go after him when he got out of his truck but her tether wouldn't reach.

"That's quite a watchdog you got there. Where did you get him?"

"Her," Phoebe corrected, getting a grip on Ruby's collar. "From the pound over in Herston."

Now that Jesse knew more than he should about their circumstances, she chose to exercise caution. Jeremy had been a good friend and she didn't want him compromised.

"Well, she's a good one, it appears. Every time I look at her she growls."

"Yes, I think she'll do. We only just got her, so you're the first real test of her alertness. They told me at the pound she'd tear the pants off anyone who came around her so she's just what the doctor ordered."

Jesse Tate looked at Phoebe then at the dog, as Judd and Bart joined them.

"Mind if I see if Curtis has an extra tappet in the machine shed? I couldn't find one at the auto parts store. He always has spare parts around and I need one urgently."

"Go ahead. We'll put Ruby inside for now but it might be a good idea for you to make friends with her," Phoebe offered, motioning for Judd to take her.

"When do you expect Curtis to come home?"

"Any day now," Phoebe defended, suddenly thinking Jesse was asking too many questions.

"Good—just in time for the harvesting."

"That's right," Phoebe answered. "Bart, why don't you go with Jesse to the machine shed and see if you can help him find that part?"

She felt badly including Jesse Tate among unknown culprits but felt the need to exercise caution, excusing her suspicious nature. Ruby growled as Bart and Jesse left for the barn.

"She won't bother Jesse will she?" Judd asked, once they were in the house.

"No. Not once they get acquainted."

Twenty minutes later, as Bart came in the back door,

she heard Jesse's truck going down the driveway.

"Did he find the part he was looking for?" Phoebe questioned Bart.

"I guess so. I don't know a tappet from a teaspoon but he seemed satisfied. He said he'd come over tomorrow to have a look at the well pump. If he can fix it, we'll get started on putting the fencing back the next morning, Judd."

"It looks like Ruby is going to be a very good watchdog, doesn't it?" Judd said, as the dog sidled up to him. "Way to go, Ruby girl."

CHAPTER NINE

In the following days Ruby became an integral member of the family. Her instincts proved to be invaluable, constantly alerting them to anything out of the ordinary. She growled when the postman pulled up at the post box at the end of the driveway, if a car moved past too slowly on Digbert Road or at the sound of a truck motor in the woods. They decided she had enhanced hearing like Superman. Phoebe had to admit she felt safer with Ruby near, and Curtis was happy she'd gotten the dog. Judd made a special bed for her in the pantry. He would like to have had her sleep with him but, although Ruby had free range of the house during the day, Phoebe insisted she stay in the kitchen at night while they slept. A true test of Ruby's watchdog skills came within days.

They'd had a long, hard day of work. Jesse had fixed the well pump, making friends with Ruby in the process. Once he was finished the boys immediately got busy refencing. It was a lot of work. The kids went to bed shortly after eating supper. Phoebe was exhausted. Instead of going directly to bed, however, she treated herself to a nice, long, leisurely bath. Ruby curled up on the floor next to the tub and went to sleep, but jerked her head up and started to growl as Phoebe stepped out of the tub. By the time Phoebe had put on her robe to go investigate, Ruby was downstairs, standing at the back door barking her fool head off. Grabbing the shotgun from the closet, Phoebe went to the door.

"What's going on?" Bart called, as he and Judd ran down the stairs and into the kitchen.

"Get back upstairs, boys," Phoebe ordered.

"Yes ma'am," Bart answered, backing around the corner into the hallway. Unwilling to move out of sight of their mother wielding a shotgun, he stood just outside the kitchen with Judd and Lily behind him.

"Whoever is out there, I'm letting my dog out. Do you

hear me?" Phoebe called through the kitchen window.

Shadows moved against the moonlight but she couldn't see who it was or what they were doing. When she opened the door a crack, Ruby bolted through at a run. A couple of yelps were heard, a man screaming then footsteps running toward the woods. Phoebe stepped outside the back door and fired a blast from the shotgun into the night sky. Running steps quickened and soon she heard the remote sound of a truck engine. Only after it was again silent, did she call to Ruby. It took a few seconds for Ruby to appear, enough time to induce the fear that she might have been hurt or abducted. Back in the kitchen, Phoebe found her children slack-jawed and staring. She put the gun back in the pantry closet as Ruby trotted into the kitchen. Despite the dire circumstances, they all broke into laughter upon seeing her. She had a patch of kaki cloth in her mouth and, on closer inspection, they discovered a piece of white cotton with small blue and red triangles on it, presumably from the boxer shorts of the intruder.

"Who do you think it was?" Judd asked.

"Probably just a bum looking for some food or whatever else he could scavenge."

"I thought I heard a truck. A bum wouldn't be driving a truck."

"That must have been Ruby growling," Phoebe lied. "We'll check tomorrow to see if Jesse had a visitor as well. It's possible he made the rounds to all the farms."

Jenny had slept through the entire episode. After a late night snack, Phoebe urged everyone back to bed. She sat up a while longer, until she knew they'd be asleep. Then she got the flashlight and went with Ruby to where she presumed she'd intercepted the intruder—to the gas tank near the woodshed. Ruby growled and sniffed the ground. Sure enough, the tank had been tampered with, the cap was off. A rag had been stuffed into the opening and a book of matches lay on the ground. Thanks to Ruby another catastrophe had been averted. Phoebe removed the rag, threw it in the tool shed, replaced the cap on the tank and went to bed.

Tallying in her mind the suspicions concerning Harley Weils, Phoebe stopped at the gas station on a trip into town shortly after the incident.

"Hi, Jeremy. How are you doing?" Phoebe sang out, as Jeremy came out of the station, a horrified look on his face. When he got close enough to her, she made a reassuring gesture that let him know she wasn't there to make trouble for him.

"Could you fill it up and wash the windshield, please?" she spoke in a loud voice. "That Ruby is a gem, thanks," she whispered.

Harley Weils came out through the garage doors of the station. He wiped his hands on a red cloth, looking around like a prairie dog sticking up from his hole. His red pickup truck sat over to the side of the building. Phoebe noted how dirty it was, wondering if it was mud from the road in the woods next to their farm.

"Hello, Harley," she called, knowing it was a useless gesture.

Watching him turn to go back into the garage, she thought she detected a slight limp in his step.

"Something wrong with Harley?" she questioned.

"Yeah. I don knows what but it pains him ta sit, parently—must be hemratoads. I gotsa same problem sometime. I axe him what was the truble but he won talk non."

The rest of the summer went better around the Higgins farm. Once in a while Ruby would bark, setting off an investigation, but no further troubles arose that kept the operation of the farm from continuing. Phoebe and the kids counted the days until Curtis would be home.

A week before his return, Jenny turned nine. Trying to make it a fun and memorable birthday, despite the absence of her dad, Phoebe threw a small party for her. Three of her friends from school were to come to spend the afternoon, riding Tess and having ice cream and cake. Lily baked two dozen white cupcakes, frosted them in pink, Jenny's favorite color, then added pink decorations and put a pink candle on each, arranging them on a tray to form a crude pony.

The girls arrived around two o'clock. Their mothers were to pick them up in three hours and then Rachael would stay to have supper and spend the night. Lily and Phoebe watched from the fence as Jenny led each girl, one at a time and squealing with delight, around the riding ring on Tess' back. Then Jenny showed her friends a few tricks she'd taught Tess, like counting to four and taking a bow. In the stable she demonstrated how she took care of Tess, allowing each of them a turn with the currycomb. While Phoebe waited out by the stable for the girls to get done grooming Tess, Lily went ahead into the house with Ruby to pour the lemonade.

Phoebe rounded up the girls and, several minutes later, they heard Lily scream. Bart and Judd did as well, arriving in the kitchen along with everyone else to find Lily sitting on the floor, laughing. Ruby was cowering in the corner with frosting all over her face, the crime scene evident— two dozen half-eaten cupcakes strewn across the kitchen table.

"I went to the bathroom and when I came back, Ruby had been a very busy girl," Lily confessed.

It was so funny that no one cared the cupcakes had been ruined. They all sat around the table laughing, drinking lemonade, and eating the peanut butter and jelly sandwiches Lily quickly prepared.

Lily was to leave the last week of August to register for another year of school, resume work, and get her apartment organized. She'd be home for the next weekend, however, for her dad's homecoming. Her boyfriend, Keith, came late in the day to drive her to the city. At the end of the driveway he nearly collided with a red pickup truck flying out of the woods. The driver swerved to the left, narrowly missing the post box, then roared down the road. Neither Lily nor Keith were aware of all that had happened so didn't assign any significance to the incident, concerned only with getting out of the way.

With Curtis due home very soon, the family doubled their efforts in getting the farm to look and function its best. Occupied with farm chores, say nothing of keeping up with the calamites they knew about, they had matured beyond their years—too busy to single out a calf to raise for show at the county fair, too busy to get Tess ready for the 4-H Horse and Pony Show. Phoebe, having neglected her soap making, didn't have anything new and interesting to exhibit, and Lily had decided that any new pie recipes would be for Keith or her family, not wasted on those who didn't fully appreciate her efforts. They unanimously agreed to skip the county fair when it arrived the next month.

The last day of the month, Phoebe was up and showered early. She prepared ribs and sauerkraut in the slow cooker, made brownies, got breakfast then drove to Dirkville to pick up Curtis. Fears had persisted for days that Morray would find a way to keep him in longer. The morning before his release, Phoebe called the sheriff's office, telling him she'd notified the state police that Curtis was due to be released and getting their assurances that if he was further detained, they would get involved. It wasn't true, but worked. The papers were signed that day.

"Phoebe, you really look rough," Curtis commented, taking her into his arms when he met her at the front desk.

"You cut close to the bone, don't you? You don't look so great yourself."

"Yes, I know. Things have been difficult, haven't they, but we're back together now and we'll make it through this," Curtis consoled, guiding her to the car.

He opened the passenger side door and Phoebe got in. Seeing Curtis take the steering wheel, more in charge again, suddenly unleashed three months of tears. It felt like the end of a long nightmare. Though the family, under her guiding hand, had managed against all odds to keep things going in his absence, the stress had been enormous. Now, with Curtis home, she hoped to get back to normal and, with the promise of an inheritance in a couple of months, move again toward solvency. But something had changed in Phoebe. She was not the same woman that had lectured Curtis about the wages of drinking, that had optimistically rallied to meet every problem they'd faced in their marriage. Holding her, Curtis wondered if that innocent piece of her former self that seemed so damaged, could be retrieved.

There were two flaws in Gaylan Morray's plan to undo the Higgins family. First, he didn't control the weather—a great surprise even to him. In June, the weather had been ideal for getting the crops going after planting. While July was hot and dry at times, there was plenty of rain. August rains were overly abundant but the crops grew well and there were enough days in between rainstorms to get the cultivating and spraying done. Second, was his underestimation of Phoebe's will and the strength of her family. He never would have thought for a moment that the Higgins family would be able to keep the farm operational. It must have killed him to see the farm thrive despite his best, or worst, efforts to the contrary. So, not to be outdone and hell bent on acquiring that farm at all costs, he stepped it up a notch.

When Curtis and Phoebe drove down the driveway of their farm early afternoon, they were met by all their children—and Keith. After intense hugs, Keith was pushed to the front and introduced. Ruby barked and barked. When Curtis tried to get in the kitchen door, she lunged at him. It would take time for her to consider him someone other than a stranger. Curtis exercised patience, happy they had a good watchdog, eager to get to know her.

Keith helped Lily clean up the kitchen after supper while the rest of them showed Curtis around. Jenny had cleaned Tess' stable to spotless, unable to wait a minute longer to show it to her dad. They went there first and his praise met her expectations. The barns were in good repair, the tractor and planter washed and ready for use, the remaining corn crop looked as good or better than any he'd grown and the livestock were content and healthy. The granary was stuffed full of grain, the barn full of hay, silo bulging with silage, and the hogs and feeder cattle ready for market, assuming they could find a place to sell them. Surveying all that had been done on the farm, he grew very emotional.

They spent the weekend celebrating with special meals and lots of quality time together. Phoebe had packed up the rest of Lily's things to take to her apartment, clearing the way for Bart to take over her room. Lily and Keith loaded the car then left to go back to the city on Sunday afternoon, while Judd and Curtis helped Bart move his things.

It didn't take long for Ruby to warm to Curtis, as the family settled back into normalcy. Curtis was incredibly happy to be home. Watching him, secure in the knowledge her partner was once again by her side, Phoebe gradually unburdened herself, relating all the incidents she'd shouldered alone. Though inordinate, the relief was not total, her psyche holding the memory of all that had happened. The three long months Curtis was gone had felt like an eternity but, now that the time had finally passed, it seemed like only a blink.

He didn't waste any time getting back to farming—out the door, onto the tractor, and into the field before anyone was up Monday morning. When he came in for breakfast the rest of the family was seated at the table. He couldn't conceal his contentment, a broad grin widening on his face as he joined them. After breakfast Jenny and Judd caught the bus to school. Judd was a sophomore and Jenny in third grade. It would be another week before Bart started community college, commuting back and forth each day and living at home. Once he finished the prerequisites of the two-year program, he'd enroll at the university in Lynchford and study engineering. Until then he would continue to assist Curtis on the farm when he wasn't hitting the books.

A week later the family decided to attend the last night of the county fair together. After the stock car races there was to be a concert by Croaking Frogs, a regional band, and then fireworks. Instead of having supper at home they ate hot dogs, sodas, and curly fries at the fair, joining Keith and Lily at the concession stand. Afterward, Jenny got a cotton candy and Judd, a funnel cake. Bart went with his new girlfriend, Cynthia to the rides. Phoebe and Curtis walked around hand in hand, unable to believe they were finally back together. Occasionally they bumped into Keith and Lily, also holding hands.

The stock car race was a success but, before the concert could get underway, it started to rain. Actually, it poured—thunder and lightening so intense no one dared leave the shelter of the grandstand. By the time the rain lightened enough for the crowd to disperse and get to their cars, everyone was soaked to the skin. There was a mad scramble to get out of the parking lot that took much longer than if it had been an organized exit. Everyone wanted to be first, butting in line, making a longer wait for those who had attempted to line up.

Keith and Lily went on to the city, giving Cynthia a ride, and Bart rode home with the rest of the family. The blinding rain was so heavy that, at times, Curtis couldn't see out the windshield and had to stop until it lightened up. When they got home everyone ran for the house between strikes of lightning. Ruby met them at the door, appearing quite agitated. They found deep scratches on the inside of the back door. She'd not experienced a thunderstorm alone before so they assumed that was the source of her angst. Inside they discovered the storm had knocked out their electricity. Phoebe brought out some candles while Curtis, flashlight in hand, located a kerosene lamp in the basement.

After drying off, Jenny got her pajamas on and crawled into bed. She could read most any book by herself but, since Curtis had come home she craved his attention, asking him to read one of her favorite books to her. He happily complied, sitting with her and reading by candle-light. Since being home, he had enthusiastically immersed himself in all aspects of family life. Later he, Bart and Judd lit candles and talked in the kitchen while Phoebe put on her night clothes. When she joined the group they sat together in the flickering glow, chatting. It was quite late when they went to bed. Curtis and Phoebe lay awake a long time, talking about all that had happened, their family, and how glad they were to have their lives back.

"When it rains, it pours," Curtis quipped, the following morning.

"It's still raining?" Phoebe sleepily asked, from bed.

"Cats and dogs. I'm really itching to get on the tractor and cut the rest of that corn but I guess it will have to wait. I only hope it will. No one will be working outside in that downpour. The electricity still isn't on either. When the rain lightens up, I'll go out and do chores. I told the boys last night I'd do them this morning. They need to settle into a more normal existence now that I'm back, and with school starting."

At the allotted time, the boys were up and ready to go. Jenny was the last one organized but managed in time. After tossing down an unconventional breakfast of pork and bean sandwiches, Judd and Jenny took the lunches Phoebe had packed for them and waited for the bus on the front porch with Ruby. Hearing it coming, they ran down the lane with books tucked under their raincoats and hoods pulled up over their heads. Bart took the car to begin his daily commute to college. He would pick the other two kids up after school on his way home. Curtis got the generator going and Phoebe used the opportunity to make some tea. It was good to sit together at the kitchen table talking, as had been their habit for years.

"Have I told you lately how much I missed you, Phoebe?" Curtis began, patting Ruby's side as she devotedly lay next to him.

"Are you talking to Ruby or me?" Phoebe returned, smiling. "I'm sure I—we—missed you even more. I really hope, now that you're back, we can get things on a more even keel around here."

"We will," Curtis reassured, taking her hand. "I know you're exhausted after all your responsibilities. I'll make it up to you one of these days, I promise."

"The corn crop isn't in jeopardy with all the rain we've been getting recently, is it?" Phoebe questioned, noting that it was of less concern with her husband at her side.

"No, it should be fine. The corn is fully grown. We just need some sunny days to finish getting the crop harvested. We'll get it done just as soon as it quits raining."

But it didn't stop raining. It was as though Gaylan Morray controlled the weather after all. By the second day without electricity, Jenny and Judd eagerly went to school. It had been fun to camp out with candles, kerosene lamps, and the limited hours of light the generator provided for a time, but it had become an inconvenience. The first day of the storm, when Bart drove to school, he had noticed that the electricity seemed to be on everywhere but Digbert Road. The next day he saw that it was on for the farms along Digbert Road as well—everywhere but on their farm. He made a mental note to talk with his father about it when he got back home that afternoon.

Curtis and Phoebe remained inside the farmhouse as the storm continued to rage outside and Ruby paced the floor. Besides the usual housework, Phoebe read and tended the accounts. Curtis caught up on various aspects of running the farm that had been neglected in his absence. He and Ruby went to the barn each day, dodging lightening, but stayed only long enough to feed the hogs and replenish the feed lot. Their generator worked but had a limited amount of fuel and, after two days of running constantly, threatened to quit. Late afternoon Curtis decided he needed to go into town for more fuel. On the way, he noticed that everyone had electricity except them. Fearing foul play, he made a U-turn and came back to the farm. Checking the electrical meter, his fears were realized—wires were cut and fuses taken out.

"I don't know why we didn't think of it two days ago," he blustered, relating the situation to Phoebe. "You might know he couldn't let things ride for long."

"I bet that's why Ruby has been so ill-at-ease. They must have come while we were at the fair and she was locked up in the house. Is there electricity to the barns? The well pumps may not be running. The rain has probably filled the tanks for now but then what?" Phoebe questioned.

"I'm going out to the barns again, so I'll check the pumps. Will this rain never let up? You don't suppose he has control of that as well, do you?"

"I wouldn't be surprised."

Curtis put on his slicker and Wellingtons in the mudroom and ran to the barn. The electricity had been cut there as well, the pumps out of commission. The hogs and feeder cattle had water but the supply was low. After feeding them he was about to head back to the house when he saw the larger problem. A huge tree from the woods adjacent to the granary had come down in the storm, probably struck by lightening, toppling onto the roof and crushing it. Their supply of wheat, stored within, was getting soaked and would be ruined.

"It looks like even God is on Morray's side, Phoebe," Curtis fumed, telling her of the calamity.

"You don't really believe that?"

"No, not really, but for heaven's sake—haven't we endured enough? How am I going to tell the boys that…"

"Tell the boys what?" Bart questioned, as he, Judd and Jenny came through the back door.

Curtis looked at Phoebe—a look that told her he'd rather have to tell his son just about anything else. Sensing tension in the air, Jenny went to her mother, crawling into her lap.

"A tree fell on the granary in the storm, crushing the roof. I'm afraid all the wheat is getting soaked—followed soon by mold that will quickly infect the entire crop."

Bart's shoulders slumped in defeat, his books dropped to the floor. Sitting down heavily in a kitchen chair, he put his head down on the table, his hands over his ears like he couldn't bear to hear more. Judd stood at his brother's side, looking demoralized.

"We worked really hard while you were gone, Dad. Now all our effort is for nothing," Judd offered.

"Your efforts weren't for nothing. Don't ever think that boys," Curtis assured. "The rain's sure to let up soon. I'll need some help on Saturday cutting up that tree to get it away from the granary. We'll see better then what the damage is. Maybe its not as bad as I first thought and we can salvage some of the wheat. Can I count on you?"

"Sure, Dad," Bart began, finally looking up. "By the way, I noticed on my way to school that the lights are on everywhere but here."

"Yes, we just figured that out this afternoon," Phoebe began. "The wires…"

"The wires were faulty and the lightening set off a spark that blew out the electricity," Curtis intercepted. "We'll get it all fixed so don't worry about it. I'll have everything ship shape by morning, except that tree. I'll need help with that."

Bart looked at his parents, doubtful, but let the matter drop. Shortly before supper Curtis got the electricity turned back on for the house. The kids all had homework so went to their rooms to study then to bed. Phoebe and Curtis stayed up late, talking, rather whispering, in the kitchen.

The next few days were cloudy but the thunder and lightening stopped and soon the rain drizzled down to a light mist. Saturday morning dawned more brightly. Phoebe let Jenny sleep in. Curtis had worked several hours to restore electricity to the barn, outbuildings, and wells before the boys got up. Ruby still seemed edgy but calmed in following Curtis and the boys around as they did chores. Immediately after lunch, they left to dispatch the large tree. It would probably take the rest of the day and most of Sunday to get it done. Phoebe began planning an extra special meal, knowing they'd be hungry. She heard the chain saw start up then, moments later shut off. Curtis was soon back, coming through the pantry door and stomping his wet boots. He had a look on his face that Phoebe recognized all too well. Something dreadful had happened. She visually checked him over to make sure he had all his body parts and wasn't bleeding.

"Where are the boys?" she croaked, extreme concern in her voice.

"He's done it again," Curtis blurted.

"Done what?" Phoebe urgently asked.

"That tree didn't fall down in the rain nor was it struck by lightening," Curtis continued. "It was sawed down, cut three quarters of the way through to make it fall exactly down over the apex of the granary roof."

Phoebe stood in disbelief. After all they'd been through it wasn't over yet.

"When will this end?" she rasped. "When are we going to stand up to that monster and get free from his grip?"

"All our resistance only brings more down upon us. Unfortunately, there's nothing else we can do, except fold up and leave. Is that what you want, for us to give up the farm?"

"No, of course not but can't the state police or sheriff, someone, do something?"

"Where's the proof, they'll say. We have evidence of

the damage but without proof as to who's doing it, there's nothing they can do. We'd have to catch someone doing the damage and I'm not sure, even then, they'd believe us or take our side in it."

"Do the boys know the tree was sawed?"

"They don't suspect anything. I got them busy chopping off the upper branches of the tree, far away from the base so I don't think they've seen that it was sawed. However that tree got onto the roof of the granary, we still need to saw it up. I'm going back out to help them. I need to saw the base completely through before they figure out that it wasn't lightening that felled the tree."

The wheels were turning in Phoebe's head. She'd had enough of Morray's maligning. Thinking there must be some way to find state police with integrity or get the necessary evidence to put a stop once and for all to their misery, she put the matter before her acute mind for resolution.

Over the weekend, Curtis and the boys finished sawing and cutting up the huge tree then mended the roof of the granary as best they could. The grain was soaked, however. They laid sheets of polyurethane on the barn floor then dumped loads of wheat onto them, spreading it out to see if it would dry enough to be usable. Curtis did not hold out much hope. During the week, while the boys were at school, he continued getting the corn crop in, storing it in the cribs behind the barn. By the end of September the corn was harvested and he'd gotten the seed for winter wheat. The grain they'd spread out on the barn floor had dried but was moldy and unusable. With other chores to do, Curtis left it for the time being, reluctant to face the situation. Life went on but it was stressful waiting for the other shoe to fall—and Morray would not disappoint.

With the help of the boys, before the weather started turning cold, the fields were plowed, ready for disking in the spring, and the wheat crop was planted. It was pointless to try to sell their livestock because no one was buying. Gaylan Morray had again seen to that. Enjoying a brief hiatus from catastrophe, they settled into a more normal farming routine. The wood from the tree that had fallen on the granary was chopped and stored in the woodshed. The garden's abundance had either been canned, frozen or eaten fresh and a good supply of fruit preserves, sauces, pickles, and chutney had been laid in. Though she often wondered what Gaylan Morray might have up his sleeve next, as the days passed uneventfully, Phoebe began to move within a state of grace.

"Curtis, wake up—I think something is on fire," Phoebe yelled, urging him awake with her elbow in the middle of the night in hearing Ruby barking.

They ran together to the window. The barn was on fire. Filled with bales of dry hay and piles of dry, moldy wheat, it went up like a torched wig. The fire chief responded to their frantic phone calls with assurances of help but no fire truck ever showed. Ruby wouldn't stop barking. Phoebe tried to help Curtis but, fearing she might get injured, he sent her back to the house, asking her to take Ruby with her. The boys helped Curtis by driving the feeder cattle away from the smoke and flames. The hogs squealed noisily, the hair on their backs singed, but they managed to toddle off to safety. The cattle, out in the south pasture, were unaffected by the fire—innocent to the fact that there would be no food to feed them over the winter when snow covered the ground.

Having seen the flames rising over the woods that separated their farms, Jesse came over and helped Curtis hose down the pole barn where the machinery was stored, saving it all. They watched together, helpless, as the barn continued to burn. There was no sleep for anyone the rest of the night.

By early morning light Curtis surveyed the scene with Ruby at his side. The barn was a total loss. Behind it, the corn cribs smoldered, smoke billowing from their roofs. If not entirely burned up, the crops inside would suffer smoke damage and be worthless, so he let them burn. Curtis sent Bart, Judd, and Jenny off to school at the usual time, with explanations, insisting they go, blaming the fire on a short in an electrical wire and himself for wiring it wrong. When Jesse came back over to see the extent of the damage, he exploded in rage.

"Someone oughta do in that bastard. I'd do it myself if I thought I could get away with it," he fumed. "Or if I had any guts," he added glumly.

With only their livestock remaining unscathed, Curtis was tempted to turn the hogs loose in the cornfield to scavenge but thought better of it. He wanted them close to the house where he could keep an eye on them. The inheritance Phoebe was to receive from her aunt, along with insurance money, would get them back on their feet but, if they stayed, if they persisted, one could only wonder what else lay in store for them. To what further extremes would Morray go to get their land? The question was not so much whether or not they could continue, as it was whether or not they wanted to. Thankful at least that he had adequate insurance for his outbuildings and crops, he decided he wasn't yet ready for unconditional surrender.

On Saturday, as her sons helped Curtis rake through the coals of the barn, Phoebe sat at the kitchen table. Haggard and worn from all she'd been through, managed, endured, the fire was the last straw. She never thought the day would come when she'd quit fighting and accept defeat but was finished, at least in spirit—finally that day had arrived. It would take a grand effort to start over, even with adequate funds rebuilding all they'd accomplished over the last twelve years. *If we sold the livestock and kept the insurance money*, she calculated, *along with my inheritance we could start over somewhere else*. She was ready to throw in the towel, to tell Curtis she was done. But, with the winter wheat planted, promising a harvest in the spring, she doubted he'd consider it.

Sipping a comforting cup of tea, she became distracted, stiffening as she heard a car coming down the driveway. Jenny was spending the day with her friend Rachael
and everyone else, including Ruby, was still out by the
barn ruins. Anxious about who it might be and what they
wanted, she jumped to her feet. The cream colored car did
not look familiar as it came slowly toward the house then
turned at the back and stopped. It was some comfort
knowing Curtis was close enough to help if it turned out
she needed him. When a man got out of the car then
walked toward the house, she began to panic. Locking the
door, she stood between it and the window where she
wouldn't be detected. He knocked, stepped back to wait
then knocked again. After knocking a third time, he
moved away from the door and walked toward the barn.
She could only see him from the back but something
about him was familiar, so she opened the door and called
after him.

"Can I help you with something?"

"Phoebe?"

"How did you …? Harry?"

Phoebe could hardly believe her eyes, as her brother
stood before her. She hadn't seen him for so long that she
wasn't sure at first that it was actually him but recognition
soon dawned. Though somewhat taller than she, he looked
like her twin. With no thought to the time out of touch, the
grievances or slights, she ran to him and embraced him.
He responded, reluctant to let her go.

"What are you doing here?"

"Is that any way to greet your brother?"

"No, of course not. Come on inside, Harry. Would you
like some tea?"

"Sure. I can't stay long. I just wanted to see how
you're doing."

"Can't stay long? I've written to you—and called—
but you've never responded. I didn't even know if you
were still alive. Your phone's been disconnected and late-

ly, your letters have been returned."

"I know. I'm sorry. I've been—away."

"Away where? What were you doing?"

"When the folks were killed I fell into a slump that I couldn't crawl out of," he began, sitting at the table. "I blamed them for everything that had gone wrong in my life. After college, I backpacked around Europe, did drugs—went to India for a time, did drugs. I just couldn't get a handle on things and find a direction. Back home in California, I started drinking—worse than Dad ever did. I wandered the length and breadth of the state for years, taking odd jobs, getting fired for drinking, living in slum conditions, and feeling sorry for myself. Then, about a year ago, something switched on in me. I think it was rereading one of your letters—nothing specific that you said, only that you continued to care, despite my not responding. I checked myself into rehab to take the cure."

"Rehab? Well, join the club," Phoebe said loudly, as Curtis walked in through the pantry door with the boys, Jesse Tate, and Ruby behind him.

"Well, Harry—long time no see," Curtis said, shaking Harry's hand.

"These are our sons, Bart and Judd—Harry, your uncle—my brother," Phoebe announced with pride.

"Glad to meet you boys. I met you, Bart, but you were just a toddler, so you don't remember. Your mother wrote to me about you when you were born, Judd, but I'm sorry never to have met you before now."

"This is our neighbor, Jesse Tate," Curtis said, as Jesse offered his hand to Harry. "And this is Ruby."

"Nice dog. Where are the girls?" Harry questioned, as Ruby rubbed up against his leg, immediately taking to him.

"Lily was only five when we last saw you. Now she's in college and lives in Lynchford. She should be home next weekend. Jenny, the youngest is at a friend's house. I'll call her to tell her we'll come and get her so you can meet her as well. You'll stay for a while, won't you?"

"No, I really can't. I just needed to see that you're all right—I don't want to interfere."

At this Curtis started laughing. The idea of anyone thinking they were interfering simply by their presence, after all they'd been through, suddenly seemed ludicrous.

"Of course you'll stay. You two have to catch up," Curtis stated.

"You were in rehab, Curtis?"

"It's a long story. We'll tell you all about it later."

"I best be goin'," Jesse inserted.

"Can't you stay for supper?" Phoebe offered.

"Oh, well, I…"

"You might as well. I'm sure Phoebe has made plenty of food so another mouth won't make any difference, will it Phoebe?"

"Not at all."

"Besides, we're so grateful for your help."

"Awright then. Is there somewhere I can warsh up?"

"Sure, right through that door—turn left," Bart offered.

While Phoebe finished preparing supper, everyone sat around the table talking. The barn burned to the ground, their cash crops up in smoke—all forgotten for a time. When Phoebe pulled the roast pork from the oven, serving it with homemade apple sauce, potatoes, and beans grown in their garden, everyone ate heartily. For dessert there was coconut cream pie. Soon after supper Jesse returned home. The boys offered to do the chores so their parents could spend time with Harry. Lingering at the kitchen table with him, Phoebe and Curtis related the saga of the past two years.

"Can't anyone do something about this?" Harry questioned.

"We need proof and we don't have it. Each time we've made allegations or tried to do anything about it, the resultant problems have only made matters worse. We fear for the children," Phoebe whispered, as the boys came back into the kitchen and the subject was quickly dropped.

Phoebe and Harry couldn't remember when last they'd seen each other. Over multiple cups of tea and another slice of pie, they all heard the details of Harry's life. What surfaced most profoundly in their minds as they talked was the realization that family—and friends—counted most in life. Phoebe called Jenny but she wanted to spend the night. Phoebe decided she'd convince Harry to stay a while, so it would be all right—she could meet Harry soon enough.

"I'll stay a few days," Harry countered, "but I just want you to know I'm not planning on moving in or anything. I need to go back to California and try to find a job."

"You could find a job around here just as well, couldn't you?" Phoebe asked.

"Maybe—we'll see. I'm used to California."

"And I'd like to get used to you," Phoebe teased, as Harry sheepishly nodded.

"You stay as long as you'd like, Harry," Curtis offered. "We could use some extra help around here if we're going to rebuild that barn."

Phoebe shot him a memorable look, suspicions confirmed. But, even if he wanted to start over, she remained uncertain. She'd have to sleep on it, give herself some time to tell whether or not she still had enough fight to pick up the pieces and go on. Hearing Harry's offer to help them and seeing the resolve in Curtis, she found herself involuntarily entertaining the possibility more seriously. At bedtime she put Harry in Jenny's room. For however long he stayed, Jenny could sleep on the couch. When she and Curtis were in the privacy of their room, Phoebe broached the subject of starting over.

"So you really want to start over?"

"Don't you?"

"I asked you first."

"If you don't want to we can pack it in—but—we still have the land and the wheat crop has been planted—what are you laughing about?"

"You're completely predictable."

"You think you know me so well, do you," he teased, taking her into his arms.

"I can't decide if we're numb, giddy from overwork and worry or just plain stupid," Phoebe analyzed. "It's going to take a lot of work to recover from this."

"I know, but we have our family and each other. Hard work has never kept us down before."

"What if Morray has more in store for us?" Phoebe questioned. "What if he doesn't stop until we're completely wiped out?"

"We'll cross that bridge when we come to it."

"I've been thinking, Curtis."

"Oh, oh!"

"Seriously. Maybe we can find a way to get back at him, to expose his abysmal ways to the public by embarrassing or shaming him."

"You don't seriously think a man like him would know anything about shame, remorse or embarrassment, do you?"

"Everyone has an Achilles heel. What if we go over the sheriff's head and involve the state police?"

"How do we know which ones aren't associated with him? It would still be our word against his. You know how that would go."

"They already have some suspicions from their investigations—maybe we could find out who led the investigation. We don't know what evidence they might have from Ted's work. Will you think about it, Curtis?"

"Yes," Curtis reluctantly answered. "But you think about it, too, especially all feasible repercussions."

The next morning Phoebe picked up Jenny and brought her back home. When Jenny saw Uncle Harry, she was uncharacteristically shy at first.

"Hi, my name's Harry," he said, greeting her and extending his hand. "I'm your mother's brother—your uncle."

Jenny took a couple of tentative steps backward then, prompted by her mother moved forward to shake his hand.

"You don't remember me because you weren't born yet when I was here last."

"Was I just a twinkle in my dad's eyes?" Jenny questioned.

"Yes, I'd say so," Harry answered, chortling loudly. It had been a long time since he'd laughed. It felt good to be with family again.

The weekend following Harry's arrival, Lily rode home with Bart. The lovely young woman she'd grown into amazed him. She reminded him very much of his mother. On Sunday evening when Keith came to pick up Lily, Harry got a chance to meet him as well. Phoebe couldn't have been happier than when observing her entire family sitting around the kitchen table. Their camaraderie, laughing, and joking together overshadowed all other circumstances in their lives and she found her strength renewed. She did not forget Gaylan Morray for long, however, knowing he could strike again at any minute. The inability to know what he might do next or how it would affect them was nerve wracking, say nothing of exhausting.

For several weeks there were no further incidents at the farm. Harry worked alongside Curtis to clear away the rubble from the fire and bury it near the adjacent field. The boys helped weekends but, because Harry was there to help, the clean-up was accomplished in record time. They couldn't have done it without him. Jenny had taken a real shine to Harry; happily giving up her bedroom to him. Ruby adored him, following at his heels wherever he went. Much to Phoebe's dismay, he announced one evening that he would stay two more days then return to California. When she objected, trying to convince him that he should look for work in the area, he conceded that if he couldn't soon find work in California, he'd return.

"Meanwhile, you need to do something about that bastard Morray," he advised.

CHAPTER TEN

From the moment they had to sell their acre of land and mortgage their farm to Gaylan Morray, and especially after Jenny had nearly been kidnapped, along with the numerous other incidents she'd personally shouldered in protection of her children, an inchoate plan had been formulating in Phoebe's brain. She continually shoved it aside but it kept resurfacing. Finally, following the burning of their barn and stock of hay and wheat, she calculated in her mind all they'd endured, giving it full attention, justifying it as harrowing hell. It breathed new life into her resolve, her fighting spirit, and she discovered she wasn't yet ready to give up.

Several weeks after Harry left for California they received a form letter in the mail from Vincent DeMar at the bank, claiming their mortgage payments were in arrears and foreclosure proceedings on their farm had been initiated. They had made their mortgage payments so the threatened action was unjustified. That's when Phoebe began surreptitiously putting in place the preliminaries for her plan. She didn't discuss it with Curtis, knowing it would be difficult to convince him to go along with it. Over the next couple of days she called upon her friend, Agnes, saying she might need a favor one of these days. Then she called Warren, telling him they all needed a break. Knowing Curtis wouldn't take one on her advice alone, she asked Warren to call and invite them over to spend a weekend.

"Why don't you and your family come over and spend a couple of days with Doris and me," Warren offered by phone the next morning.

"No, I don't see how we can do that," Curtis responded.

"Sure you can—a nice long weekend. I think you should get things off your minds and try to size up what to do next."

"I'll talk with Phoebe but I doubt she'd go for it."

"Go for what?" Phoebe asked, entering the kitchen on cue.

"Warren wants us all to come over for a couple of days—to visit—to get our minds off all that's happened."

Looking at Phoebe, Curtis saw a smile spread across her face.

"I think that's a really good idea," she finally responded.

"You do? What about Morray? I don't think we should leave the farm."

"Give me the phone. Warren, we'd love to come over sometime. Can I call you when it's a good weekend for us to get away?"

"Sure, you'll find us here most any weekend."

"Thanks, Warren."

When she hung up the phone, Curtis was not pleased. "You could at least have asked me before making arrangements to go to Warren's."

Their arguments had become more frequent and extreme in the last few weeks as tensions built. Phoebe was not herself, frayed nerves too exposed. Curtis had grown defensive, at times argumentative, but was still the more conciliatory of the two.

"I didn't set a date. We'll go when the time is right. We need to get away for a while. Except for some livestock, our house, and scattered outbuildings, there's nothing left for Morray to ruin."

"You're probably right," he said after a long pause, "but I don't like things pushed onto me, you know."

"Yes, I know. Besides, I have a plan."

"Of course you do."

"If you're nice, I'll tell you all about it this evening after the kids are in bed."

"I like it already."

When Phoebe related her plan to Curtis later that night, he was aghast at such lunacy—even frightened for her state of mind. He could not have imagined his wife capable of thinking up such a plan, much less be serious about carrying it out.

"You're letting your anger eat away at you like emotional termites. It's a dangerous, evil plan and I want no part of it," he expounded, looking at her as an alien.

"All right. We'll just continue to let Morray walk all over us and half the rest of the county as well. You say my plan is dangerous and evil. I'd say Morray is the personification of evil."

"Count me out. I've never told you what to do, Phoebe, but I'm telling you now—DROP IT!"

But Phoebe wouldn't let go of it. In small ways, she kept the idea, her plan, under Curtis' nose by reminding him of all they'd suffered at the hands of Morray, attempting to lure him into cooperation. But even a call from Morray about a month after the foreclosure notice had arrived did not align him with her risky and frightful scheme.

"Curtis, this is Gaylan Morray. I'm afraid we're going to have to speed up this foreclosure process—and we'll have to include the house. I know it wasn't supposed to be a part of the deal but the bank can't possibly get the full amount needed to cover the mortgage out of the farm, so we'll have to take the house as well. You understand—to cover our costs and bring the farm up to its proper value. I'll give you two months to vacate, however, instead of the standard thirty days—as a favor."

"You'll get our house over my dead body, Morray."

"Oh, I'll get it all right. So be it, then."

Curtis slammed down the phone receiver so hard he nearly broke it. Once he'd related Morray's side of the conversation Phoebe had a question.

"Now, are you ready?"

"Phoebe, we can't. How can you even think of doing what you have in mind? It would put our entire family, say nothing of our farm, perhaps our lives, in jeopardy."

"In sixty days we will have no farm, no house for our children to live in. Is that the kind of jeopardy you prefer?"

Two days later Judd did not come home after Saturday morning's debate team meeting at the high school, raising immediate concerns.

"Judd has the car—maybe something happened to it on the way home—like it broke down or something," Bart encouraged, standing in the kitchen with his mother.

"Or maybe he had something going on after debate that he forgot to tell us about, that scoundrel," Phoebe asserted, urging Jenny to her room. "But he knew this morning that I was preparing a nice dinner for us. It's not like him to forget something like that."

"Do you want me to take the truck to go look for him?" Bart offered.

"No, not right now. I'm going out to get your dad. Where is he?"

"In the machine shed."

By the time Phoebe got to Curtis, suspicions about what was probably going on descended on her like the plague. Frantic, she related her concerns to Curtis.

"This can't be happening," she screamed, as Curtis held her. "That monster has him, I just know it."

"We don't know what's happened to him. There's probably a very logical explanation. I'll go and search for him, starting with the school then asking around until we find out where he is. I hope he hasn't just decided to go off with his friends without telling us."

"He's not like that and you know it, Curtis. He's in trouble. I'll call around town to see if anyone's seen him, also his debate team friends. If we still don't know where he is, we'll go look for him," Phoebe pronounced, as they walked toward the house.

Twenty minutes later, when Phoebe returned from the office, no one had to ask if she'd had any luck. Her eyes told the story.

"Bart, will you please stay with Jenny while your dad and I go look for Judd?"

"Come on Ruby," Curtis called, as he and Phoebe went out the back door.

"None of Judd's friends have seen him since the debate meeting ended at eleven," Phoebe related, as they got into the truck. They drove to town in silence, Ruby between them. When they got to school their car was sitting in the otherwise empty parking lot. It was unlocked, key in the ignition, and Curtis started it right up.

"Well, we know he didn't have car trouble, anyway."

"Curtis, I think we should go to the sheriff."

"A lot of good that will do," Curtis began, until he saw the pleading look on Phoebe's face. "But, I think we'll give it a try."

Curtis drove the truck to the sheriff's office. He knew full well it was a waste of time as he walked into the dreary, institutional office.

"When was he seen last?" Sheriff Tagwell casually questioned Curtis.

"At school, I guess. Phoebe called his friends but none of them had seen him since the meeting ended."

"I'm not sure what yer son looks like, Curtis," the sheriff offered.

"He's tall with dark hair, almost black really, and blue eyes."

"A lot like yer missus, I take it."

"Yes, I'd say so. Have you seen him?"

"She's a looker that one. I been noticing her for some time now."

"Could we stick to the subject of my son, please?" Curtis asserted, with effort, overlooking the sheriff's comment about his wife.

"Yer son? Oh—right—no, cain't say as I seen him. Could be bout anywheres. Ya know kids these days. Probably cruising around with a whole batch of em."

"Well, can you at least help us look?"

"I'd like to but I got urgent business in Dirkville."

"What about Deputy Mercer? He could help us."

"Sorry, he's busy."

"I told Phoebe it was foolish to think you'd be of any help," Curtis spit, turning to leave the office.

"Good luck finding yer kid there fella," the sheriff shot back, "an say hello to that missus a yorn."

Curtis was beet red, hot under the collar, as he strode to the truck. *Something has got to be done about that man,* he vowed within.

"Did you talk with the sheriff?" Phoebe anxiously inquired, as Curtis bolted onto the truck seat next to Ruby.

"Yes and, as I suspected he wasn't the slightest bit interested in helping us."

"He actually said that?"

"I'm paraphrasing, translating his words into English."

With no idea as to where to look for Judd, he drove around town at Phoebe's direction, one by one locating the houses of his friends and hoping to find him out in a driveway shooting hoops. Two hours later they returned to the parking lot of the school, empty handed and with no clues to follow.

"At least we know he's not driving his friends around. You take the car home and stay there Phoebe, in case he calls or someone brings him home. I'm going to search around town one more time."

Phoebe was too upset to object or even respond. Looking at her, he realized her beautiful face had aged ten years since noon. When he stopped the truck, she opened the passenger side door, slid off the seat, and walked wraithlike to the car, without saying a word. After starting the car she drove off, never looking back or waving. Watching her drive away, Curtis worried that with this latest calamity she'd finally snapped. As much as he would like to have taken the time to comfort her, his growing concern for Judd was more immediate.

With Ruby beside him, Curtis searched around the

school. He found a custodian who confirmed that the meeting had ended about eleven o'clock, but he had not seen Judd. On one more sweep across town, he spied Jesse Tate coming out of the feed mill. Pulling up next to him, he rolled down the window.

"Jesse, have you seen Judd by any chance?"

"No, not lately, Curtis. Where's he got to?"

"Don't know—he never came home from a meeting at school."

"Might coulda had car trouble, don't ya think?"

"No, our car was still at school. Phoebe took it home."

"Well, I'll be. Say," he added after a time, "what did he have on?"

"Sorry, I'm not sure. I was out in the barn when he left this morning. Phoebe would probably know. It sounds to me like you might have seen him, Jesse, or think you did. Did you?"

"I'm not sure cause I dint get a close look. There was a young boy with a red sweatshirt like hood pulled up over his head riding in Harley's truck."

"Harley Weils' red pickup truck? Judd has a red hooded sweatshirt with the school letters on it but I'm not sure whether or not he was wearing it."

"It was Harley drivin it all right. I seen him while I was drivin up to the feed mill. I noticed cause the boy was sittin in the middle and had his head back against Swifty's shoulder like he was sleepin or somethin—and I didn't think Harley Weils or Swifty had any children."

"Swifty and Harley were both in the truck?"

"Yeah."

"Which way did they go?"

"Don't know—I just seen them goin down the back street behind the bank—I noticed cause Harley was goin way too fast for town drivin."

"You didn't see which way they went? Where do you think they might be headed?"

"I don't rightly know. But I bet that was Judd in the

truck. Do you think Morray might have something to do with this? You know, both Swifty and Weils is in tight with Morray.

"Weils is involved with Morray?"

"I don't know what *involved* means but he works for Morray. I know that for a fact. Does a lot of his nasty stuff, like tellin people they gotta get outta their home."

"I didn't realize he worked for Morray."

"Sure nuf. And, course, Weils and Swifty are stuck together like glue."

"I've seen Harley's red pickup out near our place, coming and going but didn't think anything of it because his mother lives across from us. I figured he was checking on the woods for her or visiting."

"Visit his ma? That ud be the day pigs fly. They don't have nothin to do with each other. Hate each other."

"Do you think Weils and Swifty might kidnap Judd on Morray's say so?"

Recent events were intersecting in Curtis' mind faster than he could keep up, the conclusion more obvious by the minute.

"All I kin tell ya is Weils and all the rest of em has got away with too much, too long. I try to stay outta it cause I don't want no more trouble—but I don't abide a guy messin with a man's kids—always suspected Morray was behind my boy's death. Lemme throw this stuff in the truck and I'll help you look for yer son."

"Thanks, Jesse."

"Right! I'll be with ya in a jiff."

He ran to his truck and put the things he'd been carrying in the back. Then he joined Curtis, who had pulled his vehicle forward.

"Good thing I made friends with yer dog a long time ago—while you was—gone," Jesse commented, sliding onto the seat of the truck next to Ruby.

"This is one of those times I wish I had a two-way radio," Curtis said to Jesse. "I could let Phoebe know what's going on."

"You might not wanna tell her 'til we know more."

"I think you're right. It would be best if I didn't worry her any more than she is already. Where do we start, Jesse?" Curtis asked, shifting the truck into gear.

"I ain't sure but I know a coupla places where he's been seen hangin out, goin fishin or huntin: Mason's Point and Croft's Bend. Should we check them out?"

"Sounds like a plan."

Curtis and Jesse drove through town at breakneck speed then careened around a corner onto the road to Dirkville. They had driven about two miles out of town when Jesse signaled for Curtis to turn left and follow a dirt road into the woods. Eventually the road came to an end at Bullfrog Creek. Before the truck came to a full stop, Jesse jumped out. Curtis parked, got out, and signaled for Ruby to follow him.

"Which way do we go?"

"There's a big cave down thisa way. We can check that out first."

The two men, accompanied by Ruby, wound their way downstream to an area where the bank of the creek rose up higher and jutted out into the water. Ruby was all over the place, sniffing at every bush and tree. Curtis paid close attention to her, hoping she was following Judd's scent but eventually realized she was tracking animals.

"I wish I had something of Judd's for Ruby to get the scent of him but maybe she knows him anyway."

Scrambling down the rocky embankment, they came to a cave tucked back between rocks and tree roots. Squatting to look into the small cave, Curtis called to Judd, No response. Unless Judd was dead and unable to answer, he was probably not in the cave but Curtis decided to explore it further, crawling on his belly into the cave as far as he could go, hoping against hope he wouldn't find anything. Emerging moments later into daylight, he was filthy, his emotions a mixture of relief and disappointment.

"No luck, then," Jesse commented, as Curtis brushed the dirt from his jeans.

"Any other ideas?"

"There's an old shack up under yonder bluff, at Croft's Bend, along French River, south of the road to Herston. I seen him with his buddies there a coupla times," Jesse offered.

"I know of Croft's Bend but don't remember a cabin there. Let's go."

After finding their way back through the woods they climbed into the truck. Curtis flew down the rutted dirt road out of the woods so fast that Ruby and Jesse were nearly bumped out through the open window. Once back in town he turned onto Digbert Road and sped toward Croft's Bend. He'd already decided that if the sheriff or deputy stopped him for speeding, he'd slug him in the face and keep going. About three miles outside of town he turned onto a gravel road. Curtis had grown up on the farm he now owned. As a boy, he'd explored the surrounding area, but was unaware of the secluded locations Jesse was taking him to, apparently hang outs for locals with questionable reputations.

On cue from Jesse, he turned onto a dirt road that led steeply up the hill. Toward the top there was a side road which he was instructed to follow. When Jesse signaled him he stopped the truck and cut the motor. There was a shack on up ahead but no one seemed to be around. Jesse suggested Curtis should wait at the truck while he checked out the shack, but he would have none of it. Together, they quietly approached the shack. Ruby started barking, startling them. Thinking she was alerting them to trouble, they kicked in the door on the count of three. Ruby, it turned out, had detected a squirrel which scampered from the shack out through a broken window as they entered.

No one was inside the shack. A crude table and two chairs were the only furnishings. There was evidence that someone had recently been there, however, cigarette butts in a dirty ashtray and some empty beer cans. The shack had a fireplace at one end and it was obvious it had held many fires. Curtis searched the premises thoroughly, looking for any clues that might lead them to Judd, even sifting through the ashes in the fireplace. Finding nothing, frustrated in their search, they sat down in the rickety chairs, their elbows resting on the table.

"Now what?" Curtis sighed.

"I donno where to look next. I donno any other places he hangs out. I wish I paid more attention when I seen his truck before. I might coulda told ya what direction he was goin. I just didn't know it was Judd with them."

"Don't worry about it, Jesse. Maybe he's even home by now. Should we go back and see?" Curtis asked.

"I guess we might as well," Jesse gloomily replied.

Curtis whistled for Ruby and they got into the truck, heading back down the steep drive to the main road.

"It'll be dark soon anyway so we'll have to continue the search tomorrow. I hope Judd's home, otherwise I don't know what Phoebe's going to do when I come home empty handed."

When they got to the main road Curtis slowed the truck preparing to turn left toward the farm. His thoughts were of Phoebe, practicing comforting words in his mind.

"I didn't think on it before," Jesse said suddenly, "but a coupla times when I was on my way down Digbert Road to my place, I seen Harley's red pickup truck comin from the other direction."

"From Herston? What would he be doing over that way? The only thing down that road is Bishop's Woods."

"Bishop's Woods," they exclaimed in unison.

Curtis turned the truck to the right. Passing the Small's place he felt a twinge of sadness. He missed their friends, but more, it was a reminder of Ted Whartley's fate. They had lived in fear for over two years, wondering what would happen next, afraid to say anything or report the incidents for fear the reprisals would be worse. A conviction was growing that he was done being afraid, done just getting along between crises. He mentally tallied all that had happened, not only to them, and decided Jesse and Phoebe were right. Something had to be done about Gaylan Morray.

On Bishop's Woods Road Curtis turned right, following the gravel lane to the north. When he spotted the sign indicating the woods to the left, he turned onto the deeply grooved dirt road. After driving about a half mile into the woods, he stopped the truck. Ruby jumped out, over Jesse's lap, and began sniffing her way through the woods.

"Is there any kind of building in these woods, Jesse?"

"None I know of but I ain't been here in years. There's a picnic shelter that's way over yonder."

"Let's split up to search the woods. You go south and I'll go north. You circle around to the west and I'll go east. We'll meet back at the shelter in an hour. I'll take Ruby with me. It's almost three o'clock. If we haven't found anything by four, it'll be growing too dark in these woods to look any further tonight."

Curtis set out, followed closely by Ruby. Looking back, he saw Jesse head the opposite direction. Most of the trees were bare, their fall foliage piled up on the ground, making progress difficult. Frustration grew as Curtis searched under brush, moved large branches, and scoured the forest floor. Gradually, his sense of helplessness fanned his frustration into flames of intense anger. The woods were huge and there was no way two men could adequately cover the area. Near the northern end of the woods he came to swampy wetlands and could go no farther. Despite the time of year, squadrons of mosquitoes advanced, forcing him to the east. Ruby appeared to be no help at all, rummaging under leaves and running off to chase squirrels.

When the hour was up, with no clues found, Curtis waited at the shelter. Jesse arrived shortly after him, equally empty handed. The look of defeat on his face matched Curtis' scowl for scowl. They searched around the shelter for ten or fifteen minutes without finding anything.

"It's almost dark. We'll have to call it a day," Curtis finally announced.

"Yeah. We can't see much. Maybe tomorra we can git some people together to look round some more. These woods are pretty big."

"Let's head back to the truck. If you don't mind, I'd like to stop at the farm before I drive you back to town to get your truck. Phoebe needs to know what's going on. We really appreciate your help, Jesse."

"Sol right. Just sorry we didn't find him. Maybe he's home, after all."

"If only. Tonight, could you try and think of any other places to look and call us if anything comes to mind?"

"Sure thing, I will. I'll think on it real hard. I'll help ya tomorra, too, if need be and can call some other folks to help. I know a few we can trust."

"That would be great. Bart could help but Phoebe and I are trying to keep the kids out of this mess as best we can."

"Smart thinkin. Youngsters don't need to be involved with the likes of Morray."

Totally engrossed in his thoughts, Curtis went around to the driver's side of the truck and got in. Jesse slid onto the passenger's seat. When Curtis started the truck, Jesse rolled down his window.

"Where's at dog a yers?"

"Oh, for god's sake. Now we have to hunt for Ruby?" Curtis stated, exasperated.

He shut off the engine again and got out of the truck, whistling for Ruby. There was no sign of her. When she didn't come after they'd whistled and called for several minutes, they started walking through the woods toward the north. Every few steps Curtis stopped to listen then called out her name and whistled again. Soon, they heard her faint barking in the distance.

"She musta got herself in trouble or has a coon treed," Jesse offered, breathless.

Following the sound of her bark, twenty minutes later they stumbled into a slight clearing. It was no where near the woods Curtis had searched earlier, much deeper into its density and to the west.

Ruby was standing near a tree barking up a storm. Beyond her stood a small dilapidated shack that looked like it could collapse within seconds. A rotten door, ajar and barely clinging to its hinges, swayed in the breeze, creaking.

"Well, I never seen that shack afore," Jesse said. "I thought I knew about everything around here."

Curtis couldn't immediately see what Ruby was barking at, looking up into trees as he got closer to her. No matter how many times he called to her, slapping his thigh, she wouldn't come. It wasn't like her to be so disobedient but she wouldn't move an inch.

"Told ya she'd have a coon treed," Jesse chortled.

Moving closer, attempting to calm Ruby, Curtis could see that she wasn't looking up into the tree but was standing beside it. He nearly fell into a hole just in front of her trying to grab her collar. Getting down on hands and knees he peered into the hole. His hands felt the outlined perimeter of a vertical tunnel, like an old mine shaft, and he instantly knew that Judd was in there.

"Judd, Judd," he called, but there was no answer.

"He's in there, I know it. I hope we're not too late. You stay here in case you see or hear anything. I'll go back to the truck and get the flashlight and some rope. I should have thought to bring them in the first place."

"You thought you was looking fer the dog," Jesse excused.

Curtis ran to the truck faster than he knew he could move. At the truck he grabbed the rope he always kept in the back for towing then found the flashlight under the seat. Running back through the woods he tripped on a root sticking up and went down hard on his knee. Willing the pain aside, he got up and continued running until he got back to where Jesse waited.

"I can't see nothin in that dark hole—but yer right, something or someone is down there. I thought I heard breathing."

"I hope you're right."

Curtis was so nervous he dropped the flashlight twice trying to get it turned on. When he finally flashed the light in the hole, he could see Judd. His crumpled body lay on a narrow ledge about twenty feet down the shaft. His eyes were closed.

"Oh, ma God," Jesse whispered, peering over the edge of the hole.

"I think he may be unconscious—maybe from the lack of air," Curtis offered, hoping his assessment was correct. "We'll get you out of there in a minute," he assured his son, as Jesse looked on.

He paced in strides, creating a circle of stamped down leaves around the mine shaft as he tied a noose in the rope. He tightened the loop around his middle then tried to locate a secure place to fasten the other end. Jesse sat on the ground with his head between his hands, sighing deeply about every ten seconds. Periodically, Curtis called to Judd, trying to awaken him. Ruby finally quit barking. Time slowly ticked away as it grew darker.

"I think I hear something," Jesse called to Curtis.

Curtis stopped, listening intently but could only hear the rustle of leaves then a muffled sound, but it wasn't coming from the mine shaft.

"Sorry," Jesse apologized. "Must a been a deer."

"We'll get you out of there, Judd," Curtis continued to reassure, mostly himself.

With the rope secured to a tree, Curtis strategized his descent into the mine shaft. Then he thought better of it.

Jesse Tate was a much smaller man.

"Jesse, would you mind going down after Judd and I'll pull you both back up. Sorry to say so, but I think I'm a bit stronger than you are."

"No offense taken. Glad to be a some use," Jesse said, jumping up and taking the rope from Curtis. "I'll tie him onto it first then ya can throw the rope back for me."

When the rope was secure around Jesse's waist, Curtis kept it taut, slowly lowering him into the shaft. An eternity passed before Jesse gave the all clear. With strength he hardly knew, he pulled the rope holding Judd to the surface. The moment Judd was on solid ground he gently laid him down next to the hole and felt of his neck. Finding a faint pulse, he patted his cheeks, hoping to revive him but, even Ruby licking Judd's face didn't bring him around.

Once Curtis had seen to Judd, he lowered the rope to Jesse and pulled him up. Then, without a moment's hesitation, he lifted his son into his arms and carried him toward the truck with Ruby forging ahead. Jesse followed close behind, carrying the gear and lighting the path. It was difficult going in the dark, even with a flashlight, but eventually they found their way. Jesse threw their jackets into the back and Curtis laid Judd on top of them.

"Jesse, it's not too cold. Could you either ride back here to keep Judd from rolling around or drive the truck?"

"You be with yer son, Curtis. Give me them keys."

"They're still in the ignition."

Curtis climbed into the back with Ruby and Judd. Jesse had some trouble getting the truck turned around, the tires spinning on the wet leaves, so he backed the truck up the dirt road, bumping over the ruts. At the entrance he backed onto Bishop's Woods Road to the left then did a y-turn to move them forward. Though Jesse didn't drive nearly as fast as he would have, it gave Curtis time to practice the lie he would tell Phoebe in front of Bart and Jenny, so he wouldn't set off alarm bells. Jesse turned left onto Digbert Road and the farm soon came into view.

When Phoebe heard the truck she flew out the back door and stood waiting beside the driveway. Jesse honked the horn a couple of times, hoping it would indicate success and lessen her worry a little in advance of seeing they had Judd. When the truck was parked Curtis jumped down, with Ruby close behind, and went to Phoebe.

"We found him. Ruby found him. He's scratched and right now he's unconscious but I think he'll be all right."

"Oh, thank God," Phoebe wept. "Let me see him. What happened?"

Curtis led her to the truck bed and flashed the light on Judd. "We'll talk about all this later, all right?" Curtis stated, motioning with his head toward the house. Phoebe understood immediately.

"Oh, my poor baby," she exclaimed. "Bring him inside."

Curtis lifted Judd into his arms and carried him to the house, as Bart came running from the barn. Inside, Phoebe directed Curtis to the couch in the living room, where she quickly arranged the pillows. While she went off to get a blanket and wet cloth, Curtis lowered Judd onto the sofa.

"What happened? Where did you find him?" Bart demanded.

"I'll explain everything later. Right now let's just see to your brother."

Phoebe came rushing back into the room. Minutes after she placed the cold, wet cloth on Judd's forehead, he opened his eyes slightly. He tried to talk but was so disoriented they couldn't understand what he was saying. Ruby stood by his side, licking his hand then resting her nose on his shoulder.

"Don't talk, son. Save your energy. And don't try to raise yourself up." Curtis advised, as though Judd could understand him.

Jenny, who had been upstairs, came leaping down the steps two at a time and rushed to her brother's side.

"We were worried about you, Judd," she exclaimed.

"Worried you were hurt."

Judd began crying, whimpering really, and Phoebe, unable to restrain her emotions any longer, threw herself on top of him, caressing and kissing him.

"Don't cry, Judd, everything will be all right," she cried.

"You're going to suffocate him, Phoebe," Curtis scolded, pulling Phoebe back. "I'm going to call Dr. Moorling—see if he'll make a house call. Otherwise, we'll have to take Judd into town. I don't think he has any broken bones only lots of cuts, especially on his head, but he needs to be checked out."

"You'll do anything for attention, won't you Judd," Bart quipped, attempting to relieve the tension.

"Jesse, we can't thank you enough for all you've done," Curtis began, finally acknowledging Jesse standing to the side of the sofa. "We wouldn't have found him if you hadn't helped."

"Well, I'm happy to help. It was Ruby that knowed where to look, though."

"That's right it was. Way to go, Ruby, old girl,"

"Bart, maybe you can drive Jesse back to town for us, would you? He has to pick up his truck."

"Sure, Dad. Be glad to. Come on Jesse."

"Thanks once again, Jesse," Phoebe said, kissing him gently on the cheek.

He flushed ten shades of red but she could tell it was a gesture he appreciated.

"We'll have you over to supper sometime next week, if you're willing to risk my cooking. I burned tonight's meal to a crisp."

"That'd be grand," Jesse answered. "Let me know how this comes out?"

"Sure thing, Jesse." Curtis escorted Jesse to the back door while Bart got in the truck. "Please don't say anything to Bart about who we think might be involved in this. We're just going to say he was hiking, got lost and, in the dark fell into a hole."

"I understand," Jesse assured.

Jesse went out the back door and soon the truck could be heard heading up the gravel driveway. Curtis called Dr. Moorling but only got his answering service. When he came back into the living room Jenny was talking to Judd, holding his hand and chattering away. Judd was sound asleep. Phoebe went to Curtis, gave him a big hug and kiss then stayed in his arms, turning around, so she could still see Judd. They stood together, his arms around her middle, looking at their son lying on the couch, realizing that he could just as well have been lying in a coffin.

"You're shaking," Phoebe commented.

"So are you."

"Jenny, you need to get something to eat then get to bed. We have to let Judd rest now. You can talk with him in the morning."

"Good night, Judd," Jenny whispered in his ear, before leaving his side. She gave her dad a hug then followed her mother to the kitchen.

Phoebe fixed Jenny a sandwich and got her a glass of milk. She appeared attentive as Jenny talked on and on about Judd, but her mind was elsewhere—on the plans circulating in her head without relief. When Jenny had eaten Phoebe sent her upstairs to get ready for bed then got a pan of soapy water and a cloth and began washing the blood from Judd's cuts. Assuring herself there was nothing more she could do for Judd for the time being, she turned his care over to Curtis and went up to Jenny's room.

"Off you go to bed, little munchkin," Phoebe said, tucking Jenny into bed. "You can sleep in tomorrow and, by the time you get up, Judd might be ready to tell you all about his grand adventure."

When Phoebe came back downstairs, Curtis was sitting in a chair opposite the sofa, staring at Judd. She went to him, sitting in his lap. While they both watched their son for any sign of alertness, he related all the details of their search and rescue, where they'd found Judd and who was implicated in his disappearance, relying heavily on things Jesse had told him about Weils's relationship with Morray.

"I don't know what Judd will say when he wakes up but, besides Judd and those responsible, so far Jesse is the only other person who knows how we found him. I'd like to keep it that way so we don't put the kids in danger."

"I agree but Bart will be back soon looking for answers. What will we tell him?" Phoebe inserted.

"I thought a lot about it while Jesse was driving us home. I think we should just say we found him in the mine shaft, that he'd apparently been out there hiking with his friends and fell in, hitting his head and getting knocked unconscious."

"That sounds feasible, at least. What if Bart questions his friends?"

"He doesn't know which friends were with him—and neither do we, right?"

"Right."

While Judd slept, with Ruby lying on the floor beside him, Phoebe cleaned up and inspected his wounds. None of them looked as serious as the bump on his head. By the time the doctor called back, they had decided that rest was needed most. The doctor agreed, saying he'd call to check on Judd in the morning and, unless he got worse, they should bring him in Monday for examination. Bart came back about a half-hour later.

"What happened, anyway? Where did you find Judd?" he questioned. "Jesse would only say you found him in Bishop's Woods."

"Son, you want answers we can't give you," Phoebe stated matter-of-factly, "because we don't know ourselves. The only thing I know for certain is that Judd didn't come home when he was supposed to."

"But what happened?"

"He must have gone hiking with some friends at Bishop's Woods," Curtis lied. "It appears as though he got separated from them and stumbled into the mine shaft. They probably left when it grew dark and they couldn't find him, assuming he'd eventually show up."

"Do you know who they were?"

"No. We'll have to wait to hear what Judd has to say—if he remembers. The doctor said he may have a concussion which might mean amnesia. I doubt it was the gang he usually hangs out with or they would have called. It might be some of those boys from Kermit that he knows from debate, since we found the car in the school parking lot," Curtis answered, glancing at Phoebe.

"I didn't know he knew any boys from Kermit," Bart offered.

"We don't know if it was them but he's mentioned them a couple of times lately and, like I said, his usual friends would have called."

"If he has amnesia will he ever remember what happened?" Bart persisted.

"We just don't know," Curtis stated. "Time will tell. He's had quite a shock. Right now we just have to make sure he's all right physically."

"Do you think he'll be all right? Should I call some of his friends to see if they know who he was with?"

"Bart, I appreciate your concern," Phoebe started, happy that Bart was no longer in high school with Judd. "Some day we may know exactly what happened but right now you need to let it be so we can focus on getting Judd better."

Bart didn't like not knowing what happened but concluded that his parents knew little more than he did about the situation—and wouldn't, until Judd could shed some light on it. Judd was still asleep but he said good night to him anyway then headed for his room. Phoebe intercepted him at the bottom of the stairs. Though he shunned affection at his age, she took him in her arms and reassured him that everything would be all right. "We'll let you know if we learn any more about the situation," Phoebe promised.

"Okay, Mom. I'm just worried about him, that's all."

"I know you are. Thanks for all your help tonight."

"Glad to do it, Mom," he said, involuntarily melting into her embrace.

Turning around, Phoebe caught Curtis rubbing his knee, saying nothing until she heard the door to Bart's room close.

"You're hurt. What happened to your leg?"

"My leg. Oh, I cut it when I fell in the woods," he calmly stated.

"Let me see it. How did you fall?"

"I was in such a hurry to get back to Judd after going to the truck for rope and a flashlight that I stumbled over some tree roots. I should have turned the flashlight on."

"Ew! That's a nasty-looking cut," Phoebe exclaimed, examining the deep wound.

The blood had dried and it was difficult to see how bad it was so she got some fresh water and began gently washing the blood off.

"It's deeper than I thought," she soon concluded. "I'll get one of those butterfly bandages in the first aid kit. You do have a time with your legs, don't you?"

"What do you mean?"

"First rope burns or chain cuts, now a deep gash. Needing attention are you? We'll have the doctor look at it when we go in on Monday to see him."

"It'll be fine, all right?" Curtis said, sternly enough to let Phoebe know he wasn't discussing the matter further.

Phoebe went to the bathroom and got the first aid kit. Returning to the living room, she knelt next to Curtis, applying some salve then a butterfly bandage to his leg. She then cut strips of adhesive tape and fastened folded gauze over the wound to further protect it.

"Since I have you at my mercy, standing over your

gaping wound with a scissors, are you now ready to tell me how you originally got Morray to agree to exclude the house from the mortgage?"

"Might as well. I saw him one day with Sally Torrent, going into a motel in Dirkville. He saw me watching them. I told him that if he didn't exclude the house, I'd go to his wife and tell her about it."

"I've heard there's no love in that marriage and that she has tight control over him. Glad someone does. Anyway it worked, for a while."

What Curtis had just told her about Morray was the missing piece for her plan and she mentally fit it into place, like a puzzle bleb. They spent the night sleeping in chairs in the living room. Ruby never left Judd's side. By morning he was awake and asking for water so they knew he'd be all right, their thankfulness immeasurable. He wasn't talking much, however, and had no recollection of how he got to Bishop's Woods, much less into the mine shaft, or who was responsible. If his memory didn't return, without an eye witness, it meant they couldn't accuse anyone of the dirty deed. To Phoebe this meant their only remaining option was to carry out her plan, but she didn't know how to get Curtis to go along with it.

After breakfast Curtis asked Bart to start chores so he could wait for the doctor's call. Bart seemed more resigned to his ignorance of the situation when he could see for himself that Judd couldn't remember anything. If Judd didn't know, he could hardly expect his parents to solve the mystery. Dr. Moorling called around eight o'clock to see how Judd was doing. He was not surprised at his inability to remember anything.

"That's typical when someone's had a blow to the head. It's like a psychogenic fugue. He might get his memory back or remember only segments of what happened, forgetting the rest. Even if part of what happened to him was traumatic, like the blow when he fell, he might erase the entire episode from his mind in protection. Be sure to bring him in on Monday. Meanwhile let him rest. Do you know what happened?"

"Not for sure but it appears he fell down a mine shaft while hiking in the woods. It was lucky we, actually our dog, found him. Thanks for your concern. See you on Monday."

The rest of Sunday, Phoebe made an effort to appear unflappable. She made cookies then fixed pork chops, Judd's favorite. Judd slept most of the day with Jenny hovering over him. She left his side only to tend Tess. Ruby wouldn't leave him even to eat, only to go outside briefly. By late Sunday evening he was showing signs of improvement in all ways but his memory and appetite. Phoebe tempted him with supper but he would only eat a small amount.

On Monday morning Phoebe and Curtis got ready to take Judd to see Dr. Moorling. Jenny, while reluctant to leave Judd, went to school as usual. Phoebe asked her not to mention the incident or ask questions of anyone because they didn't want to get anyone in trouble for something that was unintentional. Bart, on the other hand, insisted on going to the doctor with them, following them in the car. Ruby waited patiently in the truck while they all went in to see Dr. Moorling.

The doctor confirmed that Judd had a severe concussion which he felt sure was sustained when falling into the shaft. Judd would need a great deal of sleep but was otherwise all right. He would be able to return to school in a week, if he felt up to it. The doctor cautioned Phoebe, Curtis, and Bart not to press him about what happened or expect him to remember. This satisfied Bart for the time being and he left for school. Once the doctor had looked over Judd, Phoebe directed his attention to Curtis.

"Pull up your pant leg and show him your wound," she ordered.

"That's a nasty cut. How did you get that?"

"I fell in the woods, trying to get to Judd. It's fine."

"You should have gone to emergency. The butterfly bandage helped keep the skin flaps together and minimize the opening but you're going to have a wide scar when it heals. We can open it up and then stitch it."

"No thanks, I'll be fine. I'll have to skip beauty contests in the future, is that what you're saying?"

"Something like that. With those legs, even without the scar I wouldn't count on winning any prizes."

Phoebe escorted Judd out to the truck while Curtis paid the bill.

"I hope those weren't good friends of Judd's that deserted him in the woods," Dr. Moorling commented.

"We don't know for sure who it was but I doubt it was his usual friends," Curtis responded, "and I don't think they deserted him as much as left when they couldn't find him, assuming he'd already gone home."

"So you're not certain they abandoned him?" the doctor questioned. "You don't necessarily think it was malicious?"

"I seriously doubt it. But, I guess we may never know," Curtis said.

After leaving the doctor's office, Phoebe, Judd, and Curtis stopped at the drug store and had an ice cream soda. They bought ice cream to take home then headed back. Judd went immediately to his room for a nap. Phoebe and Curtis sat at the kitchen table together, thankful Judd would be all right but not knowing what else to say. In the ensuing silence, Phoebe could see the growing anger expressed in her husband's eyes. She said nothing, letting it fester into something he could express.

While he went to do chores she went up to check on Judd. When she came back down to the kitchen, Curtis was standing at the sink, crying. Phoebe went to him, taking him into her arms.

"I thought he was dead when we found him, Phoebe," he finally offered.

"I know. It must have been horrifying. I'm so sorry."

"Waiting to hear from me, to know if we found him must have been agony for you as well. You know, of course, that without Judd knowing who did this to him, what exactly happened, we again have no proof to go to the authorities with. I swear, Phoebe, if I could get my hands on Gaylan Morray, Harvey Weils or Swifty this minute, I'd choke the life out of them all."

"My plan doesn't sound so crazy now, does it?"

"We can't let them get away with this."

"Are you ready then?"

After a long pause, Curtis mournfully responded. "I'm ready." He was shaking but she could tell he meant it.

"We're going to need some help. Will you go talk with Jesse? He can help us by keeping track of Morray."

"Do you think it's wise to involve him?"

"He's already involved—and how many times have you heard him say Morray deserves to be reckoned with? He's always saying someone should do something about that man. Now's his chance."

"That's true enough. He said it again the day we found Judd."

"We'll start putting our plan into action as soon as Judd goes back to school then," Phoebe stated, as Curtis nodded his reluctant approval.

During the rest of the week they went through the motions of normalcy. By the weekend Judd was doing much better and eager to get back to school. Phoebe convinced him not to be concerned about remembering what happened—that eventually he would sort it out. She and Curtis made sure the kids had a nice weekend, keeping to themselves the gloom in their hearts for what they planned. Sunday afternoon, at Phoebe's insistence, Bart took Judd and Jenny to a ball game in town.

While they were gone Curtis saw to the livestock and Phoebe made a series of calls. The first was to Warren.

"Warren, we'd like to come and spend next weekend."

"That would be great. We'd love to have you."

"Do you think you could possibly come and get the kids right after school on Friday? It'll just be Jenny and Judd. Then Curtis and I will come on over that night. I have all that baby furniture and clothes to give to you and Doris. If you came in your van Friday afternoon, then drove back with the kids in our car, we could get everything loaded up and bring it to you."

"Sure, that would be fine. I can help you load it."

"No—thanks, Warren. I need to take some time to sort through it all first and I won't have time until after the kids go with you."

"Well all right—if you're sure."

"We'll see you about three o'clock then on Friday," Phoebe confirmed.

She hung up the phone then called Agnes, telling her she was calling in the favor, explaining only the part of the plan that needed her involvement.

Next, she called Lily. They had let her know what happened to Judd but Phoebe gave her a quick update. After reassuring her he was doing well, and would be going back to school the next day, she asked for a favor.

"Lily, could you call Bart and see if he can spend next Friday night with you and Keith? He broke up with Cynthia, you know. I think he needs more socialization right now, to keep his mind off that, and what happened to Judd. He's been quite upset about it. Your dad and I are going to Uncle Warren's next weekend and he wouldn't have any fun with the younger kids. He needs to be here to do chores on Saturday and Sunday but I think a night out would do him good. Jenny, Judd, and Ruby will go with us."

"That sounds like a good idea. Keith enjoys spending time with Bart, too."

"You'll call then? Talk with you next week, Lily."

When Curtis came in from doing chores Phoebe suggested it was a good time for him to drive over to talk with Jesse.

"Jesse, you know all that's happened to us over the last couple of years. I think Phoebe told you about it."

"Sure nuf, Curtis."

"I've heard you say repeatedly that something ought to be done about Gaylan Morray. You've suffered at his hands, as has nearly everyone around here."

"That's true—what are you gettin at, Curtis, you're as nervous as a man about to be lynched."

"Phoebe and I think it's about time we took matters into our own hands, as far as Morray's concerned. She and I have a plan to see to it he doesn't bother any of us again and we need your help, if you're willing."

"Like I said, I'd like to a stayed out of it but what happened to Judd changed my mind—it's uncalled for—count me in."

Curtis related as much of the plan to Jesse as he needed to know, keeping most details from him for his own good. Jesse's eyes turned from startled and disbelieving to cagey then approving.

"I'll do it. You just let me know where to be and what to do—and I'll do it."

"Thanks, Jesse. I knew we could count on you."

When Curtis got back home the kids were back from town and Phoebe was busy fixing supper. He gave her the thumbs up so she'd know Jesse would help. Later that evening he told her of Jesse's willingness. Phoebe explained her phone calls to Agnes, Lily, and Warren.

"Agnes is only too willing to help and everything's in place as far as the kids are concerned. Judd and Jenny will be safe at Warren's, Bart in the city with Lily and Keith, as we carry out our plan."

"I hope we know what we're doing," Curtis replied.

CHAPTER ELEVEN

Monday morning Phoebe helped Judd and Jenny pack their lunches then watched as they ran down the lane to catch the school bus. Ruby followed, waiting for them to board the bus, returning to the house only after they'd left. Judd had improved greatly since his mishap, pretty much back to normal except for the memory loss. Phoebe prayed he would never remember what had happened to him. The down side, the inability to accuse Harley Weils, Swifty or Gaylan Morray of kidnapping or attempted murder, made their plan the only option for bringing Morray to justice.

After school Judd and Jenny did their homework then helped get supper on the table. The phone rang just as they were finishing their meal. It was for Bart. He talked for a short time then rejoined the family at the table, a mildly sad look on his face.

"Who was that," Phoebe asked, as if she didn't know.

"Lily," he began. "She and Keith want me to go to the Croaking Frogs concert with them on Friday night."

"What did you tell her?" Phoebe asked.

"That I can't go. Since you're going to be gone this weekend, I'll need to stay here to do chores."

"I think you should go," his mother suggested.

"Well, it doesn't make sense to go to school, come back here and do chores, drive all the way back to Lynchford for the concert then home again."

"You could go to the concert then spend the night in Lynchford at Lily's," Curtis suggested.

"I need to be here Friday night then again Saturday morning to do chores," Bart objected.

"I'll do the chores and feed the hogs before we leave Friday night. They'll certainly keep until whenever you get back on Saturday."

"She did invite me to spend the night. You don't mind?"

"Not at all. Go ahead and call Lily back to tell her you'll come," Curtis suggested. "You'll have to take the truck, though, because we'll need the car."

Bart didn't easily shirk responsibility but was happy to be able to attend the concert. He went to phone Lily as soon as he'd finished eating.

Phoebe and Curtis spent the next couple of afternoons while the children were in school hashing over their circumstance, all that had happened, culminating with the threatened foreclosure and harm to their son. Phoebe again carefully laid out her plan for Curtis. It was a good plot but she'd overlooked a few important details. Curtis had always thought he and Phoebe incapable of criminal thought but they were intelligent and, somewhere in the far reaches of their innocent minds, their dark sides were resurrected to fill in some necessary details of a foolproof stratagem. If they could carry it off, it would be the perfect crime.

"Bart, I'll feed the hogs the next couple of mornings," Curtis announced after breakfast Wednesday morning. "It's not anything you've done or not done but a couple of them seem off. Now that they're so close to their market weight, I'd like to monitor their feeding myself for a few days, see if I can turn them around."

"Sure thing, Dad," Bart answered, getting up from the table. "I could use a break, anyway. I've been late to my first hour class a couple of times this last month."

On Thursday, home from school, Bart questioned his father when he heard the hogs squealing in their pen.

"Did you feed the hogs today, Dad?"

"Yes, but I've changed their formula so I don't think they're very happy about it. They'll adjust in a couple of days. They should be all right by Saturday and you can have your job back. I'll explain the formula changes to you tomorrow morning."

During the evening hours Phoebe grew restless, her mind struggling with concerns while forcing a calm demeanor for her children. Fortunately, acting normal rather than being normal had become a habit with her. Since the episode with Judd there had been no further incidents and, except for Phoebe and Curtis, the family had relaxed into a quiet existence again. Curtis worried about his wife, who had become jumpy, nervous, and had a hair trigger. While their relationship remained good, she wore a vacuous look at times that took her away from him to a place he couldn't reach. After a sleepless night they rose early Friday morning, ready to execute their plan.

"You're sure you don't need help with chores this morning," Bart questioned his dad, as he was explaining the new formula to him.

"No, I'll take care of it. You hurry off to school," Curtis said, getting up from the table. "And, have a nice time with Lily and Keith."

"I will—thanks," Bart said, rushing out the door.

"Judd and Jenny, remember that Bart is going to stay in the city with Lily after school. You'll have to take the bus home today. Be sure not to miss it. Uncle Warren will be picking you up around four o'clock here at the farm," Phoebe cautioned.

"Aren't you going to Uncle Warren and Aunt Doris's house, Mommy?" Jenny questioned, concern evident in her voice.

"Yes, but we'll come later in the evening. We have some things we need to take care of here before we can leave. You'll go in our car with Warren because we're loading up some of your old baby stuff in his van to take over to them. Won't you two have fun? Jenny, I'll bet Doris would let you hold that new baby if you're careful."

"Do you really think so?"

"I know so. A new baby and a new pony to play with—won't that be grand?"

Frustration and guilt saturated Phoebe. She never thought she'd see the day she couldn't wait to be rid of her kids, but it was exhausting trying to maintain the facade of calm. Curtis was still in the barn when Judd and Jenny left to catch the bus. Phoebe felt certain their plan was a good one, trying to keep circling thoughts of the dire consequences if they failed from her mind. When Curtis finally came in they sat together at the kitchen table, going over the plan again, tweaking here and there to tighten it up. Failure was not an option. They had to succeed. Everything depended on it.

After lunch Phoebe made an apple pie. Curtis did the dishes then went over to talk with Jesse to be certain he knew his part in the plan. Phoebe called Agnes to go over the plan with her again. That done, she went upstairs, showered and got dressed. She was not worried that any of the players would not do their part or forget what to do. The problem was that each step depended on the success of the previous step. One screw up, one slip and the scheme would fail—and there was no secondary or tertiary plan to fall back on.

Warren arrived on Friday afternoon with the van about the same time the children got off the bus. Over a slice of Phoebe's fresh apple pie, they chatted about the fun weekend ahead. The children then got their stuff together and piled into the family car with Ruby and Warren for the trip to Strivet County. Judd was happy his friend Ruby was going along. Since his experience in the woods, he had become rather sullen. Phoebe hoped that the weekend of spending time with his cousin, Warren Jr., his same age, would bring him around. As Warren backed up and was pulling onto the driveway, he rolled down his window and shouted to Curtis.

"Don't you ever feed those hogs, Curtis? I've never heard such a racket."

"I know it. They don't call them hogs for nothing, though, do they? I've delayed their feeding so they won't be too hungry before Bart gets back to feed them tomorrow. You'd think they were starving to death. I was just going to feed them when you arrived."

"See you later tonight then."

Once they'd all left Phoebe and Curtis loaded the baby furniture and clothes into the light brown van along with their suitcase. Phoebe straightened the house while Curtis fed the stray cats and checked on the cattle. Chores done, they sat in the kitchen drinking tea, waiting for the call. Phoebe seemed single-minded, Curtis' attempts to distract or engage her in conversation useless. At four-thirty the phone rang and Curtis answered it. When he hung up he gave Phoebe the high sign then picked up the phone again, calling Morray at the bank. The receptionist said he was there but she wasn't sure she could get him to the phone. Curtis insisted she try, telling her it was urgent. So far the plan was holding, Morray's foul mood having been or-chestrated earlier that afternoon.

"What is it, for God's sake, Edith," Morray spouted inimically, storming into the kitchen of their home mid-afternoon Friday to find his wife seated at the table. "I've told you a million times not to interrupt my meetings. What is so damn urgent?"

"Gaylan, I've turned my head all these years regarding the affairs you've had."

"Affairs? You dragged me home to talk about affairs. I thought you'd had a heart attack or something."

"Like you'd care. I've known since the early days of our marriage that you've never loved me, even that you'd taken up with that whore, Sally Torrent, from Gertrude's place. I've kept quiet about your philandering for the sake of marital peace, but the only thing I can count on in this town is respect, and I won't have your filthy laundry aired in the newspaper, for the world to see."

"What do you mean and who told you I'd taken up with Sal...Miss Torrent?"

"It's a well known fact, Gaylan."

"If it's such a well known fact and you don't care, why suddenly, is it an issue?"

"A man called me this morning, actually it sounded

more like a woman with a low voice. He, she, let's say *she*, said you'd been seen with Sally many times and not just talking—had pictures if I wanted them—intimate details of your anatomy—something about a motel in Dirkville."

"I haven't been anywhere near Sally or any other of those—women—so there couldn't be any pictures, of intimate details or anything else."

"Don't lie to me, Gaylan," Edith interdicted, pointing a porcelain bejeweled finger in his face. "There are pictures and you know it."

"Assuming there might be, why would she send them to the newspaper?"

"To even the score a little, she said. What score is she talking about?

"I have no idea."

"It's bad enough you're a cheater and liar, now the entire world must know?"

"You're going to believe a liar and a whore over me?"

"Takes one to know one. You clean this up, Gaylan, or I'll divorce you so fast it'll make your head spin. You'll be left with nothing by the time I'm through with you. I have connections you've only dreamed of."

"Oh, don't you worry. I'll clean it up all right. I'll round up Clyde and Owen and go have a talk with Sally, make her tell me who called. I'll fix this, dear, don't you worry," he cooed, stooping to plant a kiss on Edith's cheek, as she turned her head to avoid it.

Gaylan Morray flew out of the house. He was definitely a philanderer—and he'd gotten away with it through the years because of the fear instilled in his various partners. Thinking himself not only above the law but also suspicion, he never thought he'd see the day that Sally would turn on him, revealing his escapades. *And who was that woman that called, knowing so much?* he fumed within. It was true he didn't love Edith but he couldn't afford to get on her bad side and lose everything he'd worked so hard to achieve. Just for an instant he felt an emotion so alien he couldn't identify it. It was fear. As the feeling intensified, slowly creeping across his groin, he pushed it aside to refocus. *I won't let Sally get away with exposing me*, he told himself with vehement determination. *I'll find out whose behind this if it's the last thing I do.* A man with murder on his mind, he drove to the bank at top speed and parked his Jaguar. Calming himself, he strode through the front door nearly knocking over Vincent.

"Where are Clyde and Owen?" Morray questioned him, in his angst overlooking Jesse Tate at the lobby's pay phone, dialing.

"Why, they got a call—from you, they said—then left—said they were meeting you," Vincent sputtered.

"I never called them. Meeting me where?"

"At the old Westner place east of town. Did you forget? They said..."

"Never mind. I'll be out for a while."

"You look upset. Is anything the matter?"

"Mind your own goddamn business, will you? Can't I be upset without someone meddling?"

"I was just trying to...," Vincent started with trepidation until Morray's glare made him shut up.

Morray turned on his heels, heading for the front door.

"Mr. Morray. There's a call for you," his secretary yelled across the lobby.

"Take a message."

"They said it was very important."

"Who is it?"

"I couldn't tell if it was a man or woman, and they wouldn't say, but they said they knew you'd want to take the call."

"Confound-it-all! Why does everything have to go wrong in one day?"

Morray steamed into his office and slammed the door behind him, failing to see Jesse Tate slip out the front door of the bank. Picking up the receiver, he hoped his hunch was correct, that the person on the other end of the line was the same one that had called Edith earlier in the day. Ready to give them what for, he answered the phone.

"Gaylan Morray here, who's this?"

"This is Curtis Higgins. I guess you know you've finally got us over a barrel. We're tired of the fight—ready to sign over our farm to you."

"Well, it's about time." *At least all news today isn't bad*, he gloated within, forgetting his hunch. "You're doing the wise thing. You can start over somewhere else with what you have left."

"You mean the twenty hogs, fifty head of cattle, Jenny's pony, several mismatched cats, and a dog. That's not much to start over with."

"You've got your lives."

"Yes, and we're so grateful to you for that," Curtis sarcastically responded.

"When can you come in to sign the papers?"

"Well, here's the thing—Phoebe isn't feeling very well and we wondered if you could bring the papers out here?"

"That's a little irregular."

"You once told Phoebe you would do that any time we were ready."

"I'll come tomorrow morning then."

"Tomorrow won't do, I'm afraid. It will have to be tonight."

"I've got other business to attend to. I'll come tomorrow, first thing."

"It's tonight or not at all. Tomorrow we begin our contingency plan, if you don't want to deal with us tonight."

"What kind of contingency plan."

"Come about six o'clock—before we change our minds. You can bring all the pertinent papers with you— the papers related to our mortgage and foreclosure. I have a few questions to ask about those forms before we sign over the farm."

"What sort of questions?"

"Just a few questions."

"Oh, all right then—six o'clock," Gaylan conceded, after a long silence, pulling his watch from the fob.

"One more thing. We'd ask you to show some discretion and not say anything about this just yet. We're taking care of it before we leave town so we won't be here when the news hits the street—to save face."

"You're worried about saving face at a time like this?"

"Not me. It's my wife you know she's…"

"Oh, very well," Gaylan huffed, stuffing his watch back in its pocket. "But after tonight I can't be responsible for how fast word spreads or what is said."

Gaylan Morray hung up the phone, scratched his bald head and sat down in his desk chair. When buzzed with a transfer call, he absently picked up the receiver.

"Your wife's on the phone. What shall I tell her?" Judith, his secretary asked.

"That I'm out."

After the bank closed he paced in his office, waiting for his employees to leave. He searched his private files for the necessary papers, nervously shuffling them, then stuffing them into his brief case.

Vincent and Judith were the last to leave. When they were finally out the door, he grabbed his brief case and marched out, locking the door behind him. He waddled to his luxury car as fast as his short legs would carry him and started it up, taking a self-satisfied moment to listen to the hum of a fine engine. Instead of turning his Jaguar out of the parking lot to the east in search of his two sons, he drove west, toward Herston, to the farm of Curtis and Phoebe Higgins. Once down their long driveway, he parked behind the house as instructed. Getting out of the car, he noticed a light brown van parked near a shed.

The squealing hogs brought up images of a lonely childhood on the farm he was all too glad to have escaped, endless chores, and a farmer father, cruel and heartless. Pushing the memories aside, he strode toward the house— the argument with Edith, looking for his sons, his plans for Sally Torrent all forgotten with the sole thought occupying his greedy mind. He'd finally won. They were signing the farm over to him to beat the foreclosure and save their credit.

Clyde and Owen paced the Bullfrog Creek Bridge near the base of the driveway to the abandoned Westner place. The creek was sometimes only a trickle but late summer and fall rains had swelled it to the top of its banks. Most, if not all of the town, was in attendance at the high school football game but a couple of cars drove past as they waited. Two guys they knew from Dirkville stopped to chat a while, asking what they were doing at Bullfrog Creek.

"Waiting for our Dad," Owen answered.

"I thought bankers put in short days," one of the men quipped.

"Not our dad," Owen confessed. "He's not usually late though so I'm surprised he isn't here yet."

"When you get tired of waiting—or after you meet with him—come on over to the Dew Drop Inn. Rumor has it there's a big party there tonight."

"We just might do that," Clyde promised.

"See you later, then. Meanwhile, see if you can shut those bullfrogs up. They sure are noisy tonight. Must have active sex lives," the guy snickered.

It had long turned dark when Owen and Clyde grew tired of waiting for their dad. After much debate, knowing they'd be in deep trouble if their dad showed up and they weren't there, at Clyde's urging they adjourned to the nearby country bar to join their derelict friends. There was no party like they'd been told but they played pool and, as usual, drank excessively. By the time they stumbled to their truck and drove home, it was well past midnight. Because they went home another way, they did not see the crushed barrier on the approach to the Bullfrog Creek

Bridge nor their dad's car plunged into the depths of the roiling creek.

Phoebe greeted Gaylan Morray at the front door, a plasticized smile on her face.

"Sorry to hear you're not feeling well, Mrs. Higgins," Morray offered, as sympathetically as he could manage.

"Come on in, then," Phoebe responded, ignoring his forced concern. "Let's go into the living room."

"It sure is dark in here. You'll need more light to sign these papers—and a table to sign them on. We could go into the kitchen where there's more light. Let's all go into the kitchen."

"Let's not," Phoebe categorically stated.

Gaylan Morray, unable to explain the shivers running up and down his spine, dismissed them as merely a chill. Taking note of his rare obedience, an uncomfortable feeling started to form in his gut by implication. Phoebe indicated a chair where he was to sit, facing away from the kitchen door, and he lowered himself into it.

"As you well know, we're ruined," Curtis began, jarring Morray's thoughts. "We no longer have any alternative but to hand our farm over to the bank. We've given it every effort but know when we're done."

"It's always good to know when you're beaten. Shall we get to the paperwork then," he urged, opening his briefcase.

"I know you think you've left us without options but, once the papers are signed, I'll be working for my cousin over in Strivet County, in case you were wondering."

"Save me the details, Curtis. I'm not all that interested. You can all go to hell for all I care. Let's get these papers signed."

"Just out of curiosity, what would happen if we were not to sign the papers?" Phoebe questioned.

"Oh, that's rich! You dragged me out here to sign the papers after hours and now you ask what would happen if you didn't sign. Sign the damn things and let me get out of here. I have pressing business elsewhere."

"Can't you at least answer the question? What happens if we don't sign?"

"You want more misery is that it?" Morray questioned.

"We'd just like to hear you finally admit that you're the one behind all the disasters we've experienced, is all," Curtis responded.

"I'm surrounded by idiots. Who else around here do you think could have devised such an effective plan? If that imbecile Weils hadn't screwed up so many times, we'd have been done with all this long ago."

"Why would Harley help you against us?" Phoebe asked.

The question felt like a warning shot across the bow. Morray began to sweat, wondering why all the questions, what the innuendoes implied. But, eager to get the dirty deed done and proud of his methods, he humored them and answered.

"He stands to inherit that farm of his mother's—is just waiting around biding his time until he can get his hands on it. I assured him that if he'd help me, I'd make sure he got the farm a little sooner than might otherwise be expected. No one lives forever."

"You'd kill his mother—your sister?" Phoebe said, astounded to realize she could still be shocked by him.

"Stepsister. I'm done answering questions."

Something was chafing at him, telling him it was important to leave. As suspicions grew, he thought he heard someone in the kitchen behind him. Gnawing questions surfaced and it suddenly occurred to him that he had left the bank without telling anyone where he was going. He was beginning to piece some things together, the squealing hogs, the strange van in the driveway, the questions, the odd hour for conducting business. Before he could tally growing suspicions, Curtis again prompted him.

"Since you were so sure you were going to get this

farm, I suppose you've already completed the foreclosure proceedings, transferred title, and set the wheels in motion indicating the bank as owner," Curtis queried.

"No, but you can count on my doing it first thing Monday morning. I have all the necessary papers here," Morray answered, patting his briefcase. "I told you repeatedly that you couldn't win against me. It was pointless to fight back. Why you did is a mystery to me. It was useless from the start. You have only yourselves to blame for your misery."

"You tried to kill our son," Phoebe abruptly accused. "How are we to blame for that?"

If he had refused to answer, Gaylan Morray might have been saved.

"The intention was never to harm your son, you know—just scare you into compliance by taking him to that abandoned shed," Morray offered, in what almost sounded like a contrite tone. "Of course, Harley botched that as well. Now will you sign these damn papers so I can get going? I have to find my sons."

"I have a headache and need a glass of water," Phoebe suddenly announced. "Want one?"

"No—thank you," Gaylan Morray stammered, surprised by her hospitality.

Morray reached into his briefcase, as Phoebe disappeared into the kitchen. She was gone only seconds. Glancing past Morray, Curtis saw her standing in the doorway, wielding a cast iron frying pan in her right hand. In shock, he failed to react in time to stop her. Before Gaylan Morray could scream "sheriff" he was dead from a fulminating blow to his temple.

"There, you son-of-a-bitch," Phoebe blurted, letting the heavy pan dangle at the end of her arm.

Curtis looked at Morray then his wife. This was not part of the plan. He was the one that was supposed to have done in Morray and not with a frying pan. Sitting, with his head on his chest, running his fingers through his hair, he wondered how their lives had come to this. He had thought them to be good people. How had they been driven to such extremes? Morray's destruction had run through his mind more than once, but he'd thought himself incapable of murder until Judd had been kidnapped. A few months ago he would have thought it impossible for his sweet, innocent Phoebe to have devised the plan they were amidst, certainly not murder, but her maternal instincts had been roused by Morray's callous remarks. Now it was too late to turn back. It didn't matter that they had been forced to the very limits of civility. Together they had stepped over that line into the depths of hell. He sat up straight, with a determined look on his face, staring at the still body of Gaylan Morray slumped in the wooden arm chair.

"I told you, warned you, Morray, that if you touched one hair on the head of any of our children I'd kill you," he reprimanded the corpse.

Phoebe stood silently staring at the body in disbelief, trying to digest what she'd just done—a maw opening in her mind that would never heal. She appeared frozen to the spot, her feckless body folding in upon itself, kept from collapsing onto the floor only by Curtis' quick action. He took his wife into his arms and held her tightly against his chest, feeling the jerking sobs of a woman condemned.

"All right, Phoebe. Pull yourself together," he said after a time. "We can only go forward now. Let's get him out there before we change our minds and turn ourselves in to the state police."

Phoebe did not respond. She withdrew from Curtis, stepped back into the kitchen, dropped the fry pan and slumped onto a chair at the table. Curtis dragged Morray's body across the rug to the tiled floor. With only the light from the barnyard, he removed his glasses then unhooked his gold watch, pulled it from the fob, took his wallet from the suit pockets, and laid the items on the table. Next, he took off Morray's shoes, suit pants and coat, shirt, tie, and undershirt, rolling the clothes into a wad around the shoes and throwing it into the pantry. He wrapped a plastic bag around Morray's head to contain the blood beginning to ooze from the wound while Phoebe sat at the table, dumbstruck. Consoling her made no difference. She did not respond. It was then he knew he'd have to carry out the rest of the plan by himself. He only hoped he could.

As he went into the pantry to put on his Wellingtons, there was suddenly a knock on the door and he stopped in his tracks. Involved with the crime, he hadn't heard a car come down the driveway. Visions of prison, even execution forced their way through his mind as he quickly ducked back into the kitchen, hoping he'd not been detected. Phoebe had risen like the dead from her chair upon hearing the knock. Curtis whispered for her not to say anything, as they stood stark still in the dark. Another knock and then a voice called out.

"Phoebe, I know you're in there. Why's the house dark?"

Phoebe recognized it as the voice of her brother, Harry.

"Please, can you come back tomorrow," Curtis called out. "Phoebe's not here right now."

"Well, that's a hell-of-a welcome. I came to surprise you with my news. I've decided to move back here and have taken a job in Lynchford."

No response.

"Come on, let me in. What's going on?"

"I'm sick," Curtis lied.

"No you're not. What's going on? Whose Jag is this?"

At this, Curtis opened the door and pulled Harry inside the pantry then through to the kitchen.

"Where's Phoebe. Turn on some lights, Curtis. I think I've come up with a way to deal with Morray," Harry started, as Curtis gestured to the floor next to the table. "What the…"

"We can't turn on a light," Curtis explained, as the yard light revealed a supine, nearly naked body at Phoebe's feet.

"Who's that?"

"Gaylan Morray."

Harry slowly looked from Phoebe to Morray to Curtis then back at Morray.

"Oh, my God. What have you done? Is he dead?"

"Don't just stand there. Give me a hand, will you?" Curtis commanded.

"What are you going to do?"

"Are you going to ask questions or help?" Curtis reprimanded.

Harry immediately took off his coat and threw it on the table. While Phoebe watched, vacant of all expression, Curtis gave some instructions to Harry. Together they wrestled Morray's body out into the pantry. Curtis called to Phoebe to come and hold the door open and, surprisingly, she obeyed. The stronger of the two men, he took Morray's arms and torso, Harry the legs, and they carried the body out the door. When Harry figured out that the hog pen was their destination, he stumbled hard, gagging, and Morray's legs slipped from his grasp. Curtis fell backward with the body landing on top of him. Pushing the floppy, clammy, lifeless body off, he scrambled to his feet.

"It's too late to change the plan now, Harry."

"But who killed…"

"Phoebe. Now will you help or won't you?"

He picked up Morray's arms and motioned to Harry to hoist the legs. Harry heaved a huge sigh and picked them up. Crossing the barnyard with the heavy, dead body was slow going. The squealing of the hogs was deafening as they approached the pen. They struggled to get Morray's rather rotund and fleshy body up over the fence but finally managed to do so by bracing it against the fence and easing it upward a little at a time. After pushing the body over the top fence board, they heard it heavily splat into the mud below. By the time they'd turned and headed for the house, the hungry hogs had converged, and quieted considerably. Harry plugged his ears.

Back at the house, while Harry went to Phoebe, Curtis took the wad of clothes and shoes in the pantry to the incinerator and stuffed them in. In the pantry, he took off his boots then put on gloves, went into the living room, retrieved the briefcase, and removed all the papers inside. He tore them up without looking at them, threw them in the fireplace, lit a match and watched them burn to ashes. *Maybe someone else is also saved tonight*, he muttered within. When he got back to the kitchen, Harry was holding Phoebe's shaking body. Curtis scraped Morray's personal effects from the table into a black garbage bag then set it outside the back door. He calmly picked up the skillet from the floor, wiped it off, and replaced it on it's hanger above the stove. It was apparent that Phoebe was unable to understand or comprehend what was going on, so he suggested they all sit down for a time and compose themselves.

Sitting in the dark, he explained to Harry all that had happened since he'd left, while Phoebe sat silent. It didn't take much to convince Harry they were doing the only thing possible. Since Phoebe was so shaken, Harry agreed to drive the van instead of her.

Somnambulant, Phoebe walked through the pantry to the back door, responsive enough to comply as Curtis pulled on her jacket. Still in gloves, Curtis put on clean boots, grabbed the briefcase and flung it onto the seat of the Jaguar. Phoebe glided to the van and Harry steered her to the passenger side but Curtis, at the last minute, decided she shouldn't go because, in her stupor, she might be a liability. Escorting her back to the kitchen, he seated her at the table, telling her he'd be back soon and to stay right where she was, only leaving her when he saw comprehension dawn on her face. Returning to the van, he quickly explained to Harry what to do, where to go, then got into the driver's seat of the Jaguar. After signaling Harry to follow him, he drove out of the driveway and onto Digbert Road.

Curtis went the back way around town to Bullfrog Creek Bridge Road, passing only two cars. When he turned onto the road, Harry went straight as instructed, going a more circuitous route to the bridge. Near the bridge, Curtis opened the door of the Jaguar, stepped on the gas and aimed the car at the embankment above the creek. Just before the car went through the barrier and over the edge into the turgid waters of the River Styx, he jumped out of the car, rolled onto the embankment, and scrambled onto the bridge. Straightening himself, he brushed the dirt from his pants and gloved hands, scuffed up the gravel to erase his boot tracks then ran toward the road on the other side of the bridge that intersected Bullfrog Creek Bridge Road. Harry was waiting for him there in the van, lights off.

In silence they rode along the back roads to the farm. There they found Phoebe sitting at the kitchen table exactly as they'd left her. Turning on a light, they could see that her eyes were bloodshot and swollen. Without saying a word Harry helped Curtis pack up some additional items Phoebe had earlier put aside, placing them into the van. Then he helped Phoebe to the van while Curtis put on his Wellingtons, got the flashlight, grabbed the garbage bag, and headed for the hog pen. The satiated hogs were silent and the only signs of Gaylan Morray were some stray bones and remnants of mud-stained white boxer shorts. Relieved there wasn't more to dispose of, Curtis carefully removed the pieces of evidence from the mud, stuffing them into the black plastic garbage bag with Morray's personal effects.

When he got back to the house he put the garbage bag in the back of the van, hosed off his Wellingtons and set them just inside the door where they usually stood, took off his gloves, threw them into the incinerator with Morray's clothes and lit it up. Then he locked the door to the house and walked to the van, where Harry and Phoebe stood waiting. They all looked at each other as if to say *see you in hell* then Harry helped Phoebe into Warren's van.

"See you next week," Harry whispered to Phoebe.

Turning from her, he walked to his car and opened the door.

"I'll come over from Lynchford on Tuesday," he advised Curtis, before slamming his door shut and starting the motor.

Gaylan Morray's remains were laid to rest in the trash can of a McDonald's in Strivet County. His Jaguar was not discovered until late the following afternoon. By the time Curtis and Phoebe returned with their children Sunday night, rumors as to the cause of his death were rife, rampant, and varied.

"Did you hear about Gaylan Morray," Bart said, coming down the stairs to greet them in the kitchen when he heard them come in."

"What happened to Morray?" Phoebe queried, as noncommittally as she could manage.

"He's disappeared."

Since his body was never found, only his briefcase, no one was ever prosecuted, keeping Dirk County's record in tact. At the bank both Judith and Vincent told the sheriff that Morray had appeared upset when they left Friday night. Judith didn't know who'd called him. When the drivers of the two vehicles Curtis had passed stepped forward to say they'd seen Morray driving toward the bridge, suicide was briefly suspected but, without a body, rejected. Someone mentioned a strange tan van in town but it was never located. Clyde and Owen came under close scrutiny for a time, the witnesses that had seen them at the bridge that night giving testimony, then dismissed out of hand. There was no motive. The boys didn't stand to inherit anything from their dad, other than a modest life insurance policy. A haphazard and typically sloppy investigation was conducted by the sheriff who soon declared it an accident.

Reactions to Gaylan Morray's presumed death were wide-ranging. Edith Morray wondered who to thank. Clyde and Owen were completely emasculated and, without supervision, slid further down the food chain. They started drinking more heavily and it wasn't long before they'd gone through the insurance money. Their mother put them on a short leash and small allowance, controlling all their activities, time, and expenditures. They eventually settled into a routine of going to the Sunset Bar and Grill early evening then stumbling home just before midnight to get up and do the same thing the next day. Sometimes they mowed their mother's lawn or shoveled her walks, but could not be counted upon.

Once people in town felt released from Gaylan Morray's grip, they started talking—and never shut up. Haunted by FBI investigations and the state police, the board of cronies ceased and desisted. At Edith's insistence, the board of the bank was reorganized under the direction of Vincent DeMar who turned out to have more *chutzpah* and intelligence than had formerly been apparent. Under the liege lord, Gaylan Morray, he had been unable to use his banking and business skills and, unwilling to involve himself in the questionable affairs of the bank, had laid low. But, as head of the bank, he soon gained a reputation for fairness and good sense—quite a novelty in Between.

The judge and sheriff were dismissed then replaced, two lawyers were disbarred and the businessmen, narrowly escaping dire consequences, returned apt attention to their respective businesses. Doug Hewes, the druggist, was returned to prison. Swifty McClaire died within the year from alcohol poisoning. Harley Weils was brought up on several charges but none of them stuck because no one had actually caught him in the act of doing anything, except Jesse Tate who, to avoid implication, said nothing.

Grateful to have escaped with his life, Harley ran his gas station and kept a low profile, waiting for his mother's death—a waste of time as he was to learn when she finally died at the age of ninety-five, leaving all her money and the farm to the Methodist church.

By years end, under the watchful eye of the state police Between had settled back into a version of normalcy that was slightly upgraded from that of past decades. In actuality, it was only a trompe l'oeil. It would take years, and the new highway, to lift Between from isolation. In the absence of Gaylan Morray's heavy hand, the citizens of the community were eventually able to become more viable—to transform their vapid lives and make the transition from complete apathy to personal responsibility—to again take charge of affairs of government—to support and trust competent, honest leadership.

The Higgins children never learned or even suspected their parents' involvement in the mysterious disappearance of Gaylan Morray. In time some of Judd's memory returned. He remembered talking to Harley Weils in the parking lot of the school after the debates. Ignorant of Harley's part in the attempted ruination of his family, he had no reason to suspect foul play or implicate him in his kidnapping. He only remembered waking up in a shed in the woods with no idea where he was. Stumbling out of the shed, he'd fallen into the mine shaft and was knocked unconscious.

Harry stayed in Lynchford, going back to school and working for a small bank. He eventually became a vice-president under Vincent DeMar when his bank was bought out by the First Enterprise Bank in Between. Both he and Phoebe were happy to be near enough to see each other occasionally and, after Harry married, the families spent most holidays together.

Curtis and Phoebe were able to rescue their farm and once again lead productive lives. The bond of love between them, although weakened for a time, held. Eventually Phoebe recovered some of her former spirit and drive but a light had gone out in her. Though they never talked of the matter, Phoebe, Curtis, Harry, Jesse Tate and Agnes Warner knew well their actions were far from peccadillo. Scarred with guilt, they would forever pay the price of the battle—a shallow victory over evil that became their life-long burden.